INTERNATIONAL BESTSELLING AUTHOR
ANGELA J. FORD

D1519480

TREACHERY OF WATER

LORE *of* NOMADIA
1

TREACHERY OF WATER

LORE *of* NOMADIA
1

INTERNATIONAL BESTSELLING AUTHOR
ANGELA J. FORD

Copyright © 2021 by Angela J. Ford

Editing & Proofreading: Elevation Editoral

Cover Art: Susana Conde

Typography: Miblart

All rights reserved.

No part of this book may be reproduced in any form or by any electronic or mechanical means, including information storage and retrieval systems, without written permission from the author, except for the use of brief quotations in a book review.

To anyone in need of an adventure

Beware the child with golden tears
Trapped by sand throughout the years,
Furious from the pain endured
Woe to those whose fate insured
When her power comes to pass,
The empire will fall into her hands
For none has power to withstand
The rule of golden-teared hands

— PROPHECIES OF NOMADIA

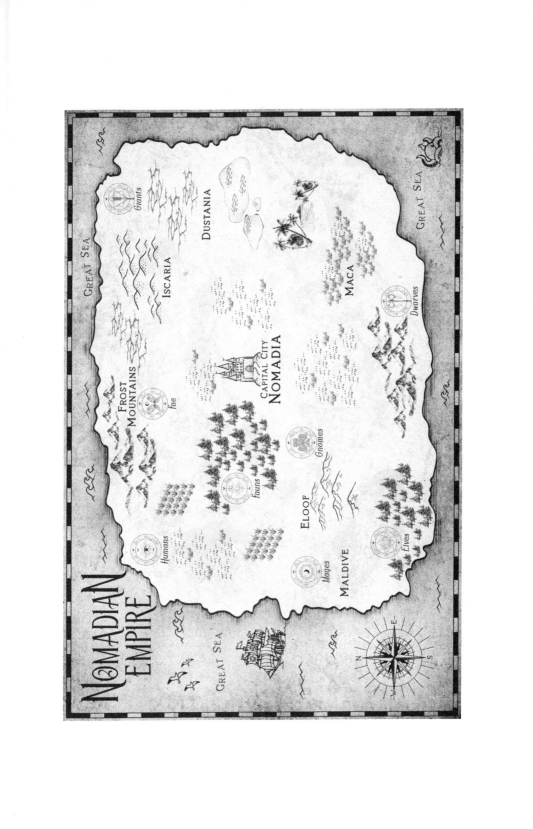

CONTENTS

1

ELMIRA

Her eyes flickered open to ripe shadows and the scent of iron. Crimson blood dripped down the manacles clasped around her ankles and settled in a shallow pool at the base of the stone. Later, the wizard who kept her locked away as a prisoner in the crypt would come to take the blood for his arcane rituals.

A hopeless gurgle bubbled in her throat, the beginning of a mad laugh that died away before she released it. How ironic that her own blood kept her locked in the dark, a slave to the guards who came to taunt her with their sun-bleached hair and remnants of sand in their clothes. She guessed, from their comings and goings, that she was still in the desert. It was hot, a dull oppressive heat that made her wish the rags she wore would disintegrate into dust. Her body had outgrown what had once been a dress for a child. Now, her limbs were long and skinny, and the hollows around her chest were filling out. That's how long she'd belonged to them.

She'd grown from a frightened elven child, orphaned and alone in the dark, to an elven woman. The years dragged by, one after the other, as slow as the crimson stain of blood flowing from her wounds. Every time they cut her, they wanted her to cry or scream, and if the guards failed, the wizard would use spells to torment her until at last she broke and sobbed plump, fat tears that turned to solid gold as they fell.

When they first captured her, she'd sobbed and pleaded. The gold flowed freely, and they encouraged her with small taunts and teasing, forcing her to skip a meal or locking her in the dark for misdeeds. She'd once lived above, in the daylight. At least she thought she had, but now reality and dreams blended together until she could not discern what was true and what was false. Emotion had long since fizzled away into nothing but a growing hatred. It sat in her stomach like a heavy stone that expanded, day by day, as she suffered under blade and whip and arcane magic.

Each day they came to torment her, she grew stronger, able to withstand the pain longer, to hold out against their tricks and ploys to get her to succumb, to submit to them. Once she'd been wholly theirs, body and soul, ashamed and embarrassed by how they treated her and hoping someone would save her or have mercy on her soul and kill her. But now she was older, and understood that those who held her had black souls, unable to sympathize with her plight.

How could she change their minds when they believed the words of an oracle? She was a child of prophecy whose actions, should she gain her freedom, would bring about the rise of the dark lord. He would raise the dead to life and bring misery across the empire of Nomadia. She hated the wizard and his guards for believing she was a tool for devastation, although darkness swam within her, especially when the wizard came near with his magic.

She was drawn to the pull of his arcane magic and what he could do when he stood in front of her, holding his staff and chanting. Those words brought fierce pain to her body, made her writhe and scream as though her flesh were on fire. How could he do such things with words? How did he possess such power? She wanted to learn; she wanted to wake up her chains and beseech them to let her go, for she knew it was only by a powerful magic that he held her.

Footsteps brought her out of her well of thoughts and she opened her eyes, blinking in the semidarkness. She lay on her back, arms stretched out and above her head, iron manacles securing her to a slab of stone. The unforgiving roughness of the stone dug into her flesh, and it heated and cooled to the whim of the wizard, sometimes burning her, other times making her shake with cold as though she were lost in a blizzard high in mountain ranges she could not name.

Her eyes darted across the room. The slab she lay on was tilted so that blood and tears would run downward to be collected in the basins that surrounded her, but the room itself was a wide expanse.

The wizard spoke to her sometimes, in his own dark, demented way. He explained why he had to torture her and told her why she was there, but she knew why. Kymeria had hid her in the crypt, then died years ago at the treachery of her own army. She still remembered the beating of the drums and the sick feeling of blood that had filled her mouth. She'd been so young and innocent when first abandoned to the grave because of the fear of what might happen.

Why did the mortals hold so tightly to old prophecies from the ancients? Back then, the world was young. Superstitions and strange beliefs led it. Because of a tale from hundreds of years ago, she was buried alive in the tomb of a great master of ink, sealed beneath a great pyramid. She'd seen the collection of treasures: trinkets of gold, carvings of gilded birds and odd-looking creatures with curved noses and abnormally large heads, and vivid paintings in royal purples and blues of strange sacrifices, pleasure, torture, and war. She'd even seen the wall of scrolls, covered in sand, and somewhere, in another room, the sacred tomb of the King of Sand himself: King Horus.

He'd ruled the empire of sand for decades and was buried in the glory of the days of old, with all the pomp and circumstance due to a great and beloved king. Buried with him were his wives and concubines, along with a fraction of his wealth and the scrolls and prophecies of that era. A recent addition to the tomb was one of the greatest terrors known to Nomadia.

She only knew about it because of the wizard. He liked to torment her with the idea of it, saying how one day he'd raise the great jinn and use three wishes to unleash untold horror on her. As though she were not already living in hell itself.

The stone doors opened and torchlight filled the room as the wizard strode in, followed by his assistant. A linen tunic swept to the wizard's knees, sleeveless because of the heat. He wore a turban on his head and carried a staff made of thick wood. It curved around his arm like a snake. Sometimes, depending on the spells he used, the staff moved like a snake too, coming to bite her legs and fill her with venom.

She lifted her chin, black eyes flashing. Thick lines weathered his face, and his mouth was turned up in a permanent sneer. Golden eyes bored into her own as he stood at the edge of the basin between her legs, which were held open by the merciless chains. He stared down at the basin, watching the slow trickle of blood, then met her eyes. "Elmira." He shook his head as though gravely disappointed with her. "You know what you have to do to make this all stop. You can make the pain go away, all you need to do is . . ."

"Cry!" she hissed, her voice low and hoarse from disuse. She was thirsty, powerfully thirsty, but it was only another tool they used over her. Keeping her hanging in the balance between thirst and hunger, driving her to the brink of insanity and then death, again and again, and laughing at her pain and misery.

"Ah." The wizard took his staff in both hands, as though warding off her very words. "Cry. It is easy. Let the tears come, let the river flow. You can feel it behind your eyes, can't you? The tang, the taste of sweet salty tears, forming to gold as they fall. Just let it flow, let it come, give in to your rage, your hate, and let the pain fade into tears."

He continued in his singsong voice, but she'd had enough of his games. She wanted him to get on with it, to poke and prod her, to drive her wild with his dark desires, for he enjoyed the blood, the sound of her cries, and the way she spat and struggled. She'd seen his eyes turn to dark gold as her blood flowed, as her body spasmed under his hands. He liked her raw and wild, with her tangled hair, unwashed, unbrushed, and her dry skin and hawkish features stretched over bone. He enjoyed the games, the misery, and the fact that it was his power that caused her unfathomable agony.

The assistant had his own share of pain; the youth's hand

was mangled from old injuries, although the missing fingers had happened in recent years. One shoulder was hunched up painfully, and scars covered his face, back, and shoulders from where the whip had smacked into him. He kept his eyes cast down as he carried the tools for the wizard. The wizard was unforgiving to all, but he held the tomb with his dark power, which was why the guards did his bidding. No one turned a sympathetic eye toward her, Elmira the captive. No one except the assistant.

She closed her eyes as the wizard gestured to his assistant. "Bring the knives."

She sniffed. There was an unfamiliar scent in the air; it itched at her scalp. She hadn't noticed it before, hadn't had clarity as she waited for the pain she'd soon endure. But she sensed it now, as she pressed her palms flat against the stone and opened her eyes.

Two words burst into her mind. *Let go.*

Suddenly, she was the stone, and the stone was her. The iron grip of the chains slid away and she bolted upright, kicking out.

The wizard cried out, but he was too slow. The kick landed on his jaw. He stumbled back, hands grasping for his knives. A cry tore from Elmira's lips, and the stone underneath her crumbled into dust, as though it had been waiting, willing her to ask.

A frenzy came over her as she bent to grasp the chains, then swung with all her strength, smacking them into the wizard's face. She brought the heavy iron around again and again, even as he lifted his staff to ward off her blows. His face was crushed and bleeding, with one eye nothing but a bubble of blood and broken bones. But she would not relent. She swung the chains again and again, driving iron into his face until it was a mess of blood and bones and cartilage.

With a snarl, she leaped onto his body and perched on his chest, watching as he passed from life to death. Cruel satisfaction beat in her breast as she waited, savoring those final moments. His fingers twitched, and a gurgle came from his lips. Then . . . nothing.

His form went slack and soft, but a wisp of white appeared, a vapor escaping from the body. His essence. She couldn't explain why, but she opened her mouth, threw back her head, and breathed in the wizard's soul.

2

DARYA

Whispers drifted through the cool waters, humming in anticipation of the upcoming celebration. Darya swam in circles above the glimmering kingdom of the sirens, hidden deep in the currents of the sea where even the bravest landwalker dared not enter. She paused admiring her glistening scales, sea blue and lily-pad green, as a flicker of gold winked above her.

Schools of silver fish swam in clusters, their underbellies glistening white, but they hadn't caused the glitter. Darya's webbed fingers tightened into fists. In any other circumstance, she would have plunged into the school of fish, enjoying the thrill of the hunt as she scooped one up to eat. Not today. Irritation flared as she watched them continue their mindless journey through the clear waters, ignorant of her frustration.

No matter what she did, each new day seemed an opportunity for the elders who presided over the Court of Nymphs to criticize her actions.

Never chase the fish. You're wasting valuable food.

Don't talk to those lower than you.

Focus on your duty as a water nymph.

Water magic should only be used to defend the sirens.

Sirens. Darya aimed a glare at the kingdom of sirens just below her. Keeping watch was dreadfully boring, especially when she watched the sirens fight and love and feast and celebrate and explore. A surge of jealousy pinched, leaving her with a growing sense of unhappiness. She was the child of a powerful deity of nymphs, blessed with longevity and water magic, only to be reduced to serving as protector of the sirens. In reality, the title meant nothing more than standing guard and watching for predators.

It was the same task the fearsome siren warriors performed for their kingdom, which was the reason for the new alliance between the mermaids and sirens. That evening, the sirens would welcome the mermaids with a banquet, for the nymph assigned to protecting the mermaids had at long last lain down to rest in the endless slumber that eventually claimed them all. Three hundred years, and suddenly all she wanted to do was sleep. Now, the sirens would protect the mermaids.

Darya didn't blame her; the nymph had probably been bored to tears, just like Darya was now.

A blur of motion shot toward her, and Darya spun, gathering the waters to herself as she prepared to blast the intruder. Finally, something to do besides swim in a circle.

"Darya. Wait!" a gleeful voice shouted. "It's only me."

Darya dropped her hands moments before the water

sprayed out in a vortex, unsure whether to be disappointed or relieved. "Talius, I thought you were a shark."

Talius snorted as he slowed down, floating in front of her. He was one of the siren warriors. Thin black hair was slicked back from his wide forehead, and the orbs of his pale eyes reflected the waters. His face was sharp and angular, giving him a frightening appearance that intensified when he grinned, revealing a neat row of pointed teeth.

"Tal . . ." Darya hesitated, torn between telling him to go away lest she get into trouble—again—with the Court of Nymphs, but wanting him to stay to amuse her.

She and Talius had become friends after she saved him from one of the sea trenches. Foul creatures lurked there, with monstrous beaks, tentacles, and poisonous clouds of ink. Although the sirens had been warned to stay away from the trenches, Talius went to seek treasure and had become hopelessly lost. Darya heard him praying for salvation and arrived just in time to save him from becoming the meal of a giant squid. He'd thanked her, then demanded to know what had taken so long. Shocked at his attitude, and then amused, Darya had laughed. Talius wasn't afraid of the nymphs and didn't bow and simper like the other sirens. She liked him not only because of his straightforward attitude, but also because he was honest with her.

"I thought you could use some company," Talius smirked. "Since you're on guard duty and all . . ."

Darya crossed her arms over her scaled chest and moved her tail back and forth, creating ripples in the water. During guard duty, she was supposed to keep her lovely skin covered with scales, a suit of armor to protect against vicious sea creatures. "It is your duty to defend the sirens," she complained. "I don't understand why the elders make us keep watch."

Talius held up the thick spear that he carried everywhere with him. Giving Darya an exaggerated bow, he announced, "Because you can see better in the water, and because the Court of Nymphs wants us to focus on harmony. If we fight, it will lead to bloodshed, while you nymphs can use your power to manipulate the waters and drive away anyone who dares oppose us."

Darya glared down at the kingdom below her. Complaining wouldn't change anything. "How are preparations coming for the mermaids? Do you think the treaty will work?"

Talius shrugged. "As a warrior, I doubt I'll be allowed near them. I hear they are soft, don't know how to fight, and use their talents to lure their prey instead of our natural weapons." He opened his mouth wider. "Despite how hard Prince Filitis tries, I believe the mermaid princess will hate it here. We dwell much farther under the sea than they do, and we never rise to the surface. Rumor has it, they know the ways of the landwalkers and have picked up many of their traditions and mannerisms."

"It's just all very political," Darya sighed. The golden flicker came again, drawing her gaze up. *What is that?* "The mermaids want the sirens to protect them and the sirens want the gentle ways and beauty of the mermaids. I don't understand the benefits of the treaty. Isn't it better if everyone simply keeps to themselves instead of changing things? It's safer for the mermaids to stay where they are comfortable. I know the great nymph who protected the mermaids went to her eternal resting place, but my older sister, Klarya, could replace her."

Talius snorted. "You and your sisters."

Darya knew she shouldn't talk about her sister with a mere siren, but she desperately wished Klarya would go away. Maybe she should have brought it up during the last meeting of the elders—not that anyone ever took her suggestions seriously.

Klarya was a creature of the depths and took her task of protection and ensuring the well-being of the sirens very seriously. Too seriously. She was highly esteemed and had a fearsome reputation among the Court of Nymphs.

Darya also had two younger sisters who were obedient and praised in the court, leaving Darya as the oddity. She was too curious, too chatty with the sirens, too playful in the waters, and too lax with her duties. Mother claimed it was because Darya was born during a storm, and that wildness had edged its way into her.

Talius was still talking, taking a defensive position against Darya's thoughts. "There are many benefits to uniting the sea creatures. True, we are all unique, but we can gain something from each other, just as I have learned from you. If we always surround ourselves with those who agree with us, how will we ever learn to think from another perspective?"

Darya frowned. "Now you sound like the king during one of his speeches."

"Is that supposed to be an insult?" Talius laughed, unoffended by Darya's words. "It just so happens that I agree with the king. For as curious as you are, Darya, it would do you good to listen to him. He's wise, and I thought . . . well, we are friends after all, and that wouldn't have happened if you hadn't been willing to protect someone different from you."

Darya noticed he did not use the word: weaker. But she didn't like where the conversation was going. According to Mother, each race was unique and should stay in their place. If they tried to change or become greater, they'd upset the delicate balance of the sea.

"Okay." Talius raised his hands in submission. "We won't talk about this anymore, but if you can escape, come to the celebration, and wear something nice instead of your scale armor."

"I will if I can," Darya agreed, although it was more likely she'd be forced to watch over the kingdom from afar than be allowed to join the festivities, especially if one of her sisters saw her chatting with Talius. The flicker of gold came yet again, causing Darya to make up her mind. "Will you do me a favor?"

Talius groaned. "Every time you ask, it leads to trouble."

Darya playfully swatted his arm. "I won't be long. Something is winking up there, and I just want to see what it is."

"As long as you hurry," Talius begrudgingly said. "I should return to the palace and assist with the preparations."

Darya nudged his shoulder. "You just don't want to stand guard. Tell me you have a better excuse. I don't imagine you'd ever lift a finger to help with decorations or food preparations."

"No," Talius admitted, running a palm over his hair to slick it back further. "The entourage of mermaids will arrive this afternoon. I'd like to be there and see if they are as beautiful as rumored."

Darya laughed, sending a stream of bubbles dancing

through the waters. "I knew it! Stay here; I'll be right back. If anyone asks, I thought I saw a predator."

With a swish of her tail, she shot upward, using her power to send the waters surging away from her. The school of silver fish scattered, reminding her she should slow down before she frightened away every living thing. But what was the point of having water magic if she could never use it?

She'd heard tales of old when nymphs ruled the sea and used their magic to create terrible storms. They sank ships and captured the landwalkers as their prey, leaving them frightened of the sea and the monsters in the deep. Apparently, the landwalkers had told tales of the horrors they'd seen and refused to investigate the sea further.

However, in recent years, the Court of Nymphs had determined that the path forward was peace. No more violent storms or frightening landwalkers to death. Instead they stayed silent, quiet, under the sea where they protected those weaker than them and battled with words, not deeds.

Darya wasn't ungrateful for her position of power—she simply wanted more, which left her antsy and restless. Unfortunately, the Court of Nymphs had made it clear that if she continued to complain and scorn the rules, she'd be cast out.

The flicker glowed brighter as Darya swam toward the surface, ripples of blue water dancing around her. She reached the pinnacle of the mountain that hid the kingdom of the sirens and navigated it with skill, avoiding the seaweed that reached for her with eel-like fingers.

Suddenly, a radiant light overcame her vision and she shielded her eyes. *Is that sunlight?* When she spun, the glow was on the same level as her, but in the distance, and an unearthly sound came from it. Closing her eyes to heighten her senses, Darya listened.

It was music, high and sweet, that sent shivers of longing down her spine. An ache throbbed in her heart. The song flowed through her like a call, and as if lured by a spell, she moved toward it, her haste slowing to a methodical swim. When she reached the sound, she had no doubt the hollow longing inside her would be fulfilled.

As she moved, lights sparkled in the water, pearl white and rose pink; tiny bioluminescent creatures. It wasn't until she reached the waving seaweed that she realized she'd gone much farther than she intended. Talius would be grumpy she'd left him alone for so long.

The music was much louder beyond the seaweed. She wrapped herself in the greenery and crouched as colorful lights moved toward her. No, not lights—people, with scales and colorful hair in shades of bright green, vivid coral, and sunshine yellow. They brought the music with them, and she saw trumpeters playing on coral shells a song so rich and beautiful the water around her vibrated. It was a signal, a coming, meant to frighten away the predators that lurked in the water and call light and beauty to themselves. The royal mermaids were on their way to the siren kingdom.

Darya flattened herself among the seaweed and watched. It would only be appropriate to rise, introduce herself, and offer to escort them to their final destination. She rose, then immediately ducked back down when she glimpsed a familiar cloud of blue hair. Klarya was already there. A bitter lump swelled in Darya's throat. So. She'd been left to guard the kingdom while Klarya had the esteemed honor of escorting the mermaids.

A sour taste stung her tongue. Grinding her teeth, Darya turned to leave, slinking through the seaweed and back through the mountain void as though she were in trouble. Why was she surprised? Klarya always received the best of everything, and exalted in it.

Why didn't the court trust Darya with anything other than guard duty? Her throat burned as she swam, hurling through the waves without caring what creatures she disturbed. Just as the kingdom of the sirens rose below her, a wailing scream shot through the waters like a knife, and the force of it hurled Darya backward.

3

DARYA

Darya whirled, eyes widening as an inky cloud plumed from the sea floor, advancing like a swarm of snakes and wrapping around the siren's palace. Heart thumping, Darya dove toward it, uncertain how to use her water magic to stop it. Within moments, she was in the thick of the vapor-like blackness, and a foul stench stole her breath away. The sea was usually cool, but heat blazed in the cloud, causing her scales to burn as though she'd spent too much time lying on a sandy beach enjoying the sunlight. Water churned, jerking her body into its grasp.

Darya lost control, arms flailing and tail thrashing as she was sucked into a whirling vortex. Blinded by the cloud, Darya opened her other senses as she tried to resist the current. Screams and cries made her blood freeze. Summoning her power, Darya arched her body and let it go. A wave billowed out from her, briefly shattering the cloud enough for her to make out thick tentacles twice the size of her body waving below her. She also glimpsed a hint of royal purple before the cloud returned with renewed force. It whirled, recognizing her as the source of power, then pounced.

A slimy, ropelike substance wrapped around Darya's waist and tugged her down. She screamed and struggled against it, but the vapor was strong. It poured into her mouth, filling her body with a hot, achy sensation. Her insides stung and her eyes itched as she twisted, begging for relief, but it was everywhere. Around her, inside her, until she wondered if it would throttle her completely. She was a nymph—immortal, powerful. Could a bit of poisonous ink truly overcome her?

Suddenly, the mist let go of her with a loud popping sound. Darya twirled, fists clenched, ready to send another wave toward whatever had attacked her. Instead, her tail scraped against the sea floor while the palace of the sirens towered above her, stained with the dark ink. The sirens had stopped screaming and were huddled in circles, with the weak and vulnerable on the inside while the warriors floated on the outside, brandishing spears. Above them floated Darya's mother and the other nymphs, her sisters. Darya's stomach twisted into a knot, but no one was glaring at her— in fact, they stared beyond her.

Slowly, dreading what she would see, Darya turned around. The water moved in a gentle circle of submission around her. Her chest went tight as a vivid violet the color of sea urchins filled her vision. Sucking tentacles floated around the octopus-like creature, and its bulbous purple body stretched twenty feet long, longer than the green electric eels that swam in the deep, where it was always dark as night. Above the creature's body rose her waist, generous chest, scale-covered arms, and orb-shaped head. Fleshy red lips took up most of her face. Her nose was flat and tiny, and her eyes were narrow golden slits that glared with glee at the chaos erupting below her. Green hair waved above her round head, and in her purple arms she carried a staff.

Darya hugged her arms around her waist, blinking against the dizziness that threatened to consume her. *The sea witch!* Darya had heard tales about the sea witch who dwelled in the dark crevices of the sea, an area inhospitable to nearly all life. The sea witch hadn't been seen in decades and many had assumed she'd left, content to enjoy her foul play elsewhere.

The sea witch was born a beautiful nymph with purple skin and green hair, a lovely combination that had swayed the sirens and mermaids to worship her beauty. In time, the power went to her head, and in her thirst for more power and worshippers, she played with dark magic and cast a spell to make her invincible. The spell worked, but it also transformed her into a monstrous creature. The sea witch then fled the Court of Nymphs. Even Darya's mother had a few stories about her treachery.

Now, the sea witch held a ball of darkness in her hands, and her lips curved in satisfaction as though she could taste the terror leaking from the sirens. Whispers whistled through the waters as she chanted:

A curse upon your palace
A curse upon your people
Find your essence lacking
Find your favorite drowning
Death be upon your door
Death be upon your family
Plague take your blood

Plague take your life

Bile burned the back of Darya's throat and a violent shudder shook her from head to tail, but she could not rip her eyes away from the sea witch. Her heart clenched. This evil had happened during her watch. She should have stood guard instead of chasing after the twinkling. If she hadn't been so curious, none of this would have happened. Although she did not know what power she had against the sea witch—darkness incarnate—she could have warned Mother and the other nymphs. Together, they could have done something . . .

"Udine!" Mother's sharp voice boomed across the still waters. "What is the meaning of this?"

Mother looked fierce as she floated in the midst of the nymphs with bare muscular arms, pink coral jewelry at her throat, and a halo of fine hair so light it often reflected the colors around her.

The sea witch's lips curled down into a frown. "Udine. Ah. That was my name. Before." A scowl darkened her face. "Sister, you dare ask the meaning of this when you know: it is revenge, plain and simple! Your court of worshippers will die. Then you'll have nothing, and you'll know my pain. I have spoken my curse, and it cannot be undone . . . but there is a remedy. Shall I share it with you?"

Darya jerked. Sister? Udine was Mother's sister?

"Share it," Mother said through gritted teeth, crossing her arms. Her tail waved back and forth in impatience.

Udine straightened her shoulders. "All I want is to be reinstated into the Court of Nymphs, but I cannot do so with this body. You will find a way to undo the spell on my body, and in exchange, I will undo my curse."

Mother's eyes flashed. "Dare you come to my court and threaten my people? You know we are the protectors of the sea creatures, a duty you were careless with. Your return causes chaos and death. There is no promise you can give that I will believe. Curses aren't meant to be broken; that is why they are curses, and if you cannot undo the dark magic that binds you, why do you believe my court will?"

"You are clever," Udine answered, seemingly unbothered by Mother's furious words. "You will find a way, for you and I both know there are many spells hidden in the great library. If the landwalkers in the great empire of Nomadia can use magic to benefit themselves, so can you. Unfortunately, in this condition, I cannot walk on land. You know what I speak of, Sister. I shall return in three days, and you will have an answer for me then, or these innocent lives you love shall perish."

Soft sobs disrupted the taut silence that had hung as Udine delivered her speech. With a twirl of tentacles, she disappeared into a cloud of black mist. All that was left of her presence were the dark stains on the palace. Darya struggled to breathe as she tried to make sense of what had just happened. More than anything, she wanted to sink into the sea floor and hide until the Court of Nymphs decided how to save the sirens.

4

ARACELI

The soft thump of a book sliding to the carpeted floor broke Araceli out of her daydream. She watched in dismay as the book tumbled off the shelf, pages turning as it opened, then landed facedown on the carpet, crushing parchment and ink in the rudely splayed position. Araceli's hand flew to her lips as her honey-brown eyes darted across the towering shelves of the library, hoping no one had seen her indiscretion.

Putting down the heavy books she carried, she slumped to her knees, hands shaking as she studied the damage. Her heart thudded so loudly in her chest, she was sure Mistress Vina—matron of the library—would appear at any moment, soundlessly as only elves moved, brow furrowed and mouth open to scold Araceli for daydreaming when she was meant to be working.

The book gave a sigh when she picked it up, and immediately she saw that the binding was cracked and the pages were wrinkled. She smoothed them out, one by one, before closing the book. She hoped the pressure of it closed would soothe the pages back into their natural state. Using her tail for balance, she rose to her feet, her hooves brushing the lush carpet of the Great Library of Zandria.

The library was a three-story palace in Nomadia, the capital city of the Nomadian Empire. It was named for its great benefactor, Zandria the Philosopher, who built it and brought the gift of knowledge to the people of Nomadia. The library had been kept for over a thousand years, and each year it grew bigger as it was filled with more works. Many came to study under the tutelage of teachers who called themselves Zandrinites, followers of Zandria.

It was an honor to work in the grand halls of the library, where every book was seen as more precious than gold. An impossible collection of dusty scrolls and thick books rose high above Araceli's head. The scent of vellum, parchment, ink, and candlelight was always with her. Even though the wide windows of the library let in as much daylight as possible, it was still necessary for the scribes to spend long hours during the evenings, transcribing words and sealing books in dark rooms.

With shaking fingers, Araceli returned to the stack of books and held up a list, scanning it for anything she'd missed. If her luck held, the mages she was delivering the books to would be the ones blamed for the damage. She knew it was wrong, but she could not afford to pay to fix the book.

Araceli was a blue-skinned faun, one of the oppressed races in the great empire of Nomadia. She was a rare breed, with two short horns on her head instead of the long, curling horns most fauns had. Her legs were long and bow-legged with hooves at the end, but instead of being covered from the waist down in hair, she was hairless. To add insult to injury, she also had a gold birthmark shaped like a star on her head.

In her twenty years as a keeper of the books, Araceli had seen prominent scholars, kings from across the sea, mages, and wizards who used the pages to gain access to their powers. Many had come, and many had gone with the glow of knowledge shining on their faces, a light in their eyes, and a bounce to their steps.

Araceli wondered what they saw in the words, but Mistress Vina told her it depended on what they saw in their mind's eyes and what they hoped for in their heart. From there, the words they read changed them.

Araceli had tried to find words that would enlighten her and give her purpose. Each day she read, wondering if one day her heart's desire would be written in ink, and she would find her purpose. But the books did not speak to her the way they spoke to others, and so she was lost, left to wander the endless rows of books, dusting, stacking, and pulling them out and returning them as visitors to the library called for them.

She knew the history of the seven kingdoms, now united under one empire, with each kingdom paying tribute to Nomadia, the greatest power in the known world. She knew about magical creatures, wild lands, the royal lineage, the towers where the mages trained, and the ships that sunk in the sea. But the knowledge in her mind seemed worthless, because she could not find her heart's desire.

She had a purpose . . . didn't she? Why couldn't she find out what it was? Maybe she was meant to serve at the great library all the days of her life, but she'd read of adventures in books, although without a purpose she was too afraid to step into the world to touch, taste, and seek out adventure for herself.

"Araceli," came a hiss.

Araceli's eyes widened.

"What are you doing?" Mistress Vina stood at the end of a row of shelves, and although they towered above her, reaching up to the concave dome of the ceiling, she cut an impressive figure.

Mistress Vina was the oldest elf in the capital and had spent her many years at the library. Although she was perhaps a hundred years old, her face was ageless; only her wise, forest-green eyes showed her age. She carried herself with grace, her long skirts swishing the floor and her delicate fingers curled around a book.

"I was . . . I . . ." Araceli stammered and went silent.

Mistress Vina glided across the carpet, beaded necklace chiming as she moved. She wore a gold and red wrap with slippers made from deerskin. Her arms were bare, and her light brown skin, just a shade darker than the vellum kept for the scribes, was the most beautiful color Araceli had ever seen. The smell of honey and lavender drifted from her, and her thick braid of black hair rested on one shoulder. Araceli was forced to look up at the elf, who towered a head over her.

"Araceli," Mistress Vina sighed. Her tone was always just above a whisper, but her eyes were kind. "What is taking so long? The mages are waiting and have requested a few more titles. I will need you to retrieve them while I search through the forbidden texts. Will you do this small task for me?"

It was not a request. "Of course."

Mistress Vina handed her a piece of parchment with hastily inked titles on it. Araceli read the list; most of the books were long, complicated wars and histories.

Tales of the Nine Realms

The Rise of the Nomadian Empire

Elements and Enchantments

"What topics are the mages studying?" she asked, curious about the last title.

"Does it matter? Mages have a never-ending desire to understand their abilities and how they came to be. Now, do not delay. We should not keep the mages waiting."

Mistress Vina's skirts rustled as she turned away. Araceli moved down the rows of books to the history section, lifting thick tome after thick tome, all the while shooting furtive glances around as though someone could read her thoughts. And she was sure some could; after all, magical abilities were common. Spells and enchantments to change minds, guide actions, and persuade others to do what you wanted could be purchased in the marketplace. There were laws regarding magic work, but there were the lawless who did things on their own terms.

Hugging the books to her chest to keep from dropping one again, Araceli hurried down the plush carpet, swallowing hard when she reached the door. Behind it, she knew, were the mages. They'd come to study in the great library and had requested these texts especially. Her duty was to slip inside with the books, place them on the table, and leave again without making eye contact or saying a word to the others. From there, they would make use of the books, and ring a bell if they needed further assistance.

Araceli often wondered who had come up with the bell

idea, for the library was a place of quiet study. Other than hushed voices, the soft sighs of paper turning, and the faint scratches of pen against parchment, there was nothing else. Occasionally the ringing of a bell could be heard, faint and sweet; a summoning. It blended into the library like the purr of a beast, the sound sinking in the carpet, much like Araceli's hooves.

Turning her attention back to the door, she took a deep breath, turned the knob, and entered. The conversation hushed as two appraising pairs of eyes rotated to her. Curiosity slammed into her as though the door had hit her in the head. Keeping her eyes on the floor, she forced herself to take each step, counting them as she went. Six steps into the room, place the books on the table, turn, and six steps out. That was it.

As she moved, something on the table also moved, catching her attention. Even though she should have kept her head bowed, shouldn't have looked, she did. Her gaze swept up from the polished floor to the carved oak of the table, the wood a swirl of browns. In the middle, a book lay. The cover was leather, but the edges of it were curled back, as if they'd been burned. Runes covered the book, shimmering as she looked at them. A sudden longing made her throat ache.

She drew in a sharp breath, not understanding but wanting, desperately wanting the knowledge that hung in that book, full of beauty and knowledge and perhaps the answer. The answer to what, she didn't know, but she knew suddenly that having that book and understanding its power would unlock the key to her destiny and purpose. Purpose. Hadn't she asked that question a hundred times: *What is my purpose?* There must be more to life than her days at the library and stolen evenings with her friend Shyrin.

"Ah." A deep chuckle brought her back to the present. "It appears our librarian is interested in ink magic."

Araceli jumped at the sound of the mage's voice. She moved forward and hastily dropped the books on the table. They landed with an audible thud that echoed across the room. She felt their stares crawl up her spine and spun, heart thumping so loud she thought they could hear it. A warm hand captured her wrist.

A squeak of fright left her lips, and she yanked, desperately trying to escape. She shouldn't have looked, shouldn't have come! Mistress Viola was always telling her that curiosity had its dangers, and she'd dared to look upon a forbidden text. For that was what the book was: an ancient, magical tome.

"Come. There is no need to fear. Many are curious about magic, there is no harm in that."

She looked into the sharp, marble-like eyes set deep in the face of the mage. He was one of the elykin—the race who ruled Nomadia—and she also assumed he was an ink mage. His chin was covered with a neat beard and mustache, and he wore black robes with an emerald crest, depicting his allegiance to the House of Emerald.

"Leave her be, you're frightening her," the other mage said. He was an elf, wore a dark robe, and was writing. The scratch of his quill on parchment was the only other sound in the room.

Araceli's thighs quivered, and she dropped her gaze, keenly aware of her inferior position.

"It is rare that one sees a blue faun," the mage went on,

"but no matter; go on your way. We will ring if we have need of you again."

Araceli practically ran out the door. Ring? No, she'd never enter again. She scurried around the corner and hid behind a shelf to catch her breath. How stupid she'd been to look at the book, as if she could aspire to learn ink magic.

5

ARACELI

When she calmed down enough to stop berating herself, Araceli turned her mind to her work. The spring rites would begin at sundown. Once she finished at the library, she'd have just enough time to slip out, change, and meet Shyrin.

The day passed, much the same way as it always did. Books were demanded, and she found them and put others away until the golden light gracing the gilded windows of the library faded, sending a rainbow of color dancing through the shelves. For a moment, a light breeze seemed to swirl in the library.

She breathed in, and something itched her nose, causing her to sneeze. Flicking her tail, she left, making her way into the shadowed hall that connected the library to the castle. The hall led up to a bridge that arched above the city. Although the bridge was enclosed in stone and glass, Araceli's breath caught in awe each time she saw the sprawling capital below her.

The city rose on a swell of land, the castle at its center with the library to the west of it and other great buildings connected with similar glass bridges. Visitors often said the capital looked like a sundial or the spine of a compass, with the castle in its center and everything else surrounding it. Below the bridges were the cobblestone roads, stunted buildings, and people.

Ages ago, before the empire was ruled by the elykin, the varied races of Nomadia were divided into seven kingdoms, each keeping to themselves. The fauns—including blue fauns—lived in forests, the fae never came down from their mountains, the elves were mysterious and aloof, the gnomes stayed underground, and the goblins and orcs warred against each other.

In the modern era, all races had come together under one sovereign authority: the Nomadian Empire. Indeed, it was common to see nearly all the races of Nomadia in the capital, working alongside each other, although their stations varied. Still, Araceli was aware of the stigmatism regarding blue fauns and the fact that her opportunities for advancement were limited.

During the years of war as the elykin formed the empire, kingdom after kingdom had seen the benefits of uniting under one sovereign empire. Even after the fauns made an alliance with the elykin, the blue fauns stood firm in their rebellion, uniting for one last battle, which they lost. Although a century had passed since then, blue fauns were still held in contempt. Araceli assumed most of her kin still lived out in the wild lands, which were full of thick forests with trees that hid the skies. But she was a hostage, taken from her family as tribute when she was born. It was customary for the empire to demand the children of those who had lost to keep them from rebelling again. Every year, dozens of children were taken in the name of peace and given jobs in the capital, where their parents could never reach them.

Araceli earned no wages, for she served the capital. When she turned five, she was sold to the library and brought up among the matrons, groomed to become an assistant there and serve the guests who came. The patrons did not mind that a blue-skinned faun acted as a servant, and the librarians had been kind to her, teaching her to read and write so she might better serve those who came to use the library.

Araceli had never known her parents. The word "family" was foreign to her. She'd only ever known the cold walls of the castle, the merry sounds of the water fountains, the kind voice of Mistress Vina, and the giggles of her friends.

The scent of fresh bread brought Araceli out of her thoughts as she trotted down the stairs to her room. The servants' quarter for the castle was underground. It consisted of a series of tiny rooms, each with enough space for a pallet and clothes and not much else. Children shared a large room, and the older ones often roomed together, squeezed into tiny spaces. Araceli, by some miraculous turn of luck, had managed to gain her own room. Likely because no one wanted to be associated with a blue faun.

After changing out of her library uniform into a clean dress—simple, but the only other garb she owned—Araceli brushed her rich brown hair and stepped out of her room, bumping into someone standing just outside her door.

"I'm sorry—" she started before two arms were thrown around her.

"Araceli!" the hugger exclaimed.

"Shyrin!" Araceli squeezed her friend back.

Shyrin was half a head taller than Araceli and willowy, with straight white hair cropped just below her furry ears. Although she was two years younger than Araceli and one of the elykin, the two had become friends after an incident in the library.

"What are you wearing?" Araceli stepped back, admiring Shyrin's dress.

Shyrin was studying to become a priestess and spent many days at the temple or reading the books of wisdom she was supposed to memorize. It was a career Shyrin had no choice in, and Araceli knew she'd rather do something else, but elykins were meant to rule and guide the empire with their wisdom. If Shyrin did not become a priestess, she would have to marry well to meet the stipulations of her kind, and Shyrin didn't want to be married off.

Elykins lived long lives and did not rush their kind into long-term relationships such as marriage. On average, they lived about two hundred years, sometimes more. They were the ones who had decided Nomadia should be ruled under one power, one throne, then conquered the smaller kingdoms until they all pledged allegiance to the elykin crown.

Shyrin twirled in the long white dress, which offset her light purple skin and almond-shaped golden eyes. She wiggled her ears, which were shaped like wings. Sometimes, she flapped them as though one day she'd lift off her feet and fly away. "Do you like it? I'm tired of wearing my priestess clothes and the veil. I know I'm supposed to be demure and modest, but tonight is a celebration." She took Araceli's hands. "Tonight, we can leave our stations behind and enjoy being alive!"

Araceli laughed, for Shyrin's enthusiasm was contagious. "I've been looking forward to this all day," she admitted.

"Come on." Shyrin grabbed her hand and dragged her through the halls. "I don't want to miss the lighting of the fire."

"Me either," Araceli agreed, but the grin slid from her face as she thought of the magical book and the mage's hand around her wrist. She tried to ignore the memory, but longing pulsed in her heart and her fingers tingled. What would happen if she opened a magical book and looked at the ink swirling within? Would she be able to read it? Would it reveal her heart's desire?

"Why are you so quiet, Araceli?" Shyrin laughed as they burst out of the castle into the crowded streets.

Araceli laced her fingers around Shyrin's and squeezed. "I'm just excited," she said.

"You just need to relax and enjoy yourself," Shyrin shouted, leading the way down the stone streets.

The capital was full of people during the spring rites. Music blared with a melody that made Araceli long to dance. Street venders called out their wares, walking up and down the road, selling savory foods, mouthwatering sweets, and drinks that made one feel as if they could fly.

Slowly, Araceli's excitement grew, and she was grateful for Shyrin, who would ensure they had whatever they desired.

The water fountains bubbled around them, and Araceli saw a gnome laugh so hard he fell inside, upending a tumbler of sparkling liquid with him. There was a shout, and an elf,

Jarome, fell in step with them, handing them each a pile of lemon drops.

Together, the three of them made their way to the center of the city, where the bonfire would be lit to celebrate the future of Nomadia. Arms linked around her friends, Araceli relaxed further as Shyrin ordered sweet, delicious drinks. They drank fizzy water and watched a circus perform where people leaped through rings of fire and a bear danced.

Clapping her hands, Araceli laughed as her vision blurred. Then the fire was lit, and she danced. First with Shyrin, then with Jarome, round and round in circles until she was dizzy and breathless. She took a break, sitting on a low stone wall while Shyrin brought more drinks. They took turns dancing and drinking.

Eventually, Jarome disappeared, leaving Araceli with Shyrin to watch the fireworks. Sparks of blue and red and gold lit up the night sky, then fell like diamonds in the velvet curtain of night.

Araceli squeezed Shyrin's hand, and she felt a part of everything, light and floating as if nothing could ever go wrong.

When they parted ways, Araceli couldn't wipe the stupid grin off her face as she stumbled back to the palace, giggling behind her hand. Her hoof snagged against carpet, and she reached out a hand to steady herself. The elixir was delicious and had gone straight to her head.

Shyrin was right. As soon as she relaxed, she enjoyed herself. Why couldn't it always be her lot to forget about thinking deeply and simply enjoy? Her life was simple, easy. All she had to do was fulfill requests at the library. Why should she worry? Her purpose would reveal itself one day.

6

NURIMIL

The white and pink petals of the trees were in bloom, brightening the landscape as Nurimil dismounted from his horse, Bern. "Let's hope this goes quickly," he murmured, patting Bern's neck, then turned to remove the heavy saddlebag.

Stone stairs, cracked with age and embedded with furry green moss, led up to the domed throne of the guild. White flags snapped in the breeze, each displaying the illustrious emblem of the Guild of Bounty Hunters: an arrow in flight, the edges of it exploding into red and orange flame.

"Nurimil." A dry voice rang out.

Nurimil gently swung the bag onto his back before turning to give the elf a nod. "Pilous."

Pilous's curious eyes lingered on the bag. "Another successful hunt?"

Nurimil grunted, unwilling to waste time talking to a

hunter who was often jealous of his accomplishments. "I wouldn't be here if I were unsuccessful."

Pilous gave a nervous laugh. "Don't tell me, you took down the Sky Screamer alone?"

"What if I did?" Nurimil blew out his breath, anxious to end the conversation.

"Now that is a feat." Pilous grinned. "I hear the people of the Maldive Cliffs worship the bird, and don't take too kindly to others bothering it."

Nurimil froze. He'd spend months dodging the mages who were furious he'd disturbed the Sky Screamer, but he'd assumed he'd left that all behind him. "Where did you hear that?"

Pilous rubbed his hands together. "I have my sources. If I were you, I'd be more careful and have someone watch my back."

Nurimil brushed past him, trying to keep the anger out of his movements. Pilous knew better than to threaten him, but Nurimil didn't know what the threat was based on, or whether it was serious. "You know I work best alone. Now, excuse me while I collect this bounty."

"Just because magic doesn't work on you doesn't mean you have to work alone!" Pilous shouted after him. "There are benefits to working together."

"In that case, take care of my horse, will you?" Nurimil called over his shoulder.

Pilous sputtered in disgust, and Nurimil quickened his pace. At the top of the stairs, he walked into the cool shadows of the building and made his way to the guild master's quarters.

The domed building was shaped like a six-pointed star. In

the center room, the guild master held audience, sent messages, and paid out his hunters, while the rest of the building provided shelter, storage, and weapons for the hunters.

Nurimil had accidentally fallen into bounty hunting and found it suited him well. Unlike most of the inhabitants of Nomadia, for some uncanny reason, magic did not work on him, and so he had appointed himself to hunt down magical beasts and steal their treasure. Still, he did not agree with everything the guild did. They served those willing to pay the highest price and were well rewarded for hunting down dangerous or magical beings.

Voices rang out from the guild master's quarters, and Nurimil had to duck under the entrance to step inside.

Daylight streamed in from the sky window, but even so, moon lamps were lit around the circular room. Unrolling his furs on the table by the door, Nurimil spread out the treasure and waited. Across from him at a table in the middle of the room sat the guild master, deep in conversation with Tyrina, a redheaded female elf.

She scowled across the room at Nurimil, and the guild master followed her gaze and waved.

"Nurimil! Just the person I wanted to see." He leaped to his feet, his paunchy stomach smacking against the table and sending a stack of gold sliding. The guild master ignored the coins as they clattered on the floor and instead waddled across the room. The gold rings on his stubby fingers and the heavy necklaces around his thick neck jangled as he moved.

Nurimil folded his hands and bowed his head in a sign of respect, although he had little for the guild master. "Hector, Tyrina," he greeted them.

Hector beamed, his round face shining in the daylight. He had gnome blood, mixed with perhaps dwarf or human; the result being, it was difficult to pinpoint his heritage. He was only around five feet tall, but made up for his short stature in both breadth and shrewd attitude.

"I have the bounty for the Sky Screamer eggs, still warm, and feathers as requested—"

"Bah!" Hector waved his hands. "I'm sure everything is in order, as it usually is. Your purse for completing that mission is waiting, but I have another task to discuss with you." He waggled his thick eyebrows. "This is a matter of great secrecy and urgency, coming from a wizard."

Nurimil folded his arms, waiting. Hector was dramatic, and if Nurimil encouraged him, it would take twice as long to hear about the task.

"I know you work alone, but this time Tyrina would be a great asset for you."

Nurimil frowned, and Hector slapped a hand over his heart. "Hear me out before you make a decision." Waving Tyrina over, he lowered his voice. The joviality faded from his face as he snapped his fingers. "Listen well and listen close. The wizard is in search of a magical creature. It is believed she will come ashore soon, and will likely be picked up by the giants in Dustania."

Nurimil stiffened.

"You are to go to Dustania and do whatever it takes to retrieve the creature and escort her to the wizard."

"What kind of magical creature?" Nurimil asked. "You know I will not take another beast to their death."

"Yes, yes." Hector scowled. "The wizard doesn't want her

for death. Now, I'm not quite sure what she'll look like, but she'll come from the sea."

"Does she have a name? Most of the legendary sea creatures have a name, but if she's from the waters, transport will be a problem."

Tyrina spoke up, her voice low and throaty. "There's a river that runs alongside Dustania. That road can be used to transport a water creature."

"If this is a squid or whale or some other vicious water predator, it will be impossible," Nurimil countered. "What kind of magic does the wizard need? Wouldn't it be more reasonable to take the magic and deliver it to the wizard?"

Hector put his hands on his meaty hips. "Just do as you're told without arguing. You don't need the details, just know that it's a water creature."

"I don't go to battle a magical creature ill prepared," Nurimil replied coldly, glaring down his nose at Hector.

"I'm warning you." Hector wagged his finger. "The wizard is paying a hefty price for this creature. It will benefit you and the entire guild. You're the best hunter we have, so you'll go without complaint, or I'll put a bounty on your head."

Nurimil's eyes narrowed, and his irritation grew. "You wouldn't dare. Like you said, I'm the best there is. Who would you turn to for your next task?"

Hector grinned, but it was mean and hard. "Echnid. Everyone is afraid of her."

A cold shiver went through Nurimil, for he knew her. She was a she-viper, a giant woman, half human, half snake, and known for her hot temper. Unlike him, she did not hunt magical beasts only, but found the living, returned slaves to their masters, found runaway women and took them back, and, rumor was, she often fought and killed thieves. Still, it was unusually cruel for Hector to turn on him. "What is the wizard offering you?"

"Wouldn't you like to know?" Hector leered. "Now go, collect your purse, and get on the road to Dustania before I change my mind."

"My horse needs to rest," Nurimil protested. He'd been looking forward to a night relaxing after the long, hard road, perhaps even with a mug of ale before he pulled his boots off and slept soundly, without the worry of anyone sneaking up on him to steal his precious bounty. It had happened more than once, and he'd learned to be cautious and protective as he traveled. Pilous had a point. If he traveled with another hunter, they could take turns keeping watch. But then he'd have to split the wealth, and Nurimil liked his money.

"One more question. Where does this wizard dwell?"

"Go!" Hector pointed to the door. "Once you have the water creature, bring her here and I will personally take care of the delivery."

Nurimil turned to leave, and when Tyrina made a move to come with him, he waved her away. There was something off, something wrong about the task, and he couldn't quite put a finger on it. He'd received the usual vague information from Hector, the usual temper when he asked questions, and the usual looming threat of being hunted. So why did he feel so on edge all of a sudden?

Musing to himself, he went to the money keepers for his fat purse of gold and silver coins. One of the bankers tried to persuade him to store his money in the treasury, but he moved on. The guild liked to keep the hunters' money, then usually made it difficult to access. Nurimil had his own hiding spots for his gains, and one day, when he retired, he'd use them for something.

He was still deep in thought as he walked toward the entrance, aware that there were more guards than usual out. A couple of men circled, glaring at him when he passed. It wasn't until he reached the entrance that he realized they were following him. A glint of a blade was all he needed to see, and Nurimil ran, dashing down the steps to where he'd left his horse.

7

DARYA

Three days later, Darya floated in the marble white halls outside the doors of the Court of Nymphs. She ran her fingers over the sea stones in her palm, the motion intended to soothe her worries, but today it wasn't helpful. She whirled, swallowing hard, her mind dancing with ideas of what they'd do to her. Whispers drifted from the ornamental doors crafted of coral and seaweed. The Court of Nymphs was perched on the flattened top of a mountain, above the valley where the palace of the sirens sat. There, darkness lingered, a scar in the sea's beauty and a reminder of what she'd done.

Darya turned her back to it, unable to look at the destruction her carelessness had caused. She admitted to herself that she had seen a hint of shadows below, but the twinkling from above had been more exciting. Her swim and discovery of the mermaids—who had returned home, effectively ending the potential alliance between sirens and mermaids—had been her downfall. If only she'd been where she was supposed to be.

"Darya," a voice hissed.

Darya stilled. Klarya.

Klarya swam up and hovered in front of her, arms crossed, face darkened into a scowl. Around her neck an emerald glittered, a prize for her commitment and faithfulness to the Court of Nymphs. "I know what you did. I saw you."

Darya's eyes went hard and a bolt of fury shot through her. Sometimes she wanted to yank the necklace from Klarya's throat or hurl a ball of water magic at her, just to see the haughty look wiped off her perfect face. "I don't know what you're talking about," Darya retorted.

"You do," Klarya challenged. "I was appointed to lead the mermaids to the palace, and you were supposed to stand guard, to ensure nothing bad happened. Instead, I saw you spying on me. Both honors were equally great, we were both protecting people, civilizations under our rule, and now you've ruined everything."

"Me?" The shriek burst out of Darya's throat, although Klarya's words were true. "Who can stand against the power of a sea witch? Even if I was where I was supposed to be, we might not have been able to stop her."

"That's not true." Klarya shook her head. "We are powerful together, and you know this to be true. If you had sounded the alarm, we might have been able to prevent the curse. It's been three days. The waters are tainted, and the sirens are ill, cursed with a plague. This isn't the first time your careless actions have caused distress to others. If you want to remain in the Court of Nymphs, you'll have to stop thinking of yourself and learn how to sacrifice so others may live."

Bile burned the back of Darya's throat and tears pricked at her eyes. Her gut reaction was to punch Klarya for having the audacity to say such cruel words, and yet they were true. Would it be better for the nymphs is she just left? No. If she could fix her mistake, prove to the Court of Nymphs that she was worthy to preside over the mortal sea dwellers and protect them, they'd welcome her. This was only a momentary setback.

Darya met Klarya's dark gaze. "I'm going to try," she said.

"Do more than try." Klarya snapped her fingers. "Decide and make it happen, none of this 'trying' and 'maybe' and weak-willedness. Darya, if you want to be a great and powerful nymph, you have to be decisive, you have to do whatever it takes. Trying is not enough."

"Are you done?" Darya demanded through clenched teeth. "I hear you, Klarya."

"Good." Klarya moved away. "I hope it sinks in this time."

Darya pressed herself against the doors, trying not to think of what might happen. Snatches of conversation drifted to her ears.

". . . there is a way, although it contradicts the ways of the nymphs."

"Dare you make such a suggestion? To walk among them is not natural . . ."

"No, but it may present a solution to our problem . . ."

A pause followed, and the voice dropped lower, inaudible to Darya's listening ears. She drew back and waited while her sisters gathered in the hall, whispering behind their shells but staying away from her. Although none of them had been invited to the council, they would hear Darya's sentencing as an example to them all of what would happen should they fail to execute their duties. The tension in the hall thickened until Darya didn't think she could stand it a moment longer, and then the doors swung open.

Warm water surged out. "Enter, Nymphs." Mother's powerful voice welcomed them inside.

Darya shivered as she swam forward, determined to not let the elders see her trepidation. The unfairness of her situation crossed her mind, but those judging her were immortal, powerful nymphs who did not offer forgiveness for errant behavior like mortals. As a nymph, Darya was expected to know better. Heart pounding, she swam to the center of the dome-shaped room.

When she was young, she'd thought the council chambers beautiful and looked forward to her summons to court, a place where the elders whispered in secret, determining the fate of the sirens and other creatures who dwelled in their domain. Now the pearl arches, garnished with seaweed and coral, seemed to frown at her. Five thrones curved toward her, made of twisted barnacles and jewel-encrusted rock. Each throne represented one of the elders, who each focused on a particular attribute related to sea life: protection, health, food, creatures, and ecosystem.

Darya's sisters swam in behind her and each took a seat. The smaller thrones were shells, one for each of the lesser nymphs who would eventually leave to preside over other areas of the vast sea, though they had to prove themselves first. Darya perched on a shell. A river of water pooled and swirled around her, creating a harmonious sound and giving the court a sense of tranquility.

Mother cleared her throat. "This court has gathered to discuss the threat of Udine and how we will answer her demands. We have debated long and hard, for we cannot take her threats lightly, nor do we possess the power to undo a curse wrought by dark magic. Our discussion has led us to the conclusion that we must work together to prevent further damage from being unleashed on the sea. Our waters are tainted, and the curse continues to spread. We can endure, but the question is, for how long? How long until Udine returns with yet another threat? Therefore, we have determined to do three things. The first is to combine our powers to slow the poison for as long as possible. The second is to find an island and move our people there. These are only temporary solutions, and will only last for a short amount of time, or until Udine sees through our ploy, which is why we must use the magic of the landwalkers. The closest shore to us is the empire of Nomadia, and within it is a great library where books of spells are kept. If we are to overcome this threat, we need their magic remedies. I want to point out that although this is risky, it is not our only hope. We have discussed other ways to bring Udine to submission, but the power of the landwalkers is great, and there is a benefit to all of us if we can gain their knowledge and magic. We have elected to send Darya on this quest, for although she was distracted standing guard, Udine's power is strong, and I will not place all the blame on Darya's shoulders. However, in the past, Darya has shown herself to be curious, flighty, and easily distracted. This quest is an opportunity for her to prove herself, to show us she is ready to take on the task of protecting our life, our people, and our power."

Air and water whooshed out of Darya's gills as she listened to Mother's words. Her mouth opened and closed as protests rose and died in her throat. She knew better than to cross Mother while court was in session, but how could they expect her, a water nymph, to traverse the wide sea to join the landwalkers? Of course, the physical transformation would take some getting used to. Whenever mermaids, sirens, or nymphs reached land, their appearance shifted. Instead of their powerful tails, they walked on two legs like the land-walkers. Mermaids and sirens appeared more like mortals, but nymphs had a greater control over their appearance and could cover their bodies with an armor of scales to hide their nakedness.

Darya had been to the surface of the water and visited the lonely islands scattered in the middle of the sea. Walking on land was strange, and required balance and forethought. She still preferred the waters, but she did not mind the land. Still, what was Mother thinking, sending her to the empire, a vast land with many magical people and strangers she knew nothing about—not their customs, nor their language? How would she find the great library?

Mother was still speaking, but Darya had tuned her out, lost in a fog of numbness, because deep down inside, she realized she had no choice. This wasn't a chance for her to become a hero and save the sirens. Mother had said so herself: they would work on finding another solution while she was gone. No, this was punishment, a chance for them to get rid of her. Just like Klarya had said earlier, Darya had to show them she was worthy, that she was a powerful nymph who could be a protector of the people. She had to show them she was entitled to her own realm.

Swallowing hard, she lifted her chin and swam off the shell. She would not let them see how hurt she was by their words. Words meant nothing to them, only actions. "I accept," she said. "I will go to the realm of the landwalkers and find a magical remedy to save our people."

8

DARYA

"I did not expect you to agree so quickly," Mother said.

Darya stretched out on one of the shells, mind racing as she considered what she needed for her journey, while Mother floated in front of her, arms crossed.

"I have no choice." Darya could not meet her gaze, knowing what she'd see there.

Mother sighed. "For what it's worth, I hope you succeed and return. We could use the wisdom of Nomadia to guide us in our future endeavors."

"I understand," Darya said, the lie burning her lips. She just wanted the conversation to end. It was enough knowing the court did not want her around, and delaying the journey only added to her frustration.

"You don't have to travel on two legs like the landwalkers; I assume many waters connect to the great library. Once you arrive, find a water route and stick to it, and be careful. Just like here in the seas, you will have to choose between friend and enemy, and choose wisely. And don't forget, regardless of where you go and whatever form you take, great power resides within you. Use it, just as you have here. To succeed, you'll need to use your wits, your judgement, and stay vigilant. As you know, carelessness is our number one enemy. Remember what happened here as you journey forth."

Mother neared as she spoke, reaching a finger under Darya's chin to draw her gaze up. Darya tried not to sulk as she met Mother's penetrating eyes. "Always remember, your future is up to you and your choices, Darya. I see great potential in you, but great potential can only be realized if you put forth effort and focus. I hope you'll find what resonates with you during your quest."

Darya blinked, then clasped her mother's hand. "I will make you proud," she vowed.

A sad smile softened Mother's severe features. "Don't make me proud. Find what resonates with you, and everything else will fall into place."

Darya sighed. "Is it time for me to go?"

"Do you want to say goodbye to your sisters?"

Darya chewed her lower lip, then shook her head. "No. I'm ready to go now."

"If you wish it. If you meet Udine or any of her creatures as you travel, the best thing to do is swim away as fast as you can."

Darya nodded, still numb at how rapidly her future had changed. Her mind went to the sirens and how they were faring in their tarnished palace. She thought of Talius. She'd miss him and their playful banter, but it was better if she simply left, let them think what they would of her, and when she returned, changed and glorious, they'd gather round to hear her tale of might and courage.

Mother swam with Darya away from the hall of the nymphs, both moving with slow and steady strokes as they wove through the dark waters like twins, every so often moving upward toward the surface. When at last they broke it, a halo of pale moonlight stretched across the sea, and the peaceful lull of waves sent a pang of sorrow through Darya's heart.

"Here is where I leave you," Mother announced. "You'll need to use all your senses, but pay attention to smell in particular. The scent of land is earthy and spicy, a blend of exotic flavors. If you smell something different from water, head toward it. Nomadia lies west of us, so follow the path of moonlight and the setting sun, but be careful of wearing yourself out."

"I know. I will be careful," Darya said, keeping her other remarks under her tongue.

"Go with grace." Mother lifted her hands and made the symbol of the nymphs.

Darya waved and dove.

She sank beneath the silky smooth waters, hands by her side, and with a flick of her tail shot through the waters like a whirlwind. She used her arms when needed, but her powerful tail kept her moving, soaring. She fled, all her fear and anger and frustration pouring out of her, and she let it go, beating her anger into the water. Fish scattered before her. A lone turtle moved away as fast as it could, and a shark bolted in the other direction. Jaw tight, Darya used the webbing between her fingers to speed her journey and fought onward in a silent battle, just her and the waves.

Who was she kidding? She wanted to be part of the Court of Nymphs and rise to a position of reverence where others looked up to her, as they did to Mother, but the competition was too fierce. If only Klarya was out of the way. But the court still saw her as Darya, the one who ruined everything. Well. She'd show them.

She swam until her anger faded into determination, and kept on swimming as the first rays of daylight filtered through to the translucent kingdom. Darya slowed down, taking in the life that teemed around her. She swam close to the surface, and smaller creatures dove out of her way, frightened by her large shadow moving over them. A coral reef spread below her, making the blue waves shimmer with white foam, green seaweed, and pink hues. Tiny ice blue and yellow sea horses floated by, and then she saw the dome top of a transparent jelly fish. She dove lower, out of its way, her fingers gliding over the velvet back of a stingray as she did. It made her shiver as she went past, but as she watched the vivid life under the sea, a sort of peace came over her. Her frantic pace slowed, but she did not stop, for how could she allow herself bliss when the sirens lay under a curse?

The day passed, and when a crimson sunset cast its glory over the waves, Darya swam in earnest again, leaving mile after mile behind. The waves of the sea were thicker now, almost as though a film covered them, and the flavor of salt and something else hung in the air. Darya kept going, although her arms were growing weary, and she knew she should find a safe place to rest. As soon as the sun came up, she decided she'd find a crevice to hide, rest, eat, and let her strength return.

The sea changed as her journey lengthened. She could not quite explain how, exactly, but she felt it, a shifting in the waters. The waters gathered around Darya like invisible fingers and pulled her into the depths, drawing her along as though it wished to show her something. A current! Of course, she'd played in currents in her youth. She and her sisters had loved to slide into whirlpools of currents, where all control ceased. They had even created their own vortexes using their water magic until Mother put a stop to it, saying they would scare the sea life with their antics. A smile came to Darya's face at the memory. She'd been young and mischievous back then, unaware of her future. And now this? She closed her eyes, slowed, and let the current drag her along.

The sea life flew by on either side in a burst of color. A school of fish swam with her, sometimes leaping out of the water and sending crystalline drops to glisten in the beams from the sun. The crystals reminded Darya of the sea stones and gems she enjoyed collecting and creating jewelry out of. Darya realized how alone she was, out in the vast sea, and for a moment wondered if the current was carrying her in the right direction. What if she became lost and could not find her way back home?

She surfaced then, breaking out of the current to see where she was. The sun was setting on the horizon, and the water reflected the deep orange color. Darya swam toward the streaks of orange, recalling Mother's advice. Suddenly, something wrapped around her waist and squeezed.

Darya's hands dropped to her waist and gripped the thick

body of a sea serpent. Below her, a nest of sea serpents uncurled and slithered through the waters. One had already wrapped a tail around her waist, and the others were drawing near, their pink tongues flickering in and out and golden eyes studying their next meal. Darya knew the habits of predators in the sea; they waited for their food to reach a vulnerable position, and alone she was most vulnerable.

Bringing her elbow up, she drove it into the thick body of the snake. It hissed and shook, but did not let go. The others drew near, flat heads leering, and then one pounced, its sharp teeth sinking into her tail.

Darya's hands shot out and power rolled in her belly. A bubble of water swelled. She waited until it grew and pulsed, ready to burst, before she let go. Water torpedoed out of her hands and blasted into the snakes, bowling them over with a mighty sound like the clap of thunder. They were flung away from her, spinning and twisting into knots.

Without waiting to see what they would do next, Darya spun and twisted the body of the snake squeezing her waist until the creature broke its hold with a sharp hiss. Keeping hold of its tail, she rose to the surface and swung it over her head until she gained enough momentum and let go.

The snake sailed high above the waters before it plopped with a splash and sank into the depths. With a growl, Darya resumed her journey, but an itching, prickling sensation warned her something was wrong. Glancing back, a tiny trickle of red followed her. The bite on her tail was bleeding.

Drawing herself up to the surface, she looked around and noted two or three fins circling her and groaned. Sharks. She didn't want to fight them, but she'd already gone too long without resting and refreshing her power. She needed to find a place to hide and eat before she wearied herself further. The power she used to scare away the snakes had already drained her. It was best to put her head down and swim; perhaps they would leave her alone. Diving again, she swam as the shadows lengthened and an inky darkness consumed the sea.

9

NURIMIL

Nurimil ran, grateful to see that Bern was still tied up where he'd left him. Pilous had been too lazy to remove the saddle and rub him down, which would have been irritating had Nurimil not been in a hurry.

Bern snorted, tossing his head, likely expecting a bag of oats and a rubdown in the barn.

"Sorry, Bern," Nurimil muttered as two men dressed in all black ran toward him.

One threw a dagger, and Nurimil ducked. It whistled over his head and thudded into a nearby tree, shaking loose a rain of pink petals. One landed in his mouth, and Nurimil spit it out and increased his speed.

"Stop, in the name of the king!" one of the men shouted.

Out of the corner of his eye, Nurimil saw that some of the bounty hunters were peeking out from the guild windows, but Nurimil could not expect any help from them. Curious to see what was happening, they'd watch, but unless coin could be gained for assistance, they would just continue to drink and watch as though it were a game.

Nurimil leaped into the saddle. "I'm a bounty hunter of the guild," he shouted to his pursuers. "I have no quarrel with you."

"You do now," one shouted. "You stole from the Sky Screamer, an act that is forbidden in our realm. You must stand trial before the warden for insulting our people."

Curses on this day. Really? This?

He'd known the Sky Screamer was an important cultural beast for the inhabitants of the Maldive Cliffs, but he'd done nothing more than steal two eggs and ten feathers. The Sky Screamer still lived, but apparently he'd insulted the people enough to be hunted all the way to the guild. Something wasn't right.

"Take it up with the guild," he yelled over his shoulder, spurring Bern into a gallop.

He didn't need this. The guild acted as the middleman, collecting the coin from the individual or group who had put up the bounty and paying it out to the hunter. Nurimil preferred to stay out of the business aspects, as long as he got paid. This wasn't the first time he'd been chased down by angry people, though it was the first time they'd come to the guild. Hector would sort it out. He always did.

However, he was lucky that he had a horse while his pursuers were on foot. Nurimil let Bern run until the road curved away and the guild was lost from sight. Slowing, he looked back, and was relieved to see he hadn't been followed. Not far down the road was an inn he could rest at, although he debated whether he should. If they followed him, they'd likely find him there. It would be wiser to turn off the beaten path and camp in the wild.

Weighing the pros and cons of his situation, Nurimil's weariness won out at last. He took a dirt trail, following it into a crevice between two mountains. The tavern he was heading toward was where many hunters rested, usually after they'd turned in their wares and had a fat purse of coin to spend. Aside from mouthwatering food, it had the best ale and wine for miles, and women that would come down from their rooms, eager to charm the hunters and steal their coin. Nurimil had fallen prey to their charms more than once. The memory made his lips twist. Not tonight, though; he wanted to sleep.

The inn was quiet, and he left Bern in the stables to be rubbed down and fed. Inside, he took a table and sat back to enjoy a meal. Later, if there was time, he'd take a long hot bath to wash away the grime from the road. Low voices rolled through the room and he saw a few familiar faces. Tipping his hat to them, he ate heartily and washed down his meal with a hunk of bread and a mug of ale. His shoulders relaxed as he mulled over his situation.

The Maldivites who were angry at him would eventually give up. All he had to do was stay one step ahead of them. Frowning, he rolled out his map, using one of his daggers to hold it in place. Dustania was a fair distance away, even on horseback, and the most direct route was through Iscaria, a desert land where sand tribes and lizard people lived. It was hot and barren—not a place he wanted to travel through, though the constantly shifting sand would throw anyone off his track.

Scratching at the stubble on his chin, he again considered

Hector's request. Aside from the usual limited information, there was something off about it, but he couldn't figure out what. Hector had seemed almost frantic. Had the wizard threatened him? And then there was the part about sending Tyrina with him, as though Hector didn't trust him to complete the task. The more Nurimil thought about it, the more he didn't like it. Which left him with the question: Should he even bother going to Dustania? If nothing else, he could go there to gather information and leave without collecting the water creature if he didn't like what he found.

He was still mulling things over when someone kicked out the chair across from him and sat down. Nurimil grunted, lifting his head to scowl at whoever had the audacity to join him. His face relaxed into a grin when he met the gaze of his old friend.

"Silas, what are you doing here?"

Silas settled his bulk on the chair across from Nurimil and leaned forward, a frown on his grim face. He was a big man, and usually did grunt work for the guild. He and Nurimil had an easy relationship, trading stories and enjoying ale at the tavern. Silas collected old scrolls from across the empire and enjoyed sharing his knowledge, although he had no desire to travel or hunt on his own. He worked for the guild, and the guild rewarded him handsomely. No one cheated the guild when Silas was around to take them to task.

"I came as soon as I could," Silas said, slapping a piece of paper down on the table.

Nurimil glanced at it, intending to chuckle until cold dread crept up his throat. "What is this?" he demanded, snatching the paper up.

"I came to warn you," Silas went on. "Hector had these drawn up as soon as you left."

Anger surged through Nurimil, and he ground his teeth, but stopped short of ripping up the paper. "Why? I work for him. I just agreed to take on another task for him!"

"There were hunters tracking you," Silas explained. "They came to complain about your actions against their people. According to them, you insulted their culture and laws. They want revenge, so they put a purse on your head. You know how Hector likes money . . ."

Nurimil's jaw worked as he stared at the likeness of his face on the paper. That's all it took—a few people complained, and now he'd be hunted like an outlaw. He wanted to punch the table, no, even better, he wanted to pick up his chair and hurl it across the wall. "Five hundred gold coins?" He had to keep from shouting.

Silas gave him a sad nod. "I know it's not fair, but you have to go. Now. Before anyone finds out. Tomorrow, every hunter in the guild will have one of these."

Nurimil nodded, half standing. "Silas, I appreciate this. You'd better go too, before anyone finds out you warned me."

Silas nodded. "Good luck, Nurimil."

Nurimil took a deep breath. He'd need it. After leaving a few coins on the table, he headed toward the stables, his mind reeling with how quickly things had changed.

10

ARACELI

Araceli ducked into the shadows of the castle and closed the door softly behind her. The muted sound of merriment still rang in the distance, and she blinked against the darkness, trying to get rid of the fireworks that danced in front of her each time she closed her eyes. Taking a step, she flicked her tail for balance as she walked, one hand against the wall, following the way from memory. It wasn't until the light appeared, floating in front of her like the lights from the festival, that she realized she'd headed to the glass bridge instead of her room.

Pressing her hand to her mouth to stifle a giggle, she edged forward, unable to keep her hooves completely silent. Yellow and white orbs flickered as she passed until she reached the bridge, silent and lonely. The view from there was spectacular, and she drew in a sigh as a swell expanded against her heart. Below, people danced in the street, torchlight making their shadows leap and grow, and above, the sky stretched out like the wings of a great bird, peppered with a quilt of incandescent stars.

Araceli pressed her hand against the glass, her heart twisting as she watched. All was calm, bright, and beautiful. It had been a perfect night. A hint of sugar still lay against her tongue and the sweetness of the elixir tingled in her throat. Then why, oh why, was she drawn back to the library? The longing tugged at her, a scratch she could not itch enough to gain relief from, and she went, hips swaying and tail swinging as she walked across the bridge toward the library.

The moon lamps were lit, glowing a pearly white that illuminated each corner of the shadowed building. By speaking a word, one could turn them on and off, but Araceli didn't know the word. Moon lamps were one of the many technological inventions the elykin had brought to the empire of Nomadia. They were beautiful creations and shone with a brightness similar to the twin moons.

The main doors of the library were locked up at night, except for a side door, which remained unlocked for those who studied long into the night. Tonight though, given the hour, Araceli doubted anyone was around. She assumed everyone had gone to the festival and enjoyed it as much as she had. Why would anyone spend time in the depths of the library, sitting in the dark and reading, when they could sink into mindless merriment?

The scent of parchment seemed odd after the wild, tangy delights of the festival, and yet it also felt like home as Araceli's hooves sank into the rich carpet. She hesitated only a moment before striding with purpose to the room the mages had occupied earlier.

Her fingers closed on the ornamental door handle, and she closed her eyes briefly. Now was the moment to draw back and return to her sleeping quarters. She'd never dared to violate the secrecy of the library after hours, so why was she compelled to do so now? Her heart thumped so loudly, she was sure if anyone else were there, they'd be able to hear it. Still, curiosity overcame her trepidation, and she pushed open the door and stepped inside.

It was a windowless room—she'd forgotten about that—and she walked into utter darkness. The door swung shut behind her with a soft hiss, and that's when she sensed it. She wasn't alone. Araceli whirled, her tail smacking into something solid and warm. Hands grabbed her arms and yanked them behind her back, forcing her chest out. A muffled cry left her lips, and she reared back, preparing to headbutt them with her horns. Whoever held her was prepared for the move and ducked out of the way. Araceli's head smacked into nothing, and she lost her balance, tipped backward, and crashed to the floor.

The hands let her fall, and when she tried to rise, something struck her shoulders, forcing her back down. Her thoughts whirled. She hadn't learned to fight, hadn't needed to, and now this? What should she do? She wanted to resist and run away, frightened of being punished for entering the library after hours. She lashed out with her hooves.

Once again, her attacker anticipated her movements. Suddenly, something hard pressed against her throat. A blade.

Araceli stilled, but couldn't help the soft whimper that came from her lips.

"That's better," the deep male voice said. "Feisty, which is good. I had hoped to lure you back here tonight, not to fight, but because I have a task for you."

That voice. It was the mage from earlier, the one who'd touched her and looked at her with curiosity.

"A task?" Araceli repeated stupidly. She was naught but a lowly librarian; why would he have a task for her?

"If you care to listen." His voice was dangerous with the hint of a growl to it. Suddenly the blade was gone, but Araceli dared not move.

"I will listen," she whispered, because she didn't have a choice. In fact, she thought herself lucky he'd used a blade, and not magic, against her. She'd never given much thought to buying a magical rune to protect her from mages, but now, lifting a tentative hand to stroke her neck, she thought it might be wise to save and buy one.

"Good." The mage snapped his fingers, and a bluish light began to glow from his staff. Araceli blinked against its brilliance. He sheathed his knife and stepped back. She wondered if he would blast her with magic if she kicked out again and dashed toward the door, then decided it was better to wait and listen. She was only a civilian, and not trained in anything other than the simple art of carrying multiple stacks of books at once.

As the light haunted the room, Araceli realized her dress was twisted around her thighs. She sat up quickly, pushing the dress back down, and glanced at the mage. He was staring at her face and, suddenly embarrassed, she looked away from those deep-set eyes. She wondered if he was a mind reader too.

"Come," the mage said abruptly, moving to the table where the book still lay.

Araceli drew in a sharp breath as she stared at it, and again that itching sensation danced across her fingers. She wanted it, wanted to touch it, to keep it, to open the book and find the words hidden in those pages. A lump swelled in her throat, and she took a step forward as though the very book called to her.

"I thought as much." Now the mage's tone was seeped with wonder. "The book calls to you, but why? Do you know what this is?"

Araceli shook her head. Of course she didn't know. It was only a book, but she was never allowed to touch the magical books. Those, Mistress Vina retrieved herself from a room where the books were stored under lock and key and magical wards to prevent thieves. Not that anyone would dare to steal from the empire.

"It's a book of ancient spells for ink mages. A dangerous book should it fall into the wrong hands, and yet, no one will suspect if a lowly librarian, a blue faun no less, takes such a book and hides it."

Heart pounding, Araceli whipped around, wondering if she'd heard correctly. Her? She should have been insulted by the slur hidden in his words and yet, no, he wasn't suggesting what she thought he was. Was he?

"I can't take the book," her words stumbled over each other in their haste to escape her mouth. "I can't . . ."

"Can't?" the mage arched an eyebrow and his fingers tightened around his staff. "This is not an order, it is a known fact. Where I go, I cannot take this tome, for it might fall into the wrong hands—the hands of those who would use it for mischief. No, you will take this book and keep it hidden until my return. Should my errand go well, it will be out of your hands within a few months. It is not much to ask."

Araceli stared at him, her embarrassment gone. "But you have magic," she breathed, "and this is the great library. You can have it locked in the crypt with other magical books, guarded by magical wards. You can put a spell on it, and no one will be able to break it." She was grasping now because she knew nothing of magic, but he was a mage. He could do all of those things, she assumed. She glanced at the book again, and it seemed to call to her, to awaken a song in her heart. A desire.

"Perhaps I could, but that is not the way. Those who pursue me would look here to find the book, as they should. Like you said, this is the great library. But I do not want to do something expected. The best way to trick enemies is to do something unexpected. So, take the book, hide it, and say nothing of this to anyone, or I shall curse your tongue. It is a simple task. Will you do it?"

Araceli edged away, skin prickling under the determined stare of the mage. He'd asked as if she had a choice, but there wasn't really a choice, was there? He expected her to do as he said without question. She knew nothing of his enemy, but it sounded so storylike and far away. The elykin ruled the empire. No one stood against them. If there were disturbances or grievances, they were quashed with blood and broken bones.

What harm would come to her from hiding a book? It would go in her room, under her pillow or pallet, and no one would know. Just for a few months, until the mage returned. "I will take it," she heard herself saying as her eyes glided to the book.

"Good." The mage leaned his staff against the table. Producing a blue cloth, he wrapped the book tenderly in it, then crossed the room to stand in front of Araceli.

She wanted to step back, away from his presence, which filled up the room with the breath of magic. He held out the tome. "Take good care of it. I will return soon."

Araceli took it, surprised to find that, for such an enormous book, it was much lighter than she'd expected.

Without another word, the mage snapped his fingers. The friendly blue light went out and the door to the room clicked shut. Araceli was left alone in the darkness, holding a forbidden, magical book.

11

ARACELI

Back in her room, Araceli closed the door and leaned heavily on it, book squeezed to her chest, eyes closed as she breathed in and out, sober again. The events of the night had taken a turn, and she didn't know whether to be frightened or exhilarated. She had a forbidden book, a magical book! Oh, if Mistress Vina knew, she'd snatch it from under her nose. But the mage had chosen her, Araceli, a blue faun, to hide the book for him. The itching grew in her fingers, and she stumbled across the tiny room, tripping over a chair before she found the light.

Holding the candle in one hand, she sat down on the pallet, hooves stretched out in front of her, back against the wall. Swallowing hard, she balanced the candle beside her and laid the book flat in her lap. Alarm bells rang in her head as she reached for the covering and unwrapped the blue cloth. Closing her eyes, she waited for something, anything, to happen. When she wasn't struck dead on the spot, she dared to open her eyes and look.

The binding of the book was an earthy brown leather and covered with symbols. At first she thought they were mere drawings made with ink. As her fingers brushed over them, she realized they were carvings embedded in the leather. A hint of gold glistened. She gasped. Where she touched the letters, they had come alive, changing from black to gold. A light shone out, brighter than the candle, illuminating the bare, dusty room.

Mouth open, Araceli stared, hoping no one would see the odd light under her door and come to investigate. The symbols reflected off the walls, and once her initial panic died away, she stuck her tongue in her cheek, debating. The mage had only requested that she hide the book; he hadn't warned her about touching or reading it.

She closed her eyes again, giving reason a chance to over-rule her curiosity, but her fingers were already moving. Eyes squeezed shut, she opened the book and peeked one eye open.

Letters scrolled across the page, written in a fine, bold hand with elegant swirls she could not read. There. She'd done it. She'd opened the book and could not understand it. Disappointment punched through her like a kick to the back of her knees. What was she expecting? She wasn't an ink mage; it stood to reason the words would not speak to her, for she lacked magic.

With a sniff, she closed the book, wrapped it tightly in the blue cloth, tucked it under her pallet, and blew out the candle.

Would life ever change for her? She'd hoped the book

would begin her adventure, would help her understand her purpose and where she belonged in the empire of Nomadia. But she'd forgotten she was nothing, only destined to serve and never rise above her station.

THE NEXT DAY, the hours at the library dragged as Araceli pulled and returned books. Each time she entered a room she kept her eyes down, unable to make eye contact lest another mage woo her with words and entice her to do his bidding. Not that she minded, but the book was constantly in her thoughts. As soon as dusk fell, she left, hooves clacking over the crystal bridge, ignoring the way the light fell on the city, casting hues of bronze and silver off the rooftops.

Her heart pounded in her chest as she walked, and she glanced over her shoulder to confirm she wasn't being followed, sure that another magical being would read her thoughts and know where the book was hidden. After all, the mage had mentioned enemies. How would she know who they were or when they arrived in the library? Only once she was on the other side of her door did she feel safe.

The question remained: How would she unlock the secrets of the book without magic? This time, she vowed to take it slow. Once again, she sat down on the pallet and unwrapped the book. Again, her heart quickened at the sight of it. It was beautiful, and her fingers tingled as she stroked the leather.

Golden hues shone out and danced across her face. Her palms were sweaty and her fingers trembled as she opened the book. The air shivered around it, as though bowing in reverence, and symbols appeared on the blank page. Though she could not read them, her pulse quickened. The book was awake; it wanted to tell her something.

Stroking her fingers across the smooth page, she bent closer to it while warmth encased her. "Show me your secrets," she whispered, her breath hot on the page.

A hum vibrated, and then the book snapped shut with a bang. Araceli was hurled onto her back and the light faded. What had she done?

Reaching out blindly, she felt for the book, but her fingers touched only her pallet and the blanket. Then, the scent of arid smoke drifted to her nostrils. She fumbled a moment longer until she found a match, struck it, and screamed.

12

DARYA

Darya's strokes slowed as the velvet shadows of night consumed the sea. The current had spit her out a long time ago, and she was sure the bleeding in her tail had stopped. There was no pain, only a slight ache that flared up occasionally; naught but a minor wound. Darya's arms burned from swimming and her heart pounded in her throat as she slowed to a stop.

Rising to the surface, she poked her head above the waters and watched, searching for signs of life. It seemed she was all alone in the sea; the sharks had left, and at last she could sleep. She closed her eyes momentarily, her shoulders sagging. How long had it been since she left the Court of Nymphs? Three days? Four? She hadn't once stopped to eat or rest, and a wave of exhaustion passed over her. The murky waters churned as her head sank down to her chest. A splash of cold water made her eyes open, and she looked up, floating on her back as she watched the sky.

When she dwelled in the Court of Nymphs, there was not much opportunity to go to the surface and survey the passing of time by the sea currents and the sun, twin moons, and stars. But now . . . she sucked in a deep breath, and the taste of fish and dirt and citrus filled her nostrils. Land must be close, but the sky was vivid in its blue darkness, peppered with thousands of tiny lights. They twinkled, white and cold, like shimmering crystals, jewels more precious and rare than the treasures found in the sea depths. Darya gazed at them, breathless in awe. Was this what the landwalkers gazed upon each night? Is this what she missed by hiding in the depths?

Her fears regarding her journey faded, and she stretched her arms above her head. This was perfection and beauty, a reminder of how lovely nature was in all its glory. Her struggles to belong with the nymphs, to prove herself worthy, seemed insignificant, and the silence of the sea swallowed her whole. A pleasant wind blew, ruffling strands of her thick green hair. Darya pulled it over one shoulder, wringing out the water before letting it rest on her bare chest. She wanted just a moment, a pure instance of relaxation, and then she'd hunt and hide until daybreak.

Darya closed her eyes, and sleep overtook her.

SHE WOKE to the sensation of falling. Her eyes opened wide and a cry burst from her lips. The last thing she recalled was falling asleep under the hypnotic moonlight, but now everything had changed. The waters were still dark but she was falling, something that had never happened to her before, and she wasn't sure how to explain it. Her arms flailed. She tried to thrash her tail, but to no avail. She'd lost control of her limbs. Darkness flashed around her. It was still night, but she was falling, spinning, head over tail. Something smacked against her scales as she tumbled down, down, down, to the bottom of what felt like a netting. And stopped.

Gasping, Darya felt around her, and her chest clenched. She was caught in something springy that kept moving, and things kept hitting her. She lifted one of the things. A fish flopped in her hands, and she tossed it away. Okay, she was trapped, but she could deal with it; it should be a minor situation for her, a powerful nymph.

The netting moved, lifting and tightening as it went. A fresh wave of apprehension swept over Darya. Clenching her teeth, she closed her eyes and sought her power. Her fingers tingled as it rose inside of her and blasted out. She channeled it into the waters, determined to break the net, but only made the net swing violently from side to side. Darya was thrown on her face, her mouth and nose pressing into the net's hard, ropy threads. It was made of a material she knew nothing about. She gripped it with her hands, wondering if she could pull it apart.

Fish slid onto her back, their bodies writhing and twisting as they, too, tried to escape. The pressure grew as she strained, pulling with all her strength, but the rope would not give way. Now the rope pressed against her chest, ramming against her rib cage, and continued until Darya was almost bent backward, the fins of her tail so close she could touch them if she stuck her tongue out far enough.

She screamed, first yanking on the rope and then pushing with her tail. A lightheaded frenzy swept over her. She could not be caught; this wasn't how her quest was supposed to end!

Opening her mouth, she bit down on the rope. Pain radiated up her jaw and she let go, eyes wet from the exertion. Her spine screamed for relief as the net tightened and she was lifted up out of the water.

Darya blinked against a pool of yellow light as she strained against the pressure on her back. It only increased, forcing a hoarse cry out of her mouth. The snare moved, whirling her until dizziness overcame her and she closed her eyes, blinking to regain lucidity. She came down with a thump, landing hard against something that smelled both oaky and salty. A combination of raw scents assaulted her nose, and a moment later, the pressure ceased.

Darya lay on her stomach, gulping in gasps of air as the pressure faded from her back. Fish flopped off her and rough voices shouted. Curling her fingers into fists, Darya gathered the moisture in the air, preparing to strike. The ground tilted and she rolled.

Something squishy moved beneath her and a voice shouted, "Aiii look! We caught one of the prized creatures of the deep!"

"Is it a mermaid?"

"Nay, fool! Look! That's no mermaid, but a nymph."

"A nymph?"

"Watch out, she probably has magic."

"Quick, get the tourmaline!"

"Hold her steady, she'll try to escape!"

A strange tingling sensation went down Darya's spine as she wiggled. The water was gone but she wasn't on land, though she wasn't sure what to call the contraption. A vague idea struck her—but no, it could not be.

Beyond the pale yellow light, she made out shadows of

people. Low, rough voices made her assume they were male. A loud creaking sound made her jump, and she hissed, letting a cloud of water out of her palms. The ball of water she expected to gush between her fingers evaporated into mist. Her throat went dry, and she tried again, reaching for the water in the air. It was so close she could taste it on the tip of her tongue, and yet she knew as she opened her hands again that she'd exhausted herself. The magic was gone.

This had only happened a few times before, when she'd exhausted her resources and had to wait, usually a day, for her energy to return. Food and drink assisted with the recovery, but she needed magic now. A cry burst in her throat; she'd have to result to violence. Her fingers skated across the ground as the tingling sensation swelled. Her tail throbbed, then shook. She writhed, a scream of pure rage resounding as her body disobeyed her, failing her in her time of need.

"Aye!" a voice shouted.

Thumping came, and the ground trembled as one of the shadows hovered over her.

"I'll be damned, she's shifting."

"They do that, stay back. . ."

A hand locked around her wrist. Darya spat and bit down hard, her teeth sinking into flesh. The taste filled her with disgust. She followed through with a punch. Her knuckles crunched as they hit something solid—a thigh? The man roared with pain and a foot stamped down on her belly. It was heavy and held her firmly in place, pressing her against the ground.

"I told you to watch out, nymphs are dangerous!"

"She bit me! The devilish creature bit me. Hold her down, I'll show her . . ."

"You'll do nothing of the sort," a female voice interrupted. "Be careful. She'll fetch a fair price in market, and you know the giants don't like damaged goods."

The pressure increased and Darya scratched and clawed at the foot, determined to free herself. A sharp pain in her midsection made her gasp for breath, and her legs jerked. Legs. She had legs. She wasn't comfortable with using them, but she kicked and squirmed, shaking herself free.

"She's escaping!"

"Get the net!"

Shouts erupted around her as Darya stumbled to her feet, slipping and sliding on what she now could see was the deck of a boat, or ship. The landwalkers used the contraptions to navigate the seas, and she'd seen them from afar, mini floating chunks of land. All she had to do was reach the side, leap, and she'd be free. Her own folly had gotten her into the situation, and she'd get herself out.

Her foot caught in a tangle of rope and she went down hard, slamming her chin into the deck. She bit her tongue on impact, hard enough to send a river of blood dripping out. She cried out as something heavy landed on her, and then the men were upon her. There were three or four shadows, she couldn't tell, but no matter how hard she kicked and struggled they wouldn't let go. Two of them twisted her arms behind her and tied them while another sat on her legs, roping them together until she was nothing more than a bound creature. Hoarse sobs wrenched from her mouth as she fought, and then someone bent down and slid something around her neck.

Darya stilled, and everything within her went cold. She felt as if the light inside of her had faded, burned out. The thing around her neck choked and burned her scales. She twisted, yanking at her bonds to attempt to pull them off, but two more cold things were put around her wrists, and a final two around her ankles.

"Take her to the barge," the woman ordered.

They lifted her, and the last thing Darya recalled was being lowered into a box filled with water. The lid shut, and she was left in complete and utter darkness.

13

ARACELI

The flame went out as Araceli dropped it, clasping her hands over her mouth. Had anyone heard her? Would they come knocking at the door? She desperately hoped not, for she couldn't be caught with a book, practicing magic she knew nothing about. The punishment for such actions would be severe, especially because she did not have anyone who would be on her side. Even Mistress Vina would frown upon such actions.

But she'd screamed because she wasn't alone. An apparition stood by the door. Had she summoned a demon? With shaking fingers, she reached for the match. Although she did not want to see, knowing she was alone with it in the dark was much worse than being alone with it in the light.

Taking a deep breath, she struck the match again and this time willed herself not to scream.

The glow of light wasn't nearly bright enough to illuminate the room, but the apparition remained, standing against the wall, eyes boring into her. She felt that stare on her skin as she lit one candle, then another and another until all three gave off enough of a glow for her to examine her unwelcome visitor.

It wasn't a demon. Still, she backed away, pressing herself against the wall as she held a candle in one hand. It was a male, not a faun or elykin, perhaps an elf, she wasn't sure. The light showed off his bronze skin, the angles of his face—hard as marble—the slope of his cheeks, and the curve of his brows. Inquisitive brown eyes stared back at her as he shifted from one foot to the other.

Araceli's face flushed hot as she stared at his bare chest, rippling with muscles that tapered down to his waist. The muscles of his stomach moved as he shifted. A white cloth covered the lower half of his body, falling to his knees like a skirt. *What kind of garb is that?*

Squeezing her eyes shut, she wanted to melt into the floor. A half-naked male was standing in her room staring at her. Was he waiting for her to speak? Had he come from the book?

Heated moments passed, and the tension eased from Araceli's body as she realized he wasn't going to attack her. He shifted his weight again and sighed. "Well. Go ahead. I don't have all day, or all night, whatever time this is."

Araceli searched the floor for the book and found it lying in the corner. Her shoulders sagged. At least the mage wouldn't be angry that she'd lost his book.

The man tapped his bare foot on the floor, followed her gaze to the book, then frowned. "What did you do with the lamp?"

Fighting to regain her tongue, Araceli squeaked out, "I don't know what you're talking about. Who are you?"

He snorted and ran a hand through his thick hair, moving it away from his forehead. "Who am I? You're the one who summoned me."

Araceli's eyes flickered to the book again. "I . . . it's my first time using the book."

The man's nostrils flared. "You summoned me using a book?"

Where was this conversation going? "I did."

"Odd." He stroked his smooth chin, then folded his arms over his bare chest as he studied the room. "What is this place? I expected a sorcerer's lair or a queen's bedroom, but this looks like a dungeon."

Despite the man's handsomeness, Araceli bristled. "Will you just tell me who you are without insulting my room? You're in the palace of Nomadia, if you must know."

He shrugged, and dark eyes bored into hers. "And you are?"

"Araceli. I'm a librarian."

"Ah, that explains the book. You must be an ink mage."

The lie hovered on Araceli's lips. How easy it would be to nod and agree with him, but the truth won. "No." She dropped her gaze to the ground. "I'm just a librarian, nothing more. I'm not supposed to have the book, I just . . . it called to me, and I wanted to know what would happen if I looked inside."

The man bowed at the waist, his head sinking so low it almost touched the ground. "Mistress Araceli, I am Kaiden the jinn, at your service. Speak your three wishes and I shall grant them."

Araceli's mouth open and closed. A jinn. In her bedroom! What would Shyrin say? Unlike Araceli, Shyrin always knew exactly what she wanted and would likely have already rattled off three wishes to the jinn. "I don't know what I want."

Kaiden's expression soured. "It's simple. You make a wish and I grant it. There are some limitations, but if you're a librarian, you already have a wealth of knowledge at your fingertips."

Araceli's face warmed. "I've searched the library, but it hasn't given me answers. I just don't know."

"This is inconvenient," Kaiden muttered, more to himself than to Araceli. "Summoned by someone who doesn't know what they want and no lamp anywhere."

Araceli wrinkled her nose. "What's a lamp?"

Kaiden rolled his eyes, then slid down until he sat cross-legged on the floor. "Since I'll be here for a while, do you have food and drink?"

Araceli glanced at the water jug. She hadn't bothered to refill it in her haste to return to the book, and now she saw her room for what it was. Barren with dusty corners, a cobweb in the ceiling, and no windows, nothing to suggest the passage of time. No wonder the jinn had turned up his nose at it.

Scooting away from the water, she pointed at it. "I'll bring fresh water and food in the morning."

"I was afraid of that," Kaiden said, "but I am at your mercy. I shall wait."

He closed his eyes.

Araceli stared at him until she felt all hot and bothered. Was he sleeping? Merely resting his eyes? She didn't know what to do. Lying down on the pallet seemed awkward and wrong when he had nothing but the hard floor to sleep on. If she gave him a blanket, would he be insulted? How she wished she could leave the room and find Shyrin, who would know exactly what to do. Only, the jinn blocked the door.

Araceli weighed her decisions. Creep out of her room and go for water, or remain with her unwelcome guest? Somehow, even in her ignorance of magic, she'd summoned him, and she felt responsible for his well-being. Or she could ponder the fact that she had three wishes. Wealth must be a popular wish, but while piles of money brought hope to her heart, there was little use for them as a blue faun. She could not buy her freedom or lessons to learn magic. In the end she'd be the same Araceli, working at the library and going back to a room filled with useless coin.

Fine dresses, sweet drinks, and the best foods were lost on her; she had enough, and new clothes would be worthless. She dressed according to her station and aside from festivals, finery did not have a place in her life. Wishing for purpose was intangible and just as useless as wishing for love or death. Jinns did not deal with intangibles.

Araceli peeked at the jinn again, but he hadn't moved. "Are you awake?" she whispered.

His eyes opened. "Is it morning?"

"No, not for a long time. It's evening now." With a pang, she realized that she'd missed dinner.

"Ah. Will you stand there all night?"

Araceli bit her lip and gave up. "No, but I can't sleep with you here."

"Why not?"

"It's inappropriate, you're a . . . a . . . jinn, in my room!"

A wry expression crossed his face. "Why yes, that is a fact, and hardly my fault. I come when I am summoned, and the lamp I'm bound to is . . . not here. I can't disappear like I usually do, so I'm stuck here until your wishes are fulfilled. So. Have you decided?"

Fear faded into frustration. She scowled. "No, I haven't, and I'd appreciate it if you wouldn't ask again."

"I see." He closed his eyes.

Araceli sighed. "You can't sleep here."

"Where should I sleep, Mistress?"

"I don't know, can't you go back into the book?"

Kaiden stood and placed a hand on the doorknob. "If my presence is so distasteful to you, I shall sleep outside."

"No!" Araceli cried, reaching out a hand as if the movement alone would stop him. "You can't; others would see you and then you'd have to explain your presence. No one can know I have the book or that I used it."

The jinn turned away from the door. "Curious. I assumed as a librarian you knew how to use the book."

"It was a mistake. I want to learn to use the book, to read it, but I don't understand magic and I'm a blue faun. I won't be allowed to learn."

The jinn frowned, his face growing harder in the low light. "What does your race have to do with it? If you want to learn ink magic, then learn it; no one can stop you. The color of your skin, the horns on your head, the hooves on your feet, and your tail cannot stop you from becoming who you want to be. You might be a librarian now, but if you work hard enough, you can be transformed into an ink mage."

"I don't know how," Araceli replied miserably, staring at the book in the corner. The symbols were gone, and it looked like just an ordinary leather book.

"Somehow, you fail to see what is standing right in front of you. All you have to do is ask."

A rush of excitement flooded her body as she stared at him. All she had to do was make a wish, and suddenly she'd become an ink mage, able to understand the words of the book and perform magic?

"How does your magic work?" she asked, gathering time to consider her choice. "I make a wish and suddenly what I want appears?"

The jinn cocked his head at her. "Do you know what the term 'jinn' means? If you've studied, you know I can teleport. Wind and fire are the elements I can drift into, and I can take what I need from the past and bring it to you. It happens quickly, and through the years I have gathered power, and magic now dances on my fingertips. All of it is moot unless I serve a master or mistress like yourself. My magic is yours, and if you wish to learn ink magic, I can give you that knowledge. It will take time, for you still have to learn—I cannot transform your mind. Say you wanted to become royalty; I could make you look like the queen of the fauns, but looks only go so far. You would still be yourself, and you would have a part to play in the great act. For what is magic but deceit? And those who are the best at being deceitful ultimately win."

Araceli shifted from one hoof to the next. His words made her skin tingle, and suddenly what she had assumed was impossible for her became very possible. But one of his statements made another question rise in her mind. "Do you always serve a master?"

"It is the way of the jinn."

He was like her. A servant with no end in sight, ever serving, ever responding to a master to the end of his years. "How will you become free?"

"If my master or mistress wishes me free, then I shall

return to my original state, before I was cursed. Now, any more questions about me, or shall we get on with your wish?"

Araceli looked up at him, surprised she was no longer afraid or intimidated by his presence. "I wish to learn ink magic."

He grinned, showing off a row of white teeth. Araceli couldn't say his grin was happy, but rather more relieved at finally having something to do. Clasping his hands together, he stood tall. "Before we begin, you're going to need a new room."

14

ELMIRA

"This is the wizard's lair?" Elmira asked as she stepped over a dead body and squinted into the dark room.

The torches had gone out, making it impossible to see anything.

"Yes, Mistress," said the assistant.

After she'd destroyed the wizard and eaten his soul, the wizard's assistant had knelt, waiting for his turn. The blood trickling off his face had stayed her hand, so instead of striking him down she'd asked, "Are you for me or against me?"

"For you," he'd responded.

Then he'd led her out and given her food and water. For the first time in years she'd bathed and cut off her long hair, but when she tried to dress, even the softest robes rubbed against her wounds, and the heat was too oppressive. So she'd knotted a scarf around her waist and tied another around her breasts. That was as far as she got before chaos erupted.

Guards approached to recapture her, and the days slid away as she fought them off and ate their souls.

It was the souls she thrived on. They filled her body with strength, and although she should not have been able to walk after such an imprisonment, she did. Broken bones knitted together, and her skin healed slowly. Once the initial adrenaline from killing the wizard had forsaken her, the souls nourished her. She needed more if she was going to live, and she needed pure souls, for the taint from the wizards and his guards filled her body.

Now, days later, she and the assistant had grown bold enough to move up and, cautious of magic traps, toward the wizard's lair.

"I'll light the torches," the assistant announced, slipping into the darkness.

A moment later, light flared up, revealing a stone room. It was circular, with a round table in the middle that was covered with books and scrolls and maps. The assistant hunched in a corner, eyes cast down, waiting. He seemed to fear her, and she did not blame him. No one had been kind to him. Why should he expect her to be different?

Elmira strode across the room, eyeing the staffs and weapons hanging on the walls. Tools of every kind lay there, enough to torture, inflict magic, and arm a small battalion. The battalion of guards who were now dead.

Snapping her fingers, she strode to the table, glancing at the documents there. Her heart beat with a heady desire for knowledge. When she was thirteen, her schooling had stopped, but now the memory returned. She picked up a scroll and unrolled it, staring until the words transformed and sank in.

"What were the wizard's plans? He liked to boast and brag; surely he told you about them?"

The assistant shuffled forward. "Yes, he was working on finding and controlling all magic."

Elmira dropped the scroll and frowned across the room at the assistant. "Come here."

His eyes filled with fear as he lurched forward to stand at the table, hunched over, cowering as if preparing for a blow.

"You're frightened of me, aren't you?"

A nod confirmed it.

"You were forced to serve the wizard unwillingly, correct? He bullied and beat you and used his magic on you, like he did to me."

The assistant peeked up at her. Tears of pain and shame and embarrassment filled his eyes.

"He hated you because you are a hunchback, and in his eyes, your disability is ugly, shameful. In my eyes, you are beautiful, because you're just like me. Do you know what I'm going to do?"

The assistant shook his head.

"I made a vow when I was chained to that stone and left in the dark to die. Each day my tormentors came, I vowed, if I ever got free, I would do one thing: rid the world of magic. Magic made us slaves—it ruined us, allowed someone else to take us and force us to serve against our will. We aren't the only ones who have suffered under the hand of might and magic. There are others, I'm sure of it, slaves who are kept in dark holes while the people of Nomadia walk in the light, unwilling to deviate from their routine to help. They listen to prophecies and make decisions based on them and turn blind eyes to suffering, because it is dangerous to go against those with magic. But you and I don't have to be afraid any longer. We will destroy those who stand in our way, and we will free the world from magic, so everyone will have a chance to overcome their oppressors and gain freedom."

The assistant fell to his knees and clasped his hands together as if praying. "Please, Mistress, let me be a part of this plan."

"Get up!" Elmira snapped. "You are a slave no longer, nor a servant, and you do not bow to anyone, ever!"

The assistant leaped to his feet, eyes wide with shock.

"You are my right hand, and I need your strength. If we are going to do this, it will be difficult, for all the magical people will stand against us. There will be wizards and sorcerers, but if we control all the power, no one will beat us down, or shame us, or make us slaves ever again. So stand tall, lift your head, and speak up. I may be cruel to those who oppress us, but never to you. Now tell me, what is your name?"

"The wizard called me Kypho."

"Kypho." She frowned. "No, that will not do. Here's a new name for you: Vero. It means 'warrior,' and that's what you shall become. Now, let's bar the door. Surely the wizard kept food and drink here? Sit down, and let's discuss what he was going to do."

The assistant, now Vero, wiped tears away from his cheeks and scuttled away, returning with a flask of water. Elmira drank deeply before passing it back to him. "Drink," she instructed. It would take a while for Vero to outgrow his shyness, but she intended to keep her word.

Together, they organized the books and maps, and Elmira gazed at them with a sudden desire to go out into the land of

Nomadia. She longed for the sun to warm her skin, to feel the wind on her face, and to snatch away the magic that sang at the core of the empire.

"The wizard sought to control the power of Nomadia," Vero began, speaking with a hesitant lisp. "He studied the core magical powers that make up Nomadia and discovered four." He held up four fingers of his good hand and ticked them off. "The first power is the ability to control the spirit world and raise an army of souls. The wizard experimented on many using soul stones, but they all died. He couldn't do what you did. The second is the ability to control wind and fire, using it to teleport. A great and terrible jinn holds this power, and if one controls the jinn, one controls that power. The wizard read tales claiming that the jinn's lamp was buried here, in the halls of his father. When the wizard did not find the lamp, he decided to try another method to summon the jinn: ink magic, though it didn't work. Ink magic is the third power, and it allows one to use spells to summon others, open portals, and control all written words. Rumor was, there is a book within the crypt that, once read, would grant one all the forgotten powers of ink magic. It was supposedly buried here along with the jinn's lamp to keep others from abusing the items' power. The wizard found neither the book nor the lamp." Vero's shoulders slumped. "He beat me when things went wrong, when he couldn't find the answers he wanted, and then he'd go down to visit you."

"I know," Elmira said, waiting.

With every word Vero spoke, her excitement heightened. She wanted to control all magic, yet the wizard in all his madness had failed. Well, she would succeed. She already had the power of souls, and if her ability allowed her to control the spirit world, she could raise an army to do her bidding. Curling her fingers, she took another sip of water, waiting for Vero to continue.

"The final power is water and grants the bearer the ability to control the waters in the sea, in the air, and across the lakes, rivers, and pools of Nomadia. In order to do this, the wizard created a fever curse and made a deal with a sea witch. She was supposed to take the curse to the kingdom of the sirens, watched over by the great water nymphs. If she does her task correctly, a powerful nymph will come ashore to seek a remedy to counter the curse. When she does, the wizard thought it was likely the slave traders in Dustania might pick her up, so he hired the Guild of Bounty Hunters to find and bring her to him."

"The wizard must have paid a hearty sum of money for those transactions," Elmira mused.

"I think he threatened the guild," Vero said.

Elmira frowned, recalling the tears of gold he'd demanded from her. "How does he know a water nymph will come ashore? If the nymphs have the power of water, they can use it to defeat the sea witch."

"The wizard created a fever spell, the remedy to which can only be found in the Great Library of Zandria. The water nymphs will have to come ashore to find it."

"And travel to the capital," Elmira mused. The capital of Nomadia was far away. When she was young, she'd heard snatches of conversation referencing it: the seat of power of the great empire, a place where the rich dwelled with magic and wealth at their fingertips. A dangerous place for a sea creature to go. "He left a lot to chance. How long ago was the deal made with the sea witch? And when is the guild expected to deliver this powerful water nymph?"

Vero went quiet. "Soon. He expected the vulture to return with a scroll."

"Vulture?"

"The bird he used to deliver messages."

Elmira stood, determination surging through her. "We have to be sure. Where does the vulture meet him?"

"I don't know. I've never been outside because the wizard thought I might escape."

"We are going to find the way out," Elmira proclaimed. As she spoke, something twisted in the pit of her belly, a gnawing hunger for more souls.

Vero stood up, his eyes hopeful.

"We need a plan," Elmira paced, thinking out loud. "It is only fate the wizard had a plan, but he knew more of Nomadia than you and I. He could send out vultures to make treaties and deals. We are not as fortunate. In order for this plan to succeed, we will have to do the work ourselves instead of relying on others. Who knows if this vulture will return? If the water nymph is on land, we need to know where she will go. We can't hope the slave traders have her, or that the bounty hunters will deliver her here."

"The wizard spent many hours reading books," Vero suggested. "He chose this as his home because of the crypt, which stores the hidden and forgotten books."

"Yes, but he did not find the jinn's lamp or the book of ink magic here, did he?"

Vero shook his head.

Elmira shivered as a delightful thought came to her. She

licked her lips. "We should go down and search for ourselves. Perhaps other guards are hiding in the crypt."

"I'll lead the way." Vero picked up a torch.

"Good. We'll search, make a plan, and then I want to leave this cursed place."

"I agree, Mistress."

He led the way out of the room, and Elmira followed. Hope beat in her heart at the challenge set before her. She intended to be smart, ruthless, and make none of the mistakes the wizard had. If luck was with her, she would wipe the scourge of magic from Nomadia and rule. Another twinge came as she walked, reminding her not to be hasty. There was time. She still needed to heal and discover how to use her new ability to control the world of souls and raise an army of spirits.

15

ARACELI

"How old are you?" Kaiden asked when Araceli returned to her room the next evening. She was carrying a tray of food in her hands and handed it to him.

"Here, I had to persuade the kitchens I needed twice my normal share, and I'm twenty-five. Why do you ask?"

Kaiden took the tray and sat down cross-legged, placing it carefully on the floor in front of him. He sniffed the air, made a face, took the lid off a bowl, frowned, then returned the lid. When his dark eyes flickered up at her, a hot flush of embarrassment shot through Araceli. Next, she needed to find him some clothes. She couldn't have a half-naked jinn stay in her room for more than two nights. "Are lumpless bags the fashion in Nomadia? If I had to guess, I would say you're a child, but when you speak you sound much older, and you seem to have knowledge a child wouldn't."

Araceli felt she should be angry at him for his tactless words, but when she looked down at herself, she realized he was right. "This is the garb of the librarians. It is what I'm supposed to wear. I don't have a choice—"

Kaiden held up a finger. "The library doesn't own you. Do they dictate your life, what you eat and wear, and where you sleep? Have you ever considered why? And have you ever asked for more?"

"I'm not entitled to more," Araceli protested. "I'm a blue faun, a child of war, a tribute taken from the fauns of the forest. My place is here, and I was taught to obey without question."

Kaiden lifted a cup to his lips, took a sip, and spat it back out. "What is this food? Scraps they feed to the dogs?"

"It doesn't taste like much, but it's filling."

"This is what you're used to? Being overlooked and taken advantage of and being seen as less than? I will not have it," he shook his head so hard, curls sprang over his forehead.

They were black as night, thick and glossy, a perfect complement to his bronze skin. Averting her eyes, Araceli tucked away that knowledge.

"Here's what you're going to do." Kaiden kicked away the tray of uneaten food. "In the morning, you will go to whoever is in charge of the rooms and ask for a better room. No, not better. You will ask for a room with a window, a table, a pot of ink, a rug, a bed—not a pallet, make sure you specify the bed —and moon lamps. This will not do. I cannot teach you ink magic when my back is sore from lying on the floor and my belly rumbles from lack of food and my throat is as dry as the desert sands."

"I can't do that!" Araceli exclaimed, aghast. "I brought you food and water, you just don't want it."

"I have a certain standard of living." He squared his shoulders. "And it does not include eating mush and calling it food. I'd rather starve. You were the one who made a wish, and now you want to take it back, but we're stuck in this together. I must fulfill your wishes and you must ask for two more before I disappear. In the meantime, I will not be treated like an animal."

Araceli's heart pounded so hard in her chest, she thought he must hear it. If only he knew what he was asking of her. There was no way she could make such a request without being laughed at. It was impossible.

Leaning against the wall, Kaiden picked up the book and placed it in his lap. "The choice is yours. Will you fight for what you want or let everyone step on you on their way to the top?"

"That's not fair," she breathed, backing away to her pallet. "You're supposed to grant my wishes."

"Yes, but like I said before, it requires work, work you don't seem willing to do. Am I wrong?"

"Yes . . . no," she sat down, miserable. "But not like this."

"I'm giving you the easiest task first." He opened the book. "The rest will be harder. If you can't do this, well then, I will just take a walk through the palace with this book."

Horror leaped and squeezed her heart. Araceli put out a hand as though she could physically stop him. "Wait, no, I'll go. First thing in the morning. Don't leave this room, and, please, give me the book."

With a smirk, he turned the page. "Hand me a candle, will you? I'm going to read tonight."

IN THE MORNING, Araceli set out early while Kaiden was still asleep, the book in his lap. Before she went out the door, she wanted to snatch it from his hands and hide it, but she was still afraid of getting too close to his sculpted body. The fact that he slept on the hard floor and went in want of food and water because of her did not sit well on her shoulders. Summoning her courage, she took the stairs that led deeper into the palace, to the halls where the matron dwelled.

Madam Zansha was in charge of running the castle, and while she reported to someone else who reported to someone else who reported to the empress, it was Madam Zansha who arranged rooms and decided who lived where. She'd served in the castle for over forty years and still bustled around, keys around her waist, snapping orders.

Araceli was afraid of her, but more terrified of what Kaiden would do if she made him sleep on the floor again. It occurred to her that he was supposed to serve her and grant her wishes, not the other way around. Yet, she was the one who was exposing herself. A young lad dashed around a corner, almost running into her. He backed up at the last minute and lifted his hands. "You don't want to go that way," he whispered. "Madam Zansha is in a tizzy."

Araceli peered over the boy's shoulder, as if it would give her answers. "What's going on?"

"Esteemed guests are arriving from the eastern shore, but does it matter? She's always upset."

The boy jogged away, and Araceli took another step, twisting her fingers together. Every nerve in her body screamed for her to turn around and head to the library.

The stone passageway opened up into a wide atrium where sunlight flooded in from a crystal ceiling. Araceli's eyes were drawn upward, where fat white clouds drifted in a rich blue sky the color of bluebells. Araceli wasn't sure if she imagined it, but she felt a floral breeze blow by, ruffling the waves of hair that rested on her back. Even though she could see the stone beneath her feet, she felt as though she'd been transported to a meadow. A yellow butterfly flew past her, and a red bird dipped out of a cloud and hovered in the sky. Bright eyes turned on her as it dove, beak open.

Araceli ducked, throwing her hands up to block the blow that never came. Instead, a brittle voice barked, "What are you doing here?"

Araceli peered up into the frowning face of Madam Zansha.

"I came to make a request," Araceli whispered, her gaze going back to the sky.

Madam Zansha followed the direction of her eyes. "Don't be daft, it's only an illusion."

"Oh."

"Speak up, faun. What is your request?"

"I . . . it's . . ."Araceli faltered.

Madam Zansha huffed. "I don't have all day. Out with it."

"My room." Araceli swallowed hard. "It's about my room."

"What's wrong with it?"

"Nothing! That is . . . it's small and . . ."

"And?" Madam Zansha demanded.

"I came to request a different one. A bigger one . . . with a window, bed, and . . ."

Madam Zansha's face darkened. "Why, you ungrateful breed! Be gone with your requests. Back to the library. How dare you insult the crown by demanding something above your station?"

Araceli swallowed hard. What would Kaiden say? "It's not that I'm ungrateful, I wouldn't make this request if it were just me, but—"

"But what, you're pregnant? Away from me; go bother someone else with your problems, and if you come back, I'll put you to work here!"

Araceli's heart sank as she fled. What were the odds that Madam Zansha would see reason later? Unlikely. But it would be worse, much worse, if anyone found out about the book.

THE PROBLEM ATE AWAY at Araceli as she worked, pulling stacks of books and returning them while at times staring off into the distance, trying to figure out how she would appease the jinn. The idea that she should have been angry at him for threatening and blackmailing her did not enter her mind. His words had inspired her, and yet she did not see how, considering her station, she could rise above being seen as nothing more than a blue faun and a librarian's assistant. For that's what she was. She did not have the honor of reading the books, but only picking them up and handing them to others who were far too superior to enter the stacks and select a book for themselves.

At sundown, she crossed the glass bridge, shoulders slumped, wondering if the temple would accept her should she be forced to resign her position as a librarian. What kind of punishment awaited those who stole a book? No one would believe her if she told them a mage had given it to her. Honestly, she hardly believed it had happened herself. She'd been drinking the night of the festival. Had she imagined it all to make the idea of stealing a book less frightening? She'd imagined things before.

Her footsteps dragged as she approached the door to her room. What would Kaiden say when he learned of her failure? But she'd delayed as long as she could. Just before she opened the door, she realized she'd forgotten to go by the kitchen to pick up a tray of food. Not that Kaiden would eat it.

She swung open the door, and four wide pairs of eyes stared at her.

It was her room, but not her room. Instead of her pallet, four beds were in the room, two on the bottom and two stacked on top. Four blue fauns stared back at her. They were no more than ten, and they huddled together, cowering as if she might come in and strike at them.

"Oh." Breath whooshed out of Araceli's body and she closed the door. Hope sparked in her heart.

Her room had been taken over by fauns, which meant her request had been heard. She took a step, then paused. Where was she going? There was no note, no indication of her new room, and she couldn't walk around the castle opening doors.

"Are you Araceli?" An elf stepped from the shadows and bowed. In one hand he carried a light that reflected in his pale eyes.

"Yes?"

"Good." The elf moved past her, throwing his words over his shoulder. "Your valet sent me."

Araceli opened her mouth to announce she did not have a valet, then clamped it shut. What a strange night. It was better to follow the elf and ask questions when they arrived. Unless it was a trap.

The halls were long and dark but at last the elf paused in

front of a door. "Here is where I leave you. Good luck." He bowed again and padded down the halls, the light dancing on the walls as he disappeared around a corner.

Unsure whether she should knock or just go in, Araceli shifted from one hoof to the other, summoned her courage, and opened the door.

16

ELMIRA

The air was thick and humid with the perfume of death in the bowels of the pyramid. Even the torches wanted to flicker out, smothered as if they couldn't breathe. Elmira followed Vero, marveling at the power that had built such a building. The aura of mystery that surrounded it excited her, along with the idea that she might find another soul to eat.

The hunger was manageable, humming in the core of her being, but she wondered if it would grow should she abstain from souls, and also whether she could use it to tap into the spirit world. It was a shame the wizard hadn't pulled texts on that subject. She'd return to his lair and read everything she could get her hands on before venturing out into the world. Besides, she needed to grow stronger.

"Here," came Vero's whisper. He paused in front of a square opening.

Elmira's eyes widened as she looked over his shoulder. Taking the torch from his hand, she slipped inside, awed.

Inside the room, the stone felt cool beneath her feet. The air was still thick, but along the walls were runes, and tucked into the crevices of each rune were scrolls. Among the walls were shelves, and on some were old books, each of them stacked reverently. Some shelves had jars, making Elmira wonder if one of them was the lamp that contained the jinn.

She turned, taking in the tomb. In the middle was a golden sarcophagus with a carving of the great king on top. Runes covered it, likely a warning against those who would disturb the dead. Carvings of women and wealth were depicted on all sides of the sarcophagus, and Elmira walked around it. The hushed awe in the room was so strong she wanted to leave, and even her thoughts of bloodshed and destruction seemed wrong in this place.

Of course, she'd heard tales of King Horus, who could teleport and control the desert winds. He went where he pleased, and others bowed before his great power. He was a rich king, with power, wealth, and wisdom. For all his deeds, he still died without an heir to the crown. After his death, the desert region fell into chaos, warred over by those who wanted to inherit his kingdom, but none had the magic to walk in King Horus's steps.

"How does one summon a jinn from a lamp?" she asked Vero.

"By rubbing it." Vero lingered in the doorway, unwilling to enter the room. "The wizard searched and rubbed all the lamps, but even with his magic, the revelation of the jinn did not come to him."

"His own greed blinded him; even I can sense the strong counter-magic in this room. The wizard wasn't the first one here, though. I was brought to this place before his time, though never down to this level." Curses on Kymeria, who had sought to protect her by taking her to the lost pyramids. Elmira had been content with the healers who raised her, and there had been another, a half brother, who protected her. She had memories of his face, his dark skin and kind eyes.

"You think someone stole the book and the lamp?"

Vero's question jerked her out of her painful memories.

"Yes." She turned in a slow circle, scanning the shelves. They were so erratic it was hard to tell how many books had been stacked on each, or how many jars and lamps there were. "If the wizard, with his magic, couldn't find them, it makes sense that they were stolen. The question is, by whom? And why haven't they used the power? Or maybe they have, and we don't know because we are locked down here, ignorant to what goes on in Nomadia."

"The wizard also had limited knowledge of the current trends of Nomadia. He used scrying to find out more."

Elmira sighed. "I don't know scrying, so there's only one thing for us to do. We have to leave the crypt and go into Nomadia ourselves."

A look of fright crossed Vero's face, but he nodded. "When do we leave?"

"When do we leave?" Elmira repeated, crossing the room to him and pressing the torch back into his good hand. "This is what I like about you, Vero. You might be frightened, but you'll do whatever it takes. That's the kind of heart that is needed to reach our goals. First, I want to read over the wizard's books and scrolls. I don't know what we'll need for our journey, so I'll leave the provisions to you. When we leave, we go to Dustania. I want to have a word with the slave traders there."

17

DARYA

Darkness gathered around Darya whether she opened or closed her eyes. A terrible thirst burned in her body, but when she tried to reach out, there was nothing. Where had her magic gone? She was strong, powerful, and should not have been caught like a fish in the sea. Fish were a life source, no more, no less, and to become one of them, nameless, an object to be sold, made her struggle all the more.

The water in the container had drained away, leaving her in the form of the landwalkers, although a hard layer of scales covered her body. When she twisted her wrists in the rope, they moved against her scales, and she imagined they were weakening. Gritting her teeth, she kept going, shifting her arms and legs to rub the rope. It was thick, and she had no idea how long it would take, but she needed to escape, to breathe the pure sea air and continue her quest.

Klarya's flashing eyes and mocking laughter bubbled in

her memory. She could almost hear the words her sister would say: *Look at you now, Darya, trapped before you even made it to land. How hopeless you are. You'll never amount to anything in the Court of Nymphs.*

A scraping sound interrupted her thoughts, and the container Darya was trapped in moved. A sickening swinging made her stomach lurch, and bile rose in her throat. She didn't want to be sick all over herself and forced it down, struggling harder. With some effort, she brought her knees up and, by jerking her pelvis up, slammed them against the top of the container. Her knees struck with a loud thump, but the box did not give way.

"Aye!" a voice shouted. "Stop that racket in there."

"That's the creature I was telling you about," another muffled voice said. "A beautiful sea creature. A nymph, they say."

"Let's have a look," another unfamiliar voice said.

Darya stilled herself. They would open the container, and she'd flee.

Another scraping sound came, and suddenly light streamed in, brilliant, bright, and blinding. The rich, spicy scent of loam plagued her nose, so strong that combined with the light, her eyes watered. A shape hovered over Darya. She tried to spring up, but her legs wouldn't work and she could not gain any leverage with her arms tied behind her back. Gloved hands closed around her upper arms and hauled her out into the light. She blinked, trying to see as low whistles echoed around her.

"By the gods."

"She's a beauty."

"Wild and feral. Look at her."

"What's with the scales?"

"It's normal, like a turtle shell. She's frightened and will hide under her armor until she feels safe."

"You don't want her to reveal herself; she'll seduce you."

Darya's blurry vision cleared, revealing two huge men standing in front of her. They were at least two feet taller than her, with tanned skin and muscled arms. One had a gold ring in his ear and brown hair gathered at the nape of his neck. His deep-set eyes were dark as night, and a piece of straw hung from his meaty lips as he considered her. After a moment, he rubbed his bearded jaw and nudged the man standing beside him. "She'll catch a fair price in market."

"Aye," the other one agreed. He was just as tall, and had a tuft of hair that stuck up from his mostly bald head. A gold ring hung in his nose, and thick gold bands covered his bare arms. "We'll give you fifty silver for her."

Someone snorted and Darya noticed that, aside from the two men holding her, there was someone else. A woman stepped forward with a wide hat on her head, a billowing shirt, and black pants. Her stringy brown hair hung loose, and she crossed her arms over her chest. "Are you trying to cheat me? She's a magical creature from the depths; she's worth two hundred silver at least."

"Pssh. With an attitude like that, you'll cut into our profits. If you wish to sell her without the blessing of the guild, go ahead and see how much you'll make. You know, and we know, your best chance is to sell her to us. I'll give you sixty silver."

"One hundred and fifty at least," the woman protested. "We did all the hard work of catching and subduing her. Whose tourmaline do you think she wears?"

"Bah, we brought our own, but since you mentioned the work, you're right, we'll reimburse you for the time you spent catching her, even though it's your job to search for creatures in the depths. Another ten silver should cover it."

"What about damages to our ship?" the woman demanded.

"One hundred silver pieces and that's my final offer," snarled the man.

"Done." The woman held out her hand.

She and the man shook, and then he handed her a sack that jingled.

Mouth dry, it took Darya a moment to realize she'd been sold to the giants. The bracelets on her wrists and ankles were replaced, and the one on her neck taken away completely.

"Pleasure doing business with you," the woman said, tucking the bracelets into a pouch. Turning, she walked away, her men following behind her.

Darya stared after them, her mind reeling. What should she do? How would she find the sea again? Around her, the land spread out as far as she could see. There was a dusty road and a cliff, beyond which came the faint hum of waves. She was close to home. It struck her, with a pang, that her goal wasn't to return home but to reach the empire of Nomadia. She'd reached land already, which meant all she had to do was gain her freedom, find a body of water that led to the great library, and get the remedy.

"Do you have a name?"

Darya jerked to face the giant man who'd spoken to her. His lip curled as he studied her, his eyes shifting to roam down her body. Swallowing, she fought to find words, but her mouth was too dry.

"Shy?" the giant cocked a brow.

He took a step toward her, and Darya did not like the expression that darkened his face. She turned on shaking legs and tried to run, but the rope was too tight and she pitched forward. An arm caught her about the waist and lifted her off her feet. She was thrown over the giant's shoulder like a bag of seashells, kicking and writhing.

"This is a lively one," he said. "I pity the person who buys her."

The other giant laughed. "Give her a drink. That'll keep her calm until market day."

The giant dropped her and Darya fell into something soft and scratchy.

"Lie still, precious," he said as he pulled a flask from his hip and shook it.

Darya's eyes darted to the flask as liquid sloshed inside.

"Open your mouth," he leered, a glimmer coming to his eyes.

Darya's heart thudded, unsure of what she should do. She was thirsty, but she was no fool.

The giant frowned. "Fine. Last chance. You won't like it if I do it my way."

Darya bared her teeth and hissed. She wanted to struggle more, wanted to fight, but exhaustion and fear made it impossible. The man opened the flask and pressed one leg against Darya's thighs to keep her from bucking and kicking him. Still, she managed to bring her head forward to butt him. With a grunt, he pressed an arm against her throat.

"Open your mouth!" he growled.

Darya hesitated, and that hesitation cost her. Powerful fingers squeezed her jaw, forcing her mouth open. A warm liquid pooled inside, and she involuntarily swallowed. It burned as it went down. Her eyes filled with water and she choked, gasping and sobbing as the liquid continued into her body. Warmth spread from her chest and radiated down into her belly, setting her on fire. Darya bucked, but the giant holding her down was too strong. When at last he stopped, liquid dripped down her chin and spread across her neck.

"There." The giant stood. "That should keep you docile until market day."

Darya tried to move, to protest, but whatever was in the liquid had done its work. A numbness spread through her body, and an unpleasant tingling made her nauseous. The world seemed to slow and tilt. Her vision went hazy again, and she heard the giant calling, "We'll get her some clothes, and she'll make us a nice pile of money!"

The crack of a whip sounded, and Darya was dragged away, fighting to keep her wits about her.

18

ARACELI

Golden light flooded the room, erasing the shadows of night. Araceli's lips parted as she took in the floor to ceiling window. It showed off the sleeping city, along with a beautiful view of the night sky, with stars glimmering in the heavens. The room was much bigger than her previous one, with a bed large enough for two or three to sleep on comfortably, piled with blankets. Thick rugs covered the floor, a fire burned in the hearth, and a man sat at a table drinking a glass of red wine.

"Close the door behind you," he said.

The door clicked shut and Araceli stared. In the light, she could see Kaiden clearly for the first time. He was tall, lean, and now wore clothes. A black shirt, open at the neck, covered the muscles of his chest. The edges of the shirt were framed with gold, and he had loose trousers fitted around his waist. A pair of slippers hid his feet, and his black hair was slicked back from his wide forehead and curled around his neck. Araceli gawked helplessly. She'd noticed his beauty before, but in the light he was handsome, beautiful —breathtaking.

When he looked at her, long lashes framed his brown eyes, and she sucked in a breath as a fluttering began in her stomach. This was what Shyrin talked about, wasn't it? Marrow-deep attraction that made her want those eyes to stay on hers, those hands to graze her skin, and those warm lips to . . .

No, she couldn't think like a lovelorn fool. Tearing her eyes away from his profile, she studied the room again. "How?"

"I assumed your meeting this morning did not go well."

"How did you know?"

His lip curled. "Ah. I merely deducted based on what I know about you. So I took matters into my own hands. As an esteemed guest who will stay for a while, this is my room. Now, you are most welcome to join me here, seeing as your room has been taken over by others. If this new arrangement is disagreeable to you, of course, you can sleep outside the door. I doubt it will be comfortable."

"What?" Araceli sputtered. How dare he hurl her words back at her!

Kaiden leaned back in the chair and took another slow sip of wine. "Yes, I'm listening. Do you have something you'd like to say?"

Araceli crossed her arms. "But this is my new room."

He raised an eyebrow. "Is it? How strange for you to take the credit when I did all the work. We will have to agree to disagree. This is my room, and you are a welcome guest. The floor is yours. Note, I ensured that you'd have plenty of blankets and furs to replicate the experience of the pallet you so enjoyed. I'm also willing to share my food and drink with you, but first you have to take off that horrible garment."

"I'm not dining with you naked," Araceli spat.

Kaiden covered his eyes. "I should hope not."

He pointed, and Araceli followed the direction of his gesture to a screen. It was open and effectively hid a portion of the room from view.

"I took the liberty of selecting proper attire for you to wear. After you take off that lump of clothing you call a uniform, toss it in the fire. From now on, you will dress like an ink mage."

Araceli glared at him. How could she be grateful to the jinn when his tone was so disparaging—when he mocked her while sitting there, drinking wine? A covered tray of what she assumed was food rested on the table. The smell was making her mouth water and her stomach growled. Perhaps it would be worth it to follow his directions just for a taste of that food.

"Just so you know," she called from behind the screen, "I'm just doing this so you will teach me magic."

He grunted in reply.

She figured the disdain in his tone meant he would not peek over the screen, so Araceli hastily discarded the offending outfit and studied what he'd laid out for her. Hooks on the wall held a row of dresses, and beside them on shelves were folded shirts, vests, pants, belts, and a cloak. Shame washed over Araceli. It was as if she'd invited a man to live with her, except he'd turned it around and claimed she was living with him. This was wrong and deeply inappropriate, especially given their relationship. Besides, there was only one bed, and he expected her to sleep on the floor. If he were truly a chivalrous gentleman, he would have arranged for two beds. Although, from what she knew of him, he was not kind, only looking to complete the transaction between them so he could move on to another more worthy master or mistress.

"Wear the blue one," Kaiden called.

He was still telling her what to do! She reached for the only blue dress there was. The heavy gold patterning on it caught the light when she pulled it free and held it up. The material was cool and soft on her fingers, and she pressed it to her face, catching a faint earthy scent. Had he perfumed her clothes?

Even though the dress appeared too small, she pulled it on and faced the looking glass next to the hooks. The dress would have been suitable to wear to the spring rites. It wrapped around her body, slipping off her shoulders and hugging her chest. Around her waist the dress was tight, then flowed over her hips and ended just below her knees. It was the most beautiful garment she'd ever owned, and she wished she could show it to Shyrin. She looked like a different creature, and with relief she found a hole for her tail. It was perfect, even though her shoulders were bare and her hair tickled her back.

Bracing herself for Kaiden's approval, she stepped from behind the screen, hands at her sides.

Kaiden's eyes narrowed as he studied her. His gaze traveled every inch of her body, lingering on her bare skin. "At last, you look grown up. Sit." He leaned forward and poured another glass of wine. "Tell me, what is your name again?"

The budding attraction she'd felt toward him fled. She sat down, frowning across the table at him. "Are you always this forgetful?"

"It's hard to remember things when I'm uncomfortable and disoriented from being shifted out of a small space into a dark room. It's even worse when I don't have a chance to rejuvenate."

Araceli picked up the glass of wine to give her hands something to do. "But aren't you immortal? Do you need to eat and sleep and drink?"

"I have a body, don't I? If I don't take care of it, it will fall into disarray. I'm not vain, but I am treated better when I look like an immortal god. As for sleep, I enjoy it. It makes the time pass faster; no need to sit up all night, waiting for another wish, especially in your case, when it could be years before you decide."

Araceli glared at him. "It won't be years."

The way he spoke stirred feelings inside of her she didn't know she had. She wanted to spar with words and retort to every comment he made, when normally she would duck her head and remain docile.

"I certainly don't know that." He spread a white napkin on his lap and took the cover off the tray that lay between them.

The minor spat faded as Araceli stared. This was a meal meant for a lord, with cuts of a pink fish, bread, green vegetables, and fruit from the gardens. "Where did you get this?"

"Does it matter? I'm a jinn. Now eat," he commanded, serving her a portion. "Afterward, we shall begin your first lesson. I assumed you also did not bring ink and parchment."

Araceli couldn't bring herself to reply as the fish melted in her mouth. No wonder he'd turned up his nose at the mush she'd brought him. If this was what life could be like, how could she go back? Fear edged into her, and she dropped her fork, half rising from the chair. "Where's the book? Did you tell anyone?"

"No." For once, Kaiden's response was solemn. "You seemed frightened, and I intend to read the book further. True, it's a magical tome, but not what I expected you to have in your possession. I believe we'd both be in trouble if anyone discovers we have it."

Araceli noticed he said "we," then sat back down. "Then you'll keep the secret? You're on my side?"

His lips curled. "Until your wishes are fulfilled, I am your jinn. It is in my best interest to always be on your side."

Even though he spoke the truth, his words rang hollow, and Araceli dug into her meal, ignoring him for the moment.

When they finished, the moon lamps burned low and shadows crept over the walls. Kaiden wiped his mouth, poured another glass of wine, and cleared the table. Araceli watched, pretending she wasn't, but his movements were elegant, like a dancer's, and as long as he kept his mouth shut, he was beautiful. The sharp angles of his face were perfected in the shadows, and she caught herself thinking of his chest and those muscles. What would they look like close up? What would they feel like?

He laid a pot of ink, a quill, and a piece of parchment on the table. "Eventually you will need a wand, but for now I want to see your penmanship. Write your name."

Araceli did so and showed him.

"You already possess a good hand; I take it you practice?"

"I rarely have the time."

"Then you are a natural. An ink mage will have a good command of writing, but it is the language of magic you'll need to understand."

Araceli's heart swelled with pride. She was a natural.

"A good ink mage recognizes that power comes from within. They write with confidence, *knowing* the words they write will turn into spells. There are two kinds of ink mages: those who create runes and spells, and those who use them. First, I will instruct you on how to use runes and spells that have already been created."

"Beginning with the book?"

"Beginning with runes. You'll have to read them before you can cast them, and I want you to have a grasp of the introductory elements before you dive deep into the craft. This will help you avoid the mistakes that many mages have made in their pursuit of power. Patience is key, as is diligence. One mistake could mean a spell goes wrong, and that could have dire consequences."

"I see." Araceli nodded, although her tail swished back and forth in excitement.

"These are the runes you will learn." He leaned over her, breath hot on her neck as he lifted the quill from her fingers. He wrote in quick, decisive strokes, brushing out a series of runes below her name.

"Practice," he said, his voice a velvet whisper in her ear.

Araceli's entire body shivered from the contact, goosebumps pebbling on her arms as he pulled back.

"While you write, I'm going to read more of this dark book and see what ruin you've dragged us into. I've seen much in my days, but nothing like this."

Grateful for a distraction, Araceli bent her head to the parchment and copied down the runes.

When she finished filling both sides of the parchment, she leaned back, suddenly drained from the exertion. The double moons glowed through the window, and she gazed at them. Peace filled her heart. Things were changing. She had a purpose, and soon she'd learn magic. A yawn burst out of her mouth, and she wanted nothing more than to lay her head down and dream of runes.

Turning her attention to the bed, she froze. Kaiden sat in the middle of it, pillows plumped around him. The book lay open in his lap, but he was staring boldly at her, his expression blank. A chill passed through Araceli as she wondered how long he'd been staring at her. "I've finished." She stood, sealing the pot of ink.

His gaze did not flicker. "Tell me, Araceli, how did you summon me?"

The innocent question felt dangerous, hanging in the air between them like a blade. Araceli's mouth went dry. "I opened the book and brushed the runes with my fingers."

"Not possible; think back, what did you do?"

Araceli thought back to the moment: her desire, her need for the book to speak to her, for things to change. "I breathed on the words, and I begged them to work."

His fingers moved over the page. "Interesting. This book is spelled to protect it, but it also tells me you did not steal it. Someone gave you this book. I wonder why."

Araceli didn't move, her fingers rigid with fear. Part of her wanted to tell Kaiden about her encounter with the mage, but the other part of her screamed for silence. She trusted the jinn for now, but what would happen when she made two more wishes and he was gone? What then? She had to protect herself now, because one day the jinn's best interests wouldn't be hers.

He closed the book and tucked it under a pillow. "You look weary. The magic of ink can be draining; you should sleep."

"On the floor?" Araceli asked, hoping he'd changed his mind.

Kaiden's lips curled. "I am more than willing to share the bed with you. I'll stay to this side"—he scooted over—"and you take the other side. Just don't try to entrap me with your tail."

Araceli bristled. "No thanks. I'll sleep on the floor!"

19

DARYA

The scent of bitter cloves woke Darya. Opening her eyes, she fought to recall what had happened to her. When she swished her tail, heavy legs wiggled. She sat up, gasping with the effort. Her hands were tied in front of her with manacles around them.

Tourmaline, they'd called it. It itched at her scales and she wanted it off, for it seemed to block her from accessing her power. Tears pricked her eyes, but she swallowed them back. If Klarya and her other sisters could see her now they'd laugh —the folly of Darya, determined to save the sirens from the sea witch's curse only to fall into the hands of landwalkers.

She didn't know what kind of landwalkers they were; she'd only heard tales of those who lived on the land: humans, elves, fauns, and darker creatures. The ones who'd captured her seemed like humans, but she knew nothing of them, only that she had to escape and find water.

It was dark, the room small and hollow, like a cave. Fear

perched like a rod of ice over her heart, ready to slide inside. Tentatively, she stood, hunched low, relieved to find that only her hands were tied. Her green hair slid down her back as she moved to the entrance and pushed.

The door wasn't locked. She stumbled forward, legs trembling, into light. It was eerie, bright, and she brought her hand up to shield her eyes. Pale orange hues shone in, and a hot wind blew. Grit swirled around her bare feet and bit between her scales, making her itch and long for water.

Water. Where was it? She sniffed, knowing that if she followed her nose she'd reach the scent, dive in, and beat the bracelets off her arms and legs with a rock. Once her power returned, she'd drown the ones who wished her ill, who had sold her for coin and rendered her powerless.

When her eyes adjusted to the light, she took in a narrow passage full of what looked like boards stacked on top of each other. The longer she stared at them, the more she realized they were cages, some with bars, some without, but all filled with either a person or an animal. Her mouth went dry as eyes stared back at her, large, sad, and hopeless.

A wall of emotion slammed through her and unease crept up her spine, driving her forward. Gaining speed on shaky legs, she made her way down the path. It widened, and the doors to the building were open, guiding her outside. She wanted to sigh with relief, but it was too soon; she wasn't free, and the air was thick with grit, the scent of water long gone.

Outside, the ground sloped down, leading to a structure built high off the ground, like a stage or a dais for royalty. A man relaxed in a chair up there, drinking and laughing with a few others. She'd have to avoid them, and she glanced around for a place to hide, but there was nowhere. The land was wide open, showing other structures and people milling about. Far off, something brown wrapped around the structures and led away. Far away, she hoped. Hope budded in her heart like a fresh flower unfolding, and she stepped forward. What if she simply walked away, and they didn't notice her?

Tucking her head down, she walked. Laughter echoed around her, mixed in with inaudible whispers and higher cries. The sights and the sounds were too much. Her heart kicked, and she walked faster, giving the men on the platform a wide berth. She wanted to run, was desperate to be free, but everywhere she looked, people milled about casually, and she didn't want to stand out.

"Hey there!" someone shouted, and her fear kicked up a notch.

"Grog, isn't that the creature you just bought?"

A rough laugh boomed out. "She's escaping while you're drinking."

"Look at her go, thinks she can just walk away from us."

"Grog, get out of your cups and teach her a lesson."

"Aw man, should have known she'd walk. Furious little creature."

"She's not so little, if you know what I mean."

"She'd be more fun if she didn't have those scales covering her, if you know what *I* mean."

"Hush up boys, and behave; this is merchandise we're talking about."

Darya wasn't sure what all the words meant, but the tone of their banter told her she was in trouble. She burst into a run, fleeing past the platform into a wide square. Brown dust churned under her feet, kicking up gravel and grit. It stung as it hit her, but she gritted her teeth, almost falling over as she

ANGELA J. FORD

tried to really use her legs for the first time. In the end, her balance threw her off. She went down hard, sliding into the dirt as people leaped out of the way, shouting.

"Watch it!"

"What do you think you're doing?"

"Be more careful!"

Darya flailed, but unlike the water, the ground was not forgiving. Her bones jarred, and then a voice bellowed, "I'll take it from here."

Something hit her back, though the blow was more jarring than painful. She heard a whistle, and something slammed into her back again. She rolled, arms bending to protect her face, but she couldn't do a good job because of the bonds around her wrists. A man leered over her, face red, with an odd whip—if that was what it was—in his hand. It had more than one tail, and they spread out as he drew back his arm. Darya whimpered as the tails tore at her, and the man bellowed, "That will teach you, running off on my watch!"

The whip came down again and again. Darya rolled, a keening sound coming out of her mouth. She wanted to speak, but the shock of the blows was too much and the man was strong. The impact jarred her through her scales as though they weren't there, and a heat inflamed her body, spreading from every inch he struck.

A hoarse scream tore out of her mouth as the whip slashed at her arms and cut across her belly and thighs. She rolled in the dust, trying to escape it, and the grit irritated her scales even more. The whip slammed into her back. Darya arched and hissed before flinging her palms out to halt him with water magic, but the power lay dormant inside her.

She managed to regain her footing, only crying out as the whip caught one cheek. She ducked the next blow, but the man grabbed a fistful of her hair and dragged her backward. Pain shot up and tugged at her head, then rippled down her spine. Her body shook with shame and anger, more so when she caught the eyes of others. They'd stopped whatever they were doing to stare at the performance as she was shamed, whipped in front of them like a criminal. Was that what they thought she was? A common criminal?

Her breath came hot, heavy, and fast. She gasped for dust-infused air as the man dragged her to a wooden block and bent her over it, holding her down with one heavy hand. She heard him panting and smelled the stink of his breaths as he beat her. Darya's breath hitched; she couldn't breathe, and soon all she could sense was the agony swirling around her. Each strike cut through her, making her scream. Kicking her legs, she struggled to escape, but the man was too strong. Tears ran down her cheeks and curses rose to her lips. She should have listened to Mother; she never listened, and now the worst was happening to her.

Shouts echoed behind her, and then it stopped. It all stopped. The hand left her back, but she was too weak to move. She slumped against the wood, then fell back, sending fresh waves of pain shooting through her. She was trying to crawl away, forgetting that her hands were still bound, when a man lifted her up.

"Easy on the goods, Grog. She needs to sell well so we can make back our money."

"Oh, she'll make money, or else!"

"You know how buyers don't like damaged goods."

"Give her a drink and put her back to rest, and she'll be ready for market day."

Hands pulled her down, and something brown and scratchy was bundled over her head. Her bonds were cut, her hands free for the first time, and then two of them tilted her head back and poured a disgusting liquid down it. Choking and kicking, Darya succumbed to her tormentors.

20

ELMIRA

W hen Elmira stepped outside for the first time in years, the brilliance of the sunshine made tears roll down her cheeks. It was blistering hot, standing in full sunlight, and a warm wind blew. She lifted her face to the sky, wide and blue without a cloud in sight, and waved her arms in the wind. She did not care how hot it was, nor how the sand burned her bare feet when it flew over them.

She wanted to run, to cry, to roll in the sand, to hug it and hold it and throw it to the wind. She was outside; she could breathe and feel. It was like being reborn. Life had been given to her again, and the dark dreams, the torment, misery, and pain were behind her. An iron will rose inside her. If she felt this way after coming out of captivity, what might others feel when they were released from their bonds? They would fall to their knees and thank her, as Vero had, for saving them from torment and death. She would be their savior.

Vero came up beside her, dressed in white from head to

toe as if the sunlight would smother him. Elmira raised an eyebrow, and for the first time in a long time, something that wasn't hatred or anger stirred in her belly. "What are you wearing?"

"Here." Vero handed her a long white robe and another piece of material. "The wizard wore similar garb when he traveled. He said it protects from the sunlight and heat."

The very last thing Elmira wanted was to protect herself from the sunlight, but it was blistering hot, and the wizard, much as she hated him, had good reasons for doing most things. Rolling her eyes, because it was annoying to have a dead wizard still guiding her actions, she shrugged on the robe and wrapped the turban around her head.

Next, Vero handed her shoes. "To protect your feet."

With yet another heavy sigh, Elmira put them on, feeling as though she were hiding herself from the world. "Anything else for me to put on?"

Vero shook his head, even though he held two packs. Elmira glanced from his hunched shoulder to his mangled hand and snatched one. "Give me that and stop trying to protect me from everything. You're my equal, not my servant."

Vero had nothing to say, and they set off across the desert. Within an hour, Elmira was sick of it. Walking, something she hadn't been able to do for so long, was a bore. Especially because of the endless sand. Her feet sunk into it, and the warm wind blew it up around her legs, rubbing grit into her wounds, which were still healing. Her skin stung, and she wished she already had the power of the wind to blow the tiny particles away. No path led through the desert; sometimes in the distance she saw dunes, but nothing else.

Fear threatened to override reason as she walked away

from everything she knew into the heart of the desert, based on the plans of a wicked wizard. After reading the wizard's books, she knew more about ink magic, which she'd need to summon spirits. All four powers interlocked together, building on each other. It would be much easier to collect them all if she could teleport to each location, find what was needed, and use the wings of wind to take her away. Curses. It was only sheer luck that the lamp and the book had been stolen before the wizard got his hands on them, but she wished she'd been able to find them.

With that thought, she glanced back, for the lost pyramids were called lost for a reason. No one could find them, save for a desert tribe who claimed their line came from King Horus himself. Impossible, since the king died childless. His children had either died when they were young or were killed in battle. Now that she'd left, would she be able to find the pyramids again? She wasn't sure if she wanted to, even with magic.

"Who travels like this?" she announced at last, coming to a stop. Her feet were blistered, the heat was almost unbearable, she was thirsty, and that hunger, that craving for souls, felt heavy in the pit of her belly.

Vero panted beside her, dropped his pack in the sand, and pulled out a waterskin. She expected him to take a drink, but he handed it to her. "The desert tribes have camels."

Elmira tilted her head, recalling the word, and soon a memory filled her vision. Humped beasts who like to spit. She recalled giggling when she rode one for the first time. Yes, they needed camels. "How do we find a desert tribe?" She took a sip and handed the waterskin back to Vero. "Drink first, then answer."

Vero drank, wiped the back of his mouth, then pointed to

a smudge on the horizon. "Those dunes look like a place to start. The desert tribes are nomads, moving in search of water and shelter. Perhaps the dunes provide shelter for them while they travel."

Elmira leveled her gaze at him. "Did the wizard know you are smart? No, don't answer that. Your deductive reasoning will serve us well." She turned toward the dunes. "We go in search of camels, and then we need a guide to take us to Dustania."

21

ARACELI

After two nights of sleeping on the floor, despite the rugs and blankets, Araceli's neck was stiff and sore. Her back ached, and each morning she stared at the bed with envy. Kaiden woke refreshed, often before she did, and opened the heavy curtains, letting the morning light stream in. It warmed the room, along with the fire, although the palace was usually even-tempered no matter the season. Another gift of magic.

Araceli woke that morning, disgruntled, to the smell of a dark brew. Each morning, Kaiden had put together some odd mixture of water, crushed beans, and spices. It smelled devilish and whenever he drank it, she expected to see horns sprout out of his head.

"What is that?" she groaned, pressing a hand to her head, which pulsed. She ran her fingers down her neck, trying to relieve the ache.

"Coffee," Kaiden announced, pouring himself a cup. "I

can make you some, if you like. It is a delicacy, rare where I come from, but available here. I like to indulge when time allows."

Araceli assumed it was a drink for the wealthy and untangled herself from the blankets. "Exactly where do you come from?"

"The desert. I grew up near the great pyramids. Do you know the tales of the King of Sand?"

"I've heard of them." Araceli moved behind the screen to dress. "Yes, King Horus, right? He is buried in the desert of Iscaria, but legends claim the pyramids have been lost for ages."

"Yes, and many have sought them, though those who succeeded kept the secret to themselves. Regardless, it is a hot land, full of blistering sunrises, cold nights, and a dry heat that makes fire seem like a joke."

Araceli doubted that, although she'd never been outside of the capital. The lands depicted in tales seemed like dreams, although part of her was curious to see what they were really like, the forests and mountains, plains and valleys, jungles and deserts, and most of all the great sea that was peppered with islands. She'd seen it on a map once, and the vastness of the empire was impossible to wrap her mind around. "Did you like it there?"

Kaiden's voice went flat. "I was free."

Stepping out from behind the screen, Araceli studied his face. For the first time, she thought she glimpsed the truth of who he was, the person he kept buried under quips and retorts and unfriendly words. Now his eyes were on the sky, a wistful look in them as he gazed up and out. Araceli almost felt sorry for him. Almost. Until he faced her. "Ah, you look quite the librarian. No one has complained about your new clothes, have they?"

"No," she admitted begrudgingly. "The head mistress even complimented the elegance of my new uniform."

"Good. When you return this evening I want to try some spells. When is your day off? Do you work in the library every day?"

"Just six days a week, but on my day off I usually go to the city square to meet a friend."

Kaiden's eyebrows shot up. "You have friends?"

"Don't look so surprised."

"If you're going out, I'll come along."

Araceli's eyes widened. "You can't! You're a secret. No one can find out about you or the book."

His gaze flickered to the bed and back to her. "No one will. Besides, I pretended to be your valet to secure this room. No one need know I'm a jinn. It's not something you'd tell your friends. Would you?"

Araceli's retort died in her throat. She had intended on telling Shyrin, but now that she actually considered it, she'd have to explain about the mage and the book and that she was learning ink magic. Would Shyrin be able to handle the truth, and could she keep the secret?

She marched to the door, fingers trembling, and at the last minute, whirled around. "I'll think of something to explain you," she said and slipped out the door.

How long could she keep up the act? Was learning ink magic worth the secrets and fear of discovery?

When Araceli reached the library, hushed whispers filled the air. She walked past stacks of books waiting to be put away, only stopping when she reached Mistress Vina's room.

It was a reading room with plush chairs, a table covered with books, and a desk. The elf sat at her desk, writing, her quill a white poof as it moved. Araceli wondered if it was made from the feathers of a rare magical bird.

Mistress Vina looked up, pressed a hand to her heart, and smiled. "Araceli, I didn't see you there."

Araceli sat in one of the chairs, uninvited, since that's what Kaiden would have done. "I was wondering if I could have a day off. Two this week, instead of one."

Mistress Vina folded her hands delicately on the desk and pressed her lips together. "Why is that?"

She shrugged. "I just want some extra time to myself. I also wondered if there's a spare room where I might catch some sleep. My room has become uncomfortable lately and I think I need a change."

"I see what is happening here." Rising, Mistress Vina closed the door, then sat down on the chair opposite from Araceli. "You grow restless, which is not unusual. You have served for years, happily doing your tasks without question. Other than your tendency to daydream, I have had no complaints about your work. I believe an extra day can be granted, but not this week. We have unusual guests, and I'd like you to serve their needs."

Dread knotted in Araceli's belly. "Unusual?"

"Yes, humans have traveled from their city to study here. There is a lord of the land in the library. You may have heard the whispers."

Humans were rare in the empire of Nomadia. Not as rare as blue fauns, but they weren't as numerous as the other races. Many of them dwelled to the northwest of the city. Their land consisted of rolling hills where they maintained vineyards and produced wine to trade to the capital. Aside from their endeavors in wine making, Araceli knew little about humans. Hopefully they weren't the enemy the mage had spoken of, but she couldn't know for sure. "Why are they here? What are they studying?"

"That is even more curious." Mistress Vina leaned forward, her voice dropping to a whisper as if the very walls could hear her. "Unlike our other guests, they peruse the library themselves. I have set them up with a room and will see to them personally should they ring, but I want you to assist me as long as they are here. After they leave, you may take an extra day."

"Thank you." Araceli rose.

Mistress Vina held up a hand. "One other matter."

Araceli sat back down, twisting her fingers together, resolved to stay calm unless she heard bad news.

"Madam Zansha came to see me to complain about a request from you. We both know how she is. In the future, if you'd like to discuss your living arrangements, please come directly to me. You have been given what is deemed worthy for a librarian, and I wouldn't want Madam Zansha's complaints to go any further than this. She could have you reassigned to another position, and I certainly prefer you here."

Araceli's face flushed. "I . . . I meant no harm. She was so busy I didn't think she heard me."

"She forgets nothing, so consider this a warning and be more cautious of your place here next time."

With burning ears, Araceli turned. All the bravery she'd borrowed from Kaiden faded away. "Of course, I overstepped. It won't happen again."

Mistress Vina opened the door, ending their conversation, and Araceli hurried away to the stacks of books waiting for her. She'd never considered that Madam Zansha would complain to Mistress Vina, and now she wished she'd gone directly to Mistress Vina in the first place. But she'd been reprimanded, and now she realized Mistress Vina agreed with Madam Zansha. What would they do if they discovered she was learning ink magic?

Araceli considered the issue as she worked tirelessly, keeping an eye out for the humans. She wished she had someone to talk to about her predicament, aside from the jinn. He didn't understand her at all and was only waiting for her to make her wishes. If she had some sense, she would wish him free and be done with it, but she also had a feeling she'd want a second wish, at least, and needed his help before she set him free. He'd alluded to the fact that granting her wishes would take work on her part, but what career opportunities were there for a blue faun who also happened to be an ink mage?

She was so deep in thought, she didn't notice the man until he spoke. "Hello," he said, his voice as smooth as silk. "Will you be able to assist me?"

22

ARACELI

He was human, with dark hair, a scar under his cheek, a straight nose, and a strong chin covered with a week's worth of stubble. He was much older than her, but it was his eyes that arrested her, deep, old, and full of pain and memories. She sensed a tiredness from him, almost a desperation. Her heart went out to him, and she suddenly wanted to help, no matter what it was, no matter what would happen.

"How may I assist you?" she asked, remembering to bow her head. Mistress Vina said she would personally assist the humans, but they hadn't rung at all.

He smiled a smile that hovered on his lips but dropped away just as quickly. "You have worked here long?"

"All my life."

"Good, I'm looking for a specific book. I have reason to believe a mage left it here, in care of the library. He may not have mentioned it, but he intended to leave it for me. The problem is, I can't find it. Perhaps you assisted the mage when he was here and can help."

Araceli stiffened. The book! Was this the enemy who was coming for it? Her mouth went dry. "We . . . I . . . I see many books here. Do you know the title?"

The man gave a short laugh and brushed his hair back, a movement that reminded her of the jinn. "It has no title."

"A nameless book?" Araceli tried to add surprise to her voice, and was sure she'd failed miserably. The library was supposed to be her haven, but right now all she wanted to do was run away as fast as she could.

"A magic book," the man confirmed. "Leather bound with runes on it, depending on how one looks at it."

He certainly was talking about the book. She wanted to ask him why he sought it, why he needed it, but she didn't know what to say or do. "I can look for it." She shrugged. "But we have thousands of books here."

"I've noticed," he agreed. "Not all are magical, though. Surely you have a section for those?"

This was her moment. "We do. Let me escort you to Mistress Vina. She has access to the magical texts and can unlock the room for you."

The man shook his head. "No need. I will continue, but if you hear of anything, please let me know."

"I will," she breathed.

"My name is Lord Elias. If you find anything, simply ask for me."

Araceli's heart pounded as he walked away and she sagged to the carpet, taking deep breaths to still her panic. Did he know? Did he suspect she had the book? Was the residue of magic on her fingertips?

The rest of the day, she crept around the shelves and jumped at shadows. When at last the sun began to set, she almost ran back to her room, all the while looking over her shoulder to ensure she wasn't followed. She crashed into the room before slamming the door shut and bending over to catch her breath.

"Araceli?"

"He's here!" she gasped. "I saw him in the library, he's looking for the book. What should we do?"

"Sit, you look wild and panicked." Kaiden pulled out a chair.

"There's no time, we have to act, we have to hide the book. He came directly to me, as if he could read my mind."

Kaiden took her by the shoulders and steered her across the room into a chair. Setting a cup down in front of her, he poured hot water into it, followed by leaves that he pulled out of a jar. "Drink that," he instructed. "It should help. Your hair is wild and your eyes are red; I hope you didn't panic in front of the man."

Hints of peppermint drifted to her nose, growing stronger as the tea leaves seeped. Araceli took a deep breath, surprised to see her hands were shaking. Kaiden sat across from her, but the mockery was gone from his eyes. "If you are truly frightened, say the word and I will transport us far away from here."

Tempting, but would her problems disappear because she went into hiding? And what would happen if the mage returned to retrieve the book, and she wasn't there to give it back to him?

"No, I don't think that will resolve anything except delay

what will happen. What is so important about the book? Why do mages and humans want it?"

"You need to read it," Kaiden said. "From what I've read, it is a history book, but it also contains dangerous spells. I skipped some of the detailed pages, but it talks of weapons of destruction, control, and death. Though, it's no surprise that this book contains such things; the history of mages is full of war and deceit."

"Have I learned enough of the runes to read it?" Araceli took a sip of tea, and immediate relief flooded her body.

"Not remotely, but you're a quick learner, although right now you seem flustered. A beginner should not practice magic under duress. It only leads to mistakes."

"Then what should we do?"

"Nothing. They don't know you have the book. What do you think will happen if they come here and discover you have it?"

"Something terrible. I've never been in the middle of a magical dispute. What if they're looking for the book because they want to summon you? But I've already summoned you and they force me to complete my wishes so that they can use you for their plans?"

Kaiden's face darkened, and his fists clenched. "If it comes to that, promise me you'll set me free. I have seen dark things, and I don't wish to be the cause of them, no matter what the motives of mages are."

"He was human," Araceli said. "Humans rarely come here."

Kaiden rose and paced. "What do you know about old scrolls and prophecies?"

"I haven't studied those."

He faced her, eyes blazing. "Can you sneak books out of the library?"

"I shouldn't," she whispered.

"This is important." Kaiden's voice carried a note she'd never heard before. "I need an old scroll, a prophecy. It was given to the humans first, and should be kept in the old texts, in the *Prophecies of Nomadia*."

Araceli suddenly felt more wary than she had earlier, dodging the eyes of the humans. "I know what scrolls you speak of. They are kept in the great library, but hidden in the room of magical books, a room I don't have access to. Those who wish to study those books have to prove they do so as a scribe, a student, and not with evil intent. I cannot reach them for you."

Kaiden turned. "Let me mull over this tonight. I vaguely recall the words, but it would be good to read them again."

"There's more," Araceli said, and because she did not have anyone else to talk to, told him about Mistress Vina and Madam Zansha and shared her concerns about being reassigned should she draw more attention to herself.

Kaiden perched on the edge of the table, watching her while she spoke. When she finished, she looked up into his inquisitive brown eyes. He did not comment or offer condolences. Instead, he smiled. The lines around his eyes crinkled.

"You're the most interesting mistress I've ever had," he announced. "Three wishes, and I have to talk you into using one. Why don't you use another to get rid of your problems? You'll have to be crafty with it. No, on another thought, I'd like to see how this goes. Your predicaments are almost entertaining, and I have days to myself to enjoy. I can actually make plans and do what I want to do." He rubbed his hands together.

Araceli pinched the bridge of her nose and made a face.

Kaiden broke out of his musings. "Are you in pain?"

"Yes. No. You know, what pains me is you! You have no empathy. All you think about is yourself and your own amusement. This is my life, and my neck is sore, my back aches, and my head is pounding from what happened, but all you can see is that you're entertained?"

At first, Kaiden didn't react, only hovered on the table, letting her words sink in. "Perhaps the years of my life have taught me to be callous, a side effect of the curse," he admitted. "But I do have the knowledge and foresight to help you, especially since we are trapped together. Come, lie down on the bed and I will help ease your physical aches."

Araceli's shoulders tightened before remembering the jinn wasn't attracted to her. A nerve pinched in her neck as she stood. "Are you going to work magic on me?"

"Not magic. Just like the tea relaxed your body, I will do the same."

"Sometimes I don't know whether I should trust you," Araceli sighed, making her way to the bed.

"Change first," Kaiden instructed. "You'll find a robe behind the screen."

Araceli did as requested, enjoying the feel of the silk robe against her skin. Tying it in front, she approached the bed. Close up, it was much bigger and seemed to beckon to her. She lay down on her back, staying on the side the jinn had not touched.

"Lie on your stomach." Kaiden sat on the edge of the bed, and the scent of eucalyptus filled the air.

Araceli breathed deep, the combination of the peppermint tea earlier and now the eucalyptus washing away her fears. Laying her head on a pillow, she tucked her arms beneath it.

Kaiden's fingers slid up her arms, brushed her hair to one side, and pressed against her bare neck. A slight pain came, and then nothing but bliss. Parting her lips, Araceli took another shuddering breath as he continued, his hands moving to her shoulders, pressing, releasing, and repeating.

A strange sensation came over her body, as if she were awakening, coming alive under his hands. When he pulled down the robe, baring her back to him, instead of protesting, a spike of liquid heat coursed through her veins.

The knots in her neck faded, and the soreness on her shoulders and back evaporated under his touch. His fingers kneaded her muscles, sending a dozen confusing thoughts racing through her mind, and delightful tingles danced through her skin as she sank to another level of bliss. It felt as if she were racing, careening, toward the edge of pleasure. With a sigh, she closed her eyes and gave in until sleep claimed her and dreams of ink took over.

23

NURIMIL

When Nurimil first laid eyes on her he knew, beyond the shadow of a doubt, with a furious knowing, undebatable and unequivocal, that it was her, and only her, that he wanted for as long as eternity would last. The knowledge was so strong, so powerful, it threatened to physically knock him over.

He felt it in the tips of his fingers and in a tingling that went from the top of his head straight down his spine to his toes. The knowing hummed in the marrow of his being, and although magic had never worked on him, he sensed it all around him as though it were a creature standing on his shoulders, screaming in his ears to wake up and pay attention. For there she was, the one who would change his life, his fate, his destiny.

And so he did what any hot-blooded, independent, selfish human like himself would do. He pulled his hat low over his eyes, squared his shoulders, and decided to get rid of her as soon as he could.

He hadn't traveled to the heights of the Frost Mountains and defeated the Ka-Fri, the largest ice leopard in the region, for nothing. He hadn't swum to the bottom of the sea and wrestled a giant squid for the most potent magical ink in all of the seven kingdoms for fun. And he sure hadn't fought the legendary shrieker of the Maldive Cliffs only to fall in love and toss away a lifetime of building his reputation and fortune. No. He decided right then and there, even as his head buzzed with knowledge. The water nymph had to go.

And his reasoning wasn't because of the complexities of a relationship between a human and a water nymph; that was the least of his worries. It was the sole fact that she would completely and utterly devastate his life as he knew it, and he wasn't ready for yet another drastic change, especially considering what had happened with the guild. Caring about someone else held a weight, a responsibility he wasn't ready for, and someone like her would come with a set of temptations and frustrations.

Nay, he wasn't ready to turn himself in and give his heart over for her, but he also couldn't leave her standing in the slave ring to be sold like some animal. His conscience pricked at him. He would buy her, free her, and take her back to her home. Once he finished with those three things, in that order, he would continue on his merry way, forgetting about her and the irritating possibilities surrounding her.

He sighed, and his horse, Bern, bumped his shoulder. "I knew I had a bad feeling about this," Nurimil complained, rubbing his jaw. Unshaven hairs pricked his rough fingertips.

His steely gaze went back to the block where slaves were

being sold. It was rare that he traveled near the slave rings. It was an impossible evil, the buying and selling of people from all races. There was some fetish in the people who bought fauns, satyrs, nymphs, elves, and other magical creatures to fulfill some horrid wish. And then there were the humans, mere humans, men, women, and children, sold as though they were horses, although some were not treated as well.

He'd seen it all, and still had a scar on his side from the little girl he'd tried to save. Though he'd succeeded, the lesson was learned: it was not up to him to interfere with the slave traders, and he would do no good in going up against them unless he had an army to command. But the rulers of Nomadia were not interested in sparing their armies to take down the slave trade. No, the empire was content to turn a blind eye, likely because it benefited from the business in some corrupt way. He shook himself out of his thoughts. There was no use dwelling on what could be; he had a good life, a grand life, full of adventure and freedom to do anything he pleased.

"Sold!" the slave trader shouted.

The bidding for a sharp-toothed troll ended, and the water nymph was next.

Nurimil touched Bern's nose and reached for his saddle-bag. Curses on this day. He was about to lose a lot of well-earned coin.

"Next we have a delightful water nymph, a magical creature caught just off the Cliffs of Dooms Drop," the slave master announced.

His assistant pulled the nymph forward by her bound hands. She was a slight creature, standing on two legs, but moved awkwardly, as though she was not used to walking. A brown burlap smock fell to her knees. It was likely something the slave traders had tossed on her after they yanked her out of the waters.

Blue and white scales covered her exposed flesh. Thick stone bracelets were on her wrists and ankles—tourmaline, a stone that blocked the wearer from using magic. Her eyes glowed like orbs in her petite face. Hair as green as seafoam cascaded down her shoulders, but it lay flat and stiff, lacking any kind of luster or shine. The slight curve of her shoulders and the downward tilt of her head all told a wordless story of fear. What had they done to her?

"Starting bids for the water nymph," the slave master called out.

The slavers were big men, some all burly muscle, others with wide guts. The blood of giants is what made them so fearsome. The first giants who settled Dustania had thirteen children, all of whom interbred among humans, and then there were thirty-two. The numbers grew with each new generation. Throughout the years, the giants had continued to breed and carry on their family tradition of running the slave rings.

In that time, the giants had built up a reputation for themselves as nasty brutes with a streak for vengeance and a tendency to bash in brains or draw blood when cheated or insulted. Hence, the buying and selling of slaves was a civil affair. No one wanted to be seen as unfavorable in the eyes of the giants, and most dealt with them by paying up front and leaving town as soon as they completed their business.

"Ten silver coins!" someone shouted.

Nurimil inwardly groaned. Silver?

The currency of Nomadia ranged, starting with bartering

and then moving to coin. Bronze coins were used for normal wares, and silver was necessary when buying something priceless or unique. Even more rare than silver were gold coins. Because of the rare and expensive magical objects he sold, Nurimil had more gold coins than most, but he was not keen to part with them. Bidding with gold coins during the auction would make others aware of his wealth, which would lead to a robbery once he left. If he wanted the nymph, he had to be cautious, which meant he should not bid along with the others.

"Stay here," he told Bern, who wasn't going to move away.

He shouldered his way through the crowd toward the front of the slave ring while the bids continued. Once he was standing next to the block, mere feet away from the nymph, who he tried not to look at, he cleared his throat and waved to get the slave master's attention.

The slave master peered down at him, his lip curling with disdain.

Nurimil grinned and held up a bag of coins. "Will this be enough to secure the nymph for myself? Seeing as I am a man of business, I'd prefer it if you kept the amount between you and I."

The slave master raised a hand to halt the bidding and snatched the bag of coins. Opening it, he pulled out a single silver coin. His eyes lit up with greed as he weighed the bag in his meaty hand, then bellowed, "Sold! Next we have a nonmagical creature who won't put a spell on you while you sleep," he chuckled. "A gnome from the hills of Eloof . . ."

Nurimil tuned out the slave master and stepped forward to claim the nymph, who continued to stare, unseeing, at the ground.

"Careful," the giant handing her over told him. "We gave her a draft of honeyed wine to keep her calm, but you'll want to protect yourself against her magic."

Nurimil smirked. Magic. Protection. Bah. "I will keep that in mind," he said as the giant removed the tourmaline bracelets.

"I'd keep her tied up, if I were you," the giant went on. "And be gentle with her, she frightens quick. I imagine she's not used to land."

"I would not have bought her if I couldn't handle her." Nurimil paused as a dark thought crossed his mind. "Has anyone come here requesting a magical water creature?"

The giant ran a hand over his jaw. "Aye." He lowered his voice, although no one else could hear him as the auction continued. "We had word to only sell her to a bounty hunter from the guild, but Dorance said to put her up for auction to the highest bidder. It didn't sit right with me but"—he shrugged—"orders is orders."

Dread sunk like a stone in Nurimil's heart, but he wasn't about to let the giant know. "You sound as if you care what happens to her." He winked as the giant's face flushed bright red.

"Bah! Be gone, troublemaker, and take your water creature with you!"

Nurimil kept the grin on his face as he reached for the nymph's arm, pretending nothing was wrong. Hector had lied to him, sending him in search of what he assumed was a beast, when in reality it was a water nymph. Which meant Hector also knew that once Nurimil discovered it was a woman, he'd run, and the guild would have yet another reason to hunt him down.

Nurimil reached for his neck with his free hand, knowing his capture would end with the loss of his head. He had to get on the road and ahead of the hunters as soon as possible, especially now that he'd stolen the bounty they needed. When his fingers touched the smooth scales of the nymph, her eyes rolled back and she pitched forward.

The giant snorted with laughter. "Probably too much wine."

Nurimil glared at him as he caught the nymph and scooped her up in his arms. She was lighter than expected, but smelled like a slave, a mix of stale seawater, unwashed burlap, and sour wine. Her head lolled to one side, resting on his shoulder. Ignoring the way his heart raced, he wove his way through the crowd, back to his horse.

The crowd parted before him, and a few bidders gave him irritated glances, then gawked lustily at the nymph. Nurimil kept his head down, hoping no one else would recognize him. Despite his predicament, a surge of satisfaction went through him. It was only one, but he'd saved another would-be slave from a lifetime of hell.

24

NURIMIL

He laid the nymph across the saddle and swung up behind her. The burlap sack rode up, showing off more blue and white scales. Averting his eyes, Nurimil pulled her limp body against his, wrinkling his nose at the stink.

"Onward, Bern," he called to his horse, who acquiesced.

They soon left the dusty slave quarters behind. Dustania was a fitting name for the village, which was perched in the bowl of a dust ring. To the north and east of the village lay the great sea and the Cliffs of Dooms Drop, while wet lands lay to the south. If one followed the road east long enough, it ended in the sand dunes, where many a lost traveler had perished because of the heat and lack of water and shelter.

After his falling out with the guild, Nurimil had taken the desert road to Dustania for two reasons. One, he had been curious about the water creature the wizard was desperate to have; he'd even considered using the creature to bargain with the guild. Two, because he needed a tourmaline stone to hold his next prey. The stones were rare and expensive, and those who owned bracelets and rings made from the stones would not willingly part with them. Since Nurimil no longer had access to the guild's resources, he'd traveled to Dustania and purchased one for himself.

Although magic did not work on him, he intended to capture the singing ostrich of Maca, a legendary beast who could run faster than a horse, sing with the voice of a siren, and change sizes at will. Such a priceless gift would please the empress of Nomadia, and he hoped to offer it to her as a token, and in exchange earn the protection of the crown.

Thus far, he'd stayed one step ahead of his pursuers, yet he still didn't like the idea of his head being exchanged for a bag of gold coin. Five hundred gold coins, to be exact.

As soon as they reached the main road, Nurimil's worries faded as the slave ring disappeared from view. They took the King's Road, a path that led northeast and southwest across Nomadia. He planned to head south on the road, then branch off east, first toward a jungle and then the prairies of Maca to capture the magical ostrich. From the prairie, he intended to take the road northwest to the capital of Nomadia, win the empresses favor, and become a free man again.

He clucked to Bern, encouraging the horse to move into a canter. Even though he didn't want to jar the nymph too much, if he continued south he'd reach a river. Perhaps it connected to the great sea, and she could find her people. It would be a relief to get rid of her, for her body pressed against his and the sensation of change felt like a noose tightening around his neck. The less time he spent with her, the better. He hoped she'd stay unconscious until they reached the river so he wouldn't have to learn her name, the sound of her voice, or anything else that might trick him into getting wrapped up in her destiny.

The road was quiet. Slow. Nurimil passed a monk, a farmer with a wagonload of supplies, and a few hooded riders. He relaxed even further when he smelled moisture in the air. As the hour passed, they neared the river, which would be the best spot to rest, get rid of the nymph, and press on south. Pleased with himself, Nurimil was caught off guard when the nymph's body stiffened in his arms.

Nurimil led Bern away from the dusty road into the wild grass that grew along the bank. It was spring, and pink and white buds sprang up, waiting for the right moment to bloom. The landscape was flat, giving him a view of the road curving onward, leading into greener lands. The calm blue waters of the river mirrored the sky, and in the distance, a smudge of emerald green; trees. Wetlands.

Bern trotted to a stop. Nurimil swung down and reached up to help the nymph down. As Nurimil sat her gently in the grass, near the unceasing ripple of water, her eyes flew open and her nostrils flared. A high-pitched scream came from her closed lips, an eerie high sound that started in her throat. Stunned, Nurimil stepped back, holding his hands out to show her he was unarmed and did not mean her harm.

The wordless scream died away as her wide golden eyes studied him. An odd expression crossed her face, and then her hands went to her wrists and ankles. Finding the bracelets that blocked her magic no longer there, she scrambled to her feet, arms and legs waving as she stumbled and then regained her footing. With one backward glance at him, she ripped the burlap sack off her body, shredding it with an unnatural strength.

Nurimil's breath caught in his throat, and something twisted in the pit of his belly. She was covered in blue and white scales from head to toe, and yet it did not hide her womanly body. Scales glistened, highlighting every curve in the low light. Another sound came from her throat, like a moan, a longing, a wish, and then she was running.

Before Nurimil could say or do anything, she leaped from the bank and dove headfirst into the river. A slight splash followed, and Nurimil dashed to the riverbank, staring down at the ripples left behind. There was no sign of the water nymph. It seemed as quickly as she'd appeared in his life, she'd disappeared.

Nurimil sat down heavily on the bank, legs spread out before him, and stared at the water. For a moment, he wondered. *What if?* What if he'd bound her, made her stay, learned her name, and then set her free? He shook himself. What was he thinking? He was a wanted man with a quest of his own. He'd done his good deed by saving the water nymph from slavery and the dark desires of a wizard. She'd returned to the waters of her birth, to freedom.

Bern nuzzled him, a reminder that there was no time for dallying. After a brief respite to give his horse a rest, he should be on his way south. No more distractions.

"Right." He stood and removed the saddlebags, scanning the area to ensure no one was watching him. "Eat up, Bern. It's going to be a late night."

He helped himself to a waterskin, apple, and strips of dried meat. The food was not particularly appetizing, but such was life on the road. He packed light, ate sparingly, and tried not to think back to warm meals, fresh food, and what it felt like to be part of a tribe with people who cared about legacy and who wanted to change the world.

At times like this, when he was alone with his thoughts, he thought back to his childhood, the thriving vineyard, the warm farm animals, the deep-throated laugher of his father, and the giggles of his sister. What would have happened if death hadn't destroyed his family? Still, without them, he'd had experiences far beyond anything he'd ever imagined. He'd traveled to the mountain heights and the depths of the sea, and in all his forty years he'd learned much about life in the Nomadian Empire.

His adventures were great, lonely at times, but as he chewed oversalted dried meat, he decided he would not have it any other way. He'd lived well, lost, and loved. Soon, he would have his freedom and could continue on his merry way.

When the chirping of crickets began, he gathered Bern's reins. But as he stood, he felt an uncanny sensation on his neck. He swallowed hard, but he knew, without turning around, that something was staring at him. His hand went to the belt where he kept his knives, and he slowly turned to see what lurked in the dark.

25

DARYA

Darya's entire body trembled as she lay under the waters, her fingers clinging to the shallow bed of the river to keep herself from rising again. Her gills opened, sending air through her lungs, and she breathed deeply. The man had taken her away from the cruel giants.

Her body jerked in memory of the beating they'd given her, followed by the humiliation of pouring that terrible liquid down her throat. If she'd been in her watery kingdom, she would have fought, but in the empire of the landwalkers, she wanted to do nothing more than hide. Still, the man had set her free, and there was something about his face, the look in his dark eyes, that did not frighten her. It was a deep knowledge, a knowing from years of life. She didn't know where he was going, but she felt that he did not intend to hurt her. He'd even laughed at the giant when the brute had talked about her powers and told him to keep her tied up as though she were an animal.

Her limbs shook again, but a gentle ripple soothed her. Spreading her fingers, she pulled the water around her like a blanket, burying her body in it. Each stroke of water healed her bruises and took away her fears, sending them downstream. She had no idea how long she lay there, unmoving, until her quest came back to her. Now that she'd escaped the slavers, she had to continue on to the great library. Except she still did not know how to get there.

Perhaps the man, if he was still ashore, could point her in the right direction. Her fingers curled. Now she was free, and the waters were hers to control again. She could use water magic, as well as something all mermaids and sirens knew was strong against the landwalkers: the power of charm and lust.

26

NURIMIL

She was in the middle of the river with nothing more than her head and shoulders showing, yet she faced him, the orbs of her dark gold eyes luminous. Her green hair was slicked back from her head and floated like a cloud behind her. The scales on her face were gone, revealing her green-tinted skin. A tingling sensation went through Nurimil. As though under a spell, he stepped closer until his boots sank into the mud on the riverbank.

"You freed me," the water nymph's voice was as clear as a bell and as beautiful as the sound of rushing water to a thirsty man.

Nurimil's heart leaped, leaving him with a deep yearning to at least learn her name before they went their separate ways. Courteous words came to his lips. "You are free, my lady. It did not seem right to leave you in the hands of the slave traders. You should return to the waters whence you came."

The evening light cast shadows over her face, so he could not see her expression, only hear the waver in her voice, the sound of tears. "For that, I thank you. You must be a noble man indeed."

How ironic that she thought of him as noble. A sad smile came to his lips. "Not noble, only doing what I deemed as right."

"You set free a great water nymph, and so I must offer you a wish. What do you seek?"

His smile faded. Was she teasing him? Testing him? "My lady, you are kind, but magic does not work on me. Even if you were to grant me a wish, it would be in vain. If you would but give me your name, I will continue with my journey and leave you to enjoy your freedom."

"Pretty words come from your lips," she said, then dove.

When she resurfaced, she was much closer to the river-bank, mere feet from him. Now he could see her golden eyes clearly, and the way beads of water dropped from her chin. His eyes went to her full mouth and wide lips, wondering what it would be like to kiss her, claim her, and sate his lust with her. She rose halfway out of the water, coming closer still, and he could not keep his eyes from traveling down the length of her exposed body.

Scales had been replaced with skin, and he eyed her smooth green shoulders and the hint of shiny scales that flashed like silver. The water parted, and up rose the creamy swells of her breasts, those curved peaks giving way to rosebud nipples, taut in the low light with droplets dripping off them. Nurimil went hard at the sight. Desire overcame him, making him want to run his tongue across them, bite and nip at the flesh, while the nymph squirmed with pleasure beneath him.

She paused suddenly, as though she sensed his thoughts, then arched her back before sinking back down, hiding her feminine treasures from him. Nurimil's heart beat a pitter-patter in his chest as she drew nearer still.

"Ah, so you are a man, tempted by lust, yet you claim you have no wishes."

Nurimil had to calm his heartbeat before he spoke again, forcing himself to look her in the eye. He knew about creatures of the water, how they wooed men away from their right minds and drove them mad with lust. He would not allow her to seduce him, even though her golden eyes gleamed. She clearly enjoyed the power she held over him, a power she would exploit.

Suddenly, his hardness went away. A strangled curse passed from his lips. He should have left as soon as the nymph disappeared. He spun away, intent on galloping into the night and forgetting about the nymph and the strange certainty that their destinies lay together.

"It was a test," her voice came again, just as he was swinging up into the saddle.

He looked down and there she was, standing on the river-bank, her toes sinking into the mud. Her green hair trailed down, hiding the curves of her breasts but leaving the dark spot between her legs open. Hissing, he looked away. Was she trying to drive him mad?

"Lady, I have freed you," he said harshly. "Return to the waters and leave me to continue my journey."

"My name is Darya," she said. "These waters are not mine, and I need your help."

A scowl covered Nurimil's face. Help? She wanted his help? There were many people who could help her, perhaps not in Dustania, but elsewhere there were many knights, even paladins, who would consider it an honor to come to the aid of a beautiful water nymph, and they would likely enjoy a night of pleasure for their troubles. But not him.

A warning sang through his blood and his eyes tore skyward, to where the shadows lengthened and the light of Sunna, goddess of the sun, disappeared from view. Stars began to pepper the sky with a million silver lights, and he leaned back on Bern and sighed. He wanted to be on his way before night fell.

"Lady Darya, you are beholden to me in no way, and I cannot help you. I must be away from this place, and quickly."

As if to convey the haste in his words, Bern pawed the ground and snorted.

Darya held out a hand, stopping just shy of touching Nurimil's leg. "Please," she whispered, although her voice carried like music in the quiet of the night. "Please take me with you. I can't stay here; these are not my waters, not my river. I will surely die. And what if the slave traders come back? I won't survive being caught by them again."

Nurimil fumed inwardly, and his blood turned warm beneath his skin. It was a risk to take her with him, and yet the guilt of leaving her behind would stay with him as he traveled south. It was one thing if she willingly wanted to leave, but another if she was frightened for her life. He grunted, willing himself not to look down again and examine her delicious body, pushing away the thoughts of what she would taste like if he dragged his tongue from her neck to navel. "For a time then," he agreed, "until you find your waters."

It was only what he had decided at the slave ring. Buy her. Free her. And help her find her home. He could keep his guard up until then.

"You will be rewarded for your kindness, Lord . . ."

"I am no lord," he admitted. "Call me Nurimil."

"Nurimil," she repeated.

His name sounded like a blessing on her lips. Something deep inside him twitched, but he ignored it and turned to his saddlebags. "We have a long ride ahead and you cannot go naked." He pulled out his cloak, rather warm for the night's journey, but it would have to do. "Wear this," he handed it to her.

Darya took the cloak and gave it a perplexed look. "I am not naked. My skin and scales are enough clothing for me."

Nurimil softened at her confusion. A water nymph, and yet so naive? "Perhaps in the waters, but here on land, one must wear clothes or be taken advantage of. Many will mistake your nakedness for something else. Surely you know the lust of men."

"It is a tool nymphs use to accomplish our purposes," she admitted, and a flash of dismay came across her face. "Is that why the slave traders made me wear that awful sack?"

"Yes." Nurimil dismounted and took the cloak from her hands. "But my cloak is made from the finest silks and lined with fur. It will be soft against your skin, and will keep you warm should the night turn cool."

He shook the cloak out and then draped it around her shoulders, stepping closer than he would have liked to fasten it loosely around her neck. He noticed the stink from the slave traders was gone, and she smelled alluring, like sea mist with a faint spice. She was just a head shorter than him and stood as still as a tree on a windless night. Her golden eyes gazed up at him, and he saw longing and loneliness plainly written across her face. Such loneliness made his heart ache.

A breeze blew past, and her seafoam green hair stirred. It had dried with an abnormal quickness and now hung in curls and waves just past her shoulders. Her lips parted as though she might speak, and for a heartbeat he thought she might lean forward, raise herself up on her tiptoes, and claim him with a kiss.

"There." He stepped back. "I have many questions for you, as I am sure you have for me, but it will have to wait until morning. We have a long, hard ride ahead of us."

It was easier to look at her now that his dark cloak swallowed up her features, except for those eyes and the tilt of her determined chin. He swung up on his horse and pulled her up behind him. Her arms tightened around his waist, and he imagined that she'd never ridden a horse before. Her legs would be sore in the morning, but there was nothing for it. He clucked to Bern, and they set off, galloping into the night.

Darya was silent behind him, and eventually her hold loosened until he thought perhaps she had lost her fear of riding or fallen asleep. He wondered if water nymphs slept curled up underwater in gigantic seashells, and how many days she'd been on land. How had she been caught by mere traders? Why did she need his help? And more importantly, how had the wizard known of her coming?

Secretly, he was thankful she was traveling with him so he could question her. In the morning he would hunt, build a fire, and cook them a warm breakfast, although he had no idea what nymphs ate. Cooked fish? Dried fish? And why was he thinking these things?

He was a fool to think he could keep the nymph with him. The nymph. It was better than thinking of her as Darya. Although, it was clear she had to be in some kind of trouble if she was far from home, being sold on a slave block. That look in her eyes, the fear, the loneliness—he wanted to know more. So lost was he in his musing that he almost missed the sound of a rattle, then there was a hiss and the whoosh of an arrow.

"Bern!" Nurimil cried out, but too late. His horse gave a whinny of fear and pain. One moment they were upright, running along the road, the next the horse had crashed into the underbrush, bucking and screaming with pain. Nurimil lost hold of the reins, and suddenly he was airborne.

27

NURIMIL

The impact knocked all the air out of Nurimil, and a ripple of pain flared up his back.

"Curses on this day!" he groaned.

Even though he was used to the sound of a creature in pain, the cries of his trusty steed cut through him like a knife ripping through muscle. Despite the pain in his lower back, he forced himself to stand upright.

He'd fallen into a small grove of trees twisted with vines, bramble, and thorn bushes. An oddity on the way out of Dustania, but the river ended near the grove and kept it lush and fed. The trees blocked his view of the road and Bern. Another curse left his lips. Where was Darya? Nurimil's fist closed around the hilt of his trusty sword. With a grunt, he pulled it free and crept toward the road just as the rattle came again.

A shiver went up his spine. Even though he did not want to care, his eyes moved back and forth, searching the bramble and road for Darya. She was unused to his world, and the shock of being hurled from horseback might have knocked her out, or she could be injured and easy prey for the creature.

There came a whooshing sound, and Nurimil ducked as an arrow shot into the bramble, clearly missing him, which meant the creature could not see him. There was an angry cry, and he stayed low as he moved toward the road. Wild grass crept up almost knee high, but it was not enough to hide him from the beast. Another muttered string of curses left his lips as he laid eyes on his foe.

She was a woman, almost ten feet tall, and her pale skin glowed in the low light. She was naked from the waist up, her navel bare but her breasts covered with her thick, ropy black hair. From her waist down she had the body of a rattlesnake, covered with a thick collection of multicolored scales. A hiss came from her lips, and her body undulated unnaturally across the road as she jerked around, searching.

Her face was free of scales and might have been beautiful once, but there was nothing humanlike about it now. Her eyes were horizontal and yellow, wide like a snake's, and double-lidded. When she opened her mouth, a double row of sharp fangs appeared, a warning for her enemies. Nurimil knew exactly who she was: Echnid the she-viper.

She was a fearsome bounty hunter. Nurimil had come across her a time or two, when she wasn't hunting and had been on friendly terms with him, if one could call a she-viper friendly. She was one of the most fearsome, ruthless bounty hunters, and now she was after him.

Nurimil tried to think of another curse and came up empty. He moved his sword from his right hand to his left, racking his mind for a plan, although he knew that if he attempted to fight Echnid, he would lose.

Echnid gave another hiss, and her body jerked toward the trees, toward him. Nurimil's heartbeat increased in anticipation of a duel, but he ignored it. The best plan was to hide, for there was no running from Echnid. She would find him, sink her fangs into his heart, and fill it with poison until his heartbeat slowed, little by little, and he gave in to her every whim. The way she played with her victims was horrific. He would not succumb to such a death, but would Darya? And where was she? As much as he wanted to get rid of the nymph, he was also frightened for her.

And then he saw her. Darya was kneeling in the middle of the road, his cloak streaming out behind her like water. Slowly, she rose to her feet, hands outstretched as though she were walking on a balance beam. Green hair shone in the moonlight behind her as she faced Echnid. One hand came up, palm facing outward and fingers slightly bent.

Nurimil stared in surprise, unable to move as words came from her lips, a chant in what he assumed was the language of water. Was Darya casting a spell? His gaze flickered toward Echnid, who paused, her yellow-eyed gaze moving away from the trees and to the slight figure standing on the road, chanting at her.

"Darya," Nurimil whispered.

He scrambled out of his hiding place, vaguely aware he was making a mistake and going against his own code of never acting impulsively. In the past, carefully laid out plans and relying on his wits had kept him from death. Dashing toward Echnid was pure folly, yet he could not sway his actions.

Echnid fitted an arrow into the bowstring and pointed the gleaming tip at Darya, who continued to chant as though unaware of the danger. Nurimil would have bet a pouch of gold that Echnid's arrow was poisoned. They always were. Even a nick of the tip would slow down her opponent and give her an advantage. Nurimil had tried to travel with poisoned arrows once, but after accidentally poisoning himself and having to seek a healer, he'd given up on that notion. Nay, he had other skills, including swordsmanship.

Taking the hilt in both hands, he swung at Echnid's tail. She hissed and spun, swiping her tail toward him. The rattle slammed into his chest. Nurimil lost his balance and fell backward, just as Echnid twisted to face him and let the arrow go.

The poisoned shaft hurled toward his chest, and Nurimil lay on his back, gasping in horror. There was no time to move or block the arrow with his sword, although out of habit his arm was already in motion, drawing the blade up over his chest to protect himself while his feet moved, kicking the ground as he scrambled backward. But the arrow kept coming. Just before the arrowhead kissed his shirt, it shattered, pieces flying into the air and twisting apart as though it had exploded from the inside out. Nurimil threw his arm across his face to protect his eyes. When he dared look again, Echnid had turned her back on him and given her full attention to Darya.

Darya stood like a pillar of strength in the road. A singsong chant came from her lips, and her volume increased. As she spoke, a change came over Echnid. Her jerky movements slowed, a hand went to her throat, and her arm holding the bow quivered.

Nurimil scrambled to his feet, but stopped short of plunging his sword into Echnid's snake skin. It felt wrong to kill her when she was under the influence of Darya's spell.

The bow dropped from Echnid's fingers and thudded onto the road with a sickening smack. She choked as she struggled to breathe. A second hand went to her throat, as though if by holding it, air could enter her body again. She convulsed as her face turned purple. Those double-lidded eyes rolled back in her head, and then she collapsed on the road, her body arching and bucking until the rattles lay still.

Nurimil gawked, and then a grin came to his lips. Echnid. Defeated! Although he doubted she was completely dead; she-vipers had an odd way of returning to life just when he assumed their souls had left their bodies. Sheathing his sword, he stepped over the coils of Echnid's snake body toward Darya.

As soon as he was within a pace of her, he knew something was wrong. Her arms came down and her knees buckled, sending her down on the road beside their foe. Her face tilted up and she licked her dry lips. "Water," she whispered. "I need water."

He paused, bewitched somehow by her gentle eyes, the way she stared at him with complete and utter trust. The hardness in his heart softened, and he promised himself that after he helped her, he would go his own way. Perhaps his life would be better for meeting her. But whatever they did, they must do in a hurry. For now he knew the hunters had caught his trail, and they were coming for him.

28

DARYA

"I t's going to be a long night," Nurimil said in his accented voice.

The way his words flowed was rough, like the wild seas before a storm, and yet compelling. There were deep undertones in his voice that made desire thrum low in her belly. An odd sensation, because she hadn't truly wanted to seduce him; the act was only a way to get what she wanted—but now? She lay on the riverbank, back to him, one hand drawing lazy circles on the surface of the water. Water was the conductor for her strength, and slowly, her power surged back into her. She'd never spell cast on land before, and doing so had given her the awareness that she needed water to rejuvenate after expelling so much magic. She tilted her head, glancing at him.

Nurimil squatted on the riverbank, organizing his saddle bags. He frowned as he moved, and there was a weariness about him. After all, he had lost his mount. A horse, is what he'd called it. Bern. Much like the seahorses Darya rode when she was in her domain. A longing rose in her throat, blocking out words. Closing her eyes, she recalled home. The sound of trumpets, the silkiness of water, the laughter of sirens, and the gaiety of life under the sea. It was lost to her for now, but the man, Nurimil, would help her. She sat up, removed her hand from the water, and put both bare feet in instead.

"Why?" she asked, waiting for him to look at her.

His masculine face was hardened, as though he'd seen much, and there was a scar on his jaw, almost hidden by the stubble of his beard. Obsidian eyes were set deep in his face, and when those twin jewels caught her staring, the tempo of her heart increased and a flush stole up her cheeks. His arresting stare lingered on her body, as though he wanted to see more of her flesh, currently hidden behind her protective barrier of scales. Yet earlier, when she'd given him a glimpse, he seemed angry. Considering the clothing she'd seen all landwalkers wear, she supposed it made sense. They covered themselves, unlike the sea people. She needed to learn to be more like the landwalkers if she were to dwell in their world for however short a time it would be. The sooner she completed her task, the better.

He sighed and slung a bag over his shoulder before tossing the other one into the river. Darya drew in a sharp breath. Why had he thrown away so much?

"I am being hunted, Darya. I am no easy companion to travel with, and it's not safe for us here. Sooner or later, someone will find the body of the she-viper and track us down. Plus, my horse is dead." His eyes went dark with sorrow and he paused, staring at the river as though it would give him answers. "We need to put as much distance as possible between us and the she-viper before dawn."

He wanted to keep going? Darya dropped her gaze to the waters. Gods give her strength! She was unused to walking, and the day's activities had already robbed her of her energy. How was she to keep going?

Nurimil towered above her, so close she caught the faint scent of juniper. His body was intoxicating, and as he held out his hand to her, she had a sudden vision of the two of them, lip-locked, naked in the waves, a fire of passion spreading around them as their fingers explored each other's bodies. Heat spread up her cheeks as her nipples hardened under the cloak. She bit her bottom lip. Did he sense how aroused she was by him? She'd heard of nymphs who seduced humans, but she thought it might be the other way around; that nymphs couldn't help it, for they were the ones beings seduced by humans. He was tall, dark, and handsome, and she—

"Are you ready?" Nurimil asked, hints of concern puncturing his question. "You can tell me why you need my help as we travel."

Darya touched his hand, her fingers grazing the calluses and then the rough skin of his palm. Her heart kicked at the blend of sensation. She paused to control her arousal, wrapped her hand around his wrist, and allowed him to pull her upright. He was a head taller than her, and her heart thrummed at their proximity. Earlier, when he'd put the cloak around her, she thought he was going to kiss her, and she wondered what his lips would taste like. Different from her people? More earthy? Gentle? Did she want him to be gentle? Lovemaking was scorned among the nymphs and encouraged among the sirens. They needed children to carry on their bloodline, while the nymphs sought to keep their numbers low so their power would be shared among the few rather than the many. Pleasure and love were unnecessary, which was another reason for Darya's apathy toward the Court of Nymphs. But they weren't around now; they'd never know what she and Nurimil did together.

"You're not wearing shoes . . ." he sighed.

The moment broken, Darya looked down, relieved to hide the disappointment in her eyes. She'd just met this man. Why did she feel as though they had an unspoken bond? He was only a human, and although she was attracted to him, they had no future together. Besides, she had a task to complete. Her people were counting on her.

"I don't need them," she told him. With a twitch of her fingers, the scales covered her feet up to her ankles.

A brief smile came to his face. "You can cover yourself with scales at will?"

He let go of her, and Darya instantly missed the strength of his touch, especially the way it made her feel protected, safe.

He strode down the riverbank in an easy looping gait, yet all the same, his pace was too fast. She almost tripped over her feet in her rush to keep up. Gods. Was this how humans traveled all the time? Swimming was much faster. She was halfway tempted to toss off the cloak he'd given her and dive into the river.

"My scales are my skin," she explained, breathless with her attempt to keep up with him. "Like you wear those garments." She gestured to his clothes. "Or what the warriors wear."

"Armor?" he clarified.

"Yes. Armor." The word sounded funny on her tongue. She realized it was the most she'd spoken above water, and the sound resonated differently in her head. "We wear scales for protection."

He nodded, although she could only see the vague shape of his head bobbing up and down in the darkness. It was much brighter by the river, for it reflected the cool lights of the night. All the same, it was dark and her eyes kept drifting closed. A yawn opened her mouth, and she sighed. After spell casting, she always wanted to sleep, and while water gave back some of her energy, it wasn't enough.

Nurimil noticed her fading pace and adjusted his steps to match hers. "We'll find a place to rest soon." His voice was gentle, underlaid with concern.

Darya eyed his brawny arms, wishing he'd whisk her up and carry her. Why oh why did Nurimil's horse have to die?

"Why do you need my help?" he asked.

In the darkness, she saw him glance at her but was unable to read his expression.

Sorrow crept through her heart and moisture pricked behind her eyes. A tingling sensation made her wish for water, to dive in and swim and swim and swim until she was utterly exhausted. It's what she'd done before, and what got her caught by the slave traders.

She twisted her hands together, missing the buoyancy of water. "I am a water nymph from the Court of Nymphs. First and foremost, my duty is to protect the kingdom of sirens, a task I failed at. It was during my watch that the enemy of my people, a sea witch, sabotaged the kingdom and unleashed a plague. It spread quickly throughout the waters, tainting the seas. There is time before they all die, but I need a spell to purify the waters. My spell casting is not enough. I spoke to the elders, and they told me I must travel to the great library to find the cure."

Nurimil grunted. "And you need my help because . . . ?"

Darya stared. Had he not heard her? "I don't know anything of the layout of the land, nor how to get to the great library. I need your help to get there."

Nurimil halted, and Darya's heart pounded. Was he going to turn her away? Say no? She had no one else to go to, and in the hours she'd spent with him, aside from their uncanny connection, she'd come to trust him. She felt certain the fates had brought them together. He'd saved her from the slave traders, then freed her without fear of her power.

He faced her and the river cast a light over his face, chasing away the shadows. "Darya," he said in a low voice. "Traveling with me is dangerous. Back there on the road, the she-viper was after me. There's a bounty on my head for five hundred golden coins, more than enough to live comfortably for years. It's a tempting offer, which means there are many hunters coming after me. It's not safe. I am headed south to travel through the jungles to Maca. I need to hunt for a creature that will secure my freedom. If I succeed without being killed along the way, then, and only then, will I go to the capital city of Nomadia. On my way to see the empress, I will stop at the great library. But understand this: I cannot enter the city and bargain for my freedom without a priceless gift for the empress. I value my head, which is why I won't go anywhere near Nomadia without that gift. If you are desperate or in a rush, I am not the man you should travel with."

Darya's heart sank with bitter disappointment, and her lips trembled. She thought over his words, recognizing that he hadn't said no, merely explained what he needed to do before going to the city. Which meant she could still travel with him, couldn't she?

The very thought of leaving his presence made her feel bereft and lonely. Lonely like she'd been in the Court of Nymphs, misunderstood and longing for more than the simple task of standing guard and fighting off sharks and sea snakes. This was her one chance to be something else, to become a hero. More than anything, she was certain she needed him.

"How long will it take?" she asked, determined to keep the pathetic tears out of her voice. He didn't understand. Her people would die if she did not save them.

He reached out and gently touched her shoulder. "I am not much good to you dead. At the next trading post, I will acquire a horse, and perhaps there will be a traveling party striking out for the capital. You can go with them. It will be much faster than staying with me. And safer."

"My thanks are with you." She bowed her head, even as disappointment seeped through her.

She had magic, she could protect him on the road, but she sensed it was not what he wanted. He'd freed her, and now he wanted to be left alone. The thought shouldn't have made her ache, but it did.

29

DARYA

Darya tried to make sense of her feelings as they continued, especially her attraction to Nurimil. Even in the sea, she'd been warned against the bounds of love. Should the day come when the nymphs dwindled in number and needed to produce more offspring, an arrangement would be made with another court from another sea. After the male and female fulfilled their duties, they'd part ways.

Unlike the sirens and mermaids, the nymphs did not need a life mate for companionship and partnership. Water magic allowed nymphs to live unrestricted by the needs of mortals, free from relationship-related constraints. Life being as it was in the sea, Darya hadn't given a romantic relationship much thought. Even now, just the consideration made her cheeks flush hot. Tempting the landwalkers with lust was one thing, but desires she'd never had were rising, and she wanted Nurimil's dark gaze on her body, his heated touch on her skin, to see admiration in his eyes—and she didn't know why.

When the first glints of dawn kissed the sky, Nurimil cautiously moved off the road into a thicket, hand on his knife. Once they reached a thick knot of underbrush, he ducked under overhanging branches, lifting them to guide her through. "We should sleep here until midmorning."

Darya studied their surroundings, and relief loosened the knot that had tightened around her chest ever since she'd been captured. This was what she'd expected Nomadia to be like: dense with foliage, rich with the scent of life, and soothing with a low hum of creatures. Gratefulness surged within her like a wave and she turned to Nurimil, who took her arm. He guided her to the ground, and she leaned into him, partly because she was exhausted and grateful for a chance to rest, and partly because she wanted to be near him.

The ground was soft, and she sensed water running deep underground. That knowledge comforted her as she lay down and Nurimil tucked the cloak around her. "I'm sorry we had to push so hard," he murmured. "We have a good head start and I want to keep it."

Disappointment was swift when he moved away to lean against the trunk of a tree. Darya watched how his dark hair gathered around his neck, and how his jaw softened as he closed his eyes. He was unlike the nymphs and sirens, even the gentle mermaids. Somehow he was pleasant to look at, dispelling the notion that landwalkers were hideous. A faint smile came to her lips before her eyes flickered shut and she sank into a dreamless sleep.

IT SEEMED mere moments before a light touch came at her shoulder, shaking her awake. "Darya?"

Confusion and then fear made her chest tighten until her eyes flew open, and she remembered she wasn't in the slave quarters anymore. Relief did not come immediately, for pain sizzled through her. Yawning, she stared at the ground. It had been soft when she went to sleep, but now her body ached from the contact with it. A dull ache pounded in the back of her skull. Suppressing a groan, she sat up, warmth flooding her body as she remembered him.

Nurimil crouched in front of her, his dark eyes warm, a hint of lust glinting in them as he backed away and opened his bag. "I don't know what you eat," he admitted. "I intended to make a fire, but . . ."

Darya sat up straighter. Cool air kissed her bare shoulder as she re-covered herself with the cloak. Like he'd said, it was comfortable against her skin, and she wondered if all the pieces of clothing the landwalkers wore were this nice. "Seaweed," she told him. "Fish, mussels, sometimes crab if we're close to land, or shrimp. I don't suppose you have any of that here?"

He shook his head and handed her a flat substance. "If you're hungry, this dried meat will satisfy you. I can't say that it's delicious, but we'll have to make do until we reach the trading post."

Darya took the flat substance and smelled it, breathing in a smokey flavor mixed with salt. Keeping an open mind, she took a bite. It was salty and dry. She chewed, her jaw working, and chewed some more. It was very different from biting into a fish, still raw and alive, and ripping it apart with her sharp teeth. She swallowed, coughed, and made a face.

Nurimil burst into laughter. To his credit, he pressed a fist against his mouth. "No good?"

Darya coughed again, tears burning her throat. "I'm sure I'll get used to it."

Nurimil chuckled and stood, reaching out a hand to help her stand. Again, she relished their connection, her skin warming at his touch. For a moment, she wanted to cast aside the cloak and stand bare before him, but he slung the bag over his shoulder and crept toward the road.

The sun was fully in the sky, heating the ground. As they walked, Nurimil cast frequent glances over his shoulder, as though watching for someone or something. His hand occasionally strayed to the sword strapped to his back. Darya noticed that he carried other weapons in his belt. If he were in the sea, he'd be a guard or warrior, yet he called himself a bounty hunter.

"Are you afraid more like the she-viper will come?" Darya asked.

"Yes. I imagine she will recover and do one of two things, or both: either report to the guild or continue to chase us." He sighed. "Darya, I wasn't entirely truthful with you earlier."

She stiffened. "What is it?"

"There's no easy way to say this, so I hope you'll listen and reserve judgement."

Fear coiled in her belly. "What's wrong?"

Nurimil scratched the back of his neck. "I can't pretend I understand what is happening, but you should be aware that I'm not the only one who is being hunted. I work . . . er . . . used to work for the Guild of Bounty Hunters. They asked me to go to Dustania—that's where we met."

Darya had the distinct feeling he was deeply uncomfortable with what he was about to say.

"I only hunt beasts, a fact the guild is well aware of, yet they told me I had to go to Dustania to purchase a water creature for a wizard."

Darya's mouth went dry and then flames of fury sprang to life. She tightened her fists as he continued, "I assumed it was a dumb beast such as a giant fish, or sea turtle, or one of those rare starfish. I had no idea it would be you." He ran his fingers through his hair.

"What would a wizard want with me?" Darya demanded. Wizards had great power and magic. Like sea witches, they cast spells with wands and staffs. Since they were landwalkers, they also used books to carry their knowledge. In fact, a wizard might be useful in helping her find a counter-curse for the sea witch's' spell. Her tongue stumbled over her next question. "Do you mean someone is hunting me too?"

"Yes. I don't know why." Nurimil's jaw tightened. "I'm going to find out, and I'm going to clear my name."

A tension hung between them, the admission of fear, cold and icy despite the warmth of the sun. Darya studied him, taking in his broad shoulders, his long, easy gait. The charming laugh from the morning was gone, replaced with determination.

"I'm a water nymph," she assured him. "I have water magic. No one will touch us."

He nodded, but did not look at her, leaving Darya wondering what obstacles she would encounter in the empire of landwalkers.

30

ELMIRA

After they found camels and a guide, the journey was almost pleasant. The nights were chilly, dark, and starry. Elmira shivered from the cold, despite being wrapped in robes and huddled close to Vero. Eventually, the landscape changed, giving way to a long dusty road, flat plains, and occasional trees.

Once they reached the road, they set the camels free, and Elmira thanked their guide for his assistance by sucking his soul right out of his body. Vero didn't look, but she knew her power to consume souls awed him. Part of her was torn when she saw the signpost pointing the way to the capital of Nomadia. Should she turn that way and find out if ink magic was in the capital? But she needed the book, and she needed the jinn. Both could be anywhere in the world. It was best she focused on gaining water magic.

Elmira smelled water before they arrived. The vapors were so strong she wondered why everything was dusty. A river snaked along the road, the grass on its banks long and lush, and then she smelled stink. The smell of death and bowels overrode everything else, taking her back to her years of captivity. She whirled, spinning to a grove of trees. "Something dead is in there."

"It might be an animal," Vero suggested. "It happens often."

"Does it?" Elmira paused, then turned aside to look. The grove was thick, and the smell increased as she neared.

It was a dead horse. Wild animals had picked at the meat and organs, allowing white bone to show through the decaying flesh. An arrow lay on the ground near the horse's rump. The underbrush had been thrashed, and Elmira backed away, returning to the road.

"Be on your guard, Vero. I smelled blood, and there was a battle. Do people usually kill horses?"

"No. They are magnificent beasts like camels, used for riding."

Elmira cocked her head. "We should get horses, then. Let's find some in the city."

They continued, picking up the pace, but it wasn't until almost nightfall that they reached the village. Elmira paused when the row of buildings and people appeared. Wrinkling her nose, she sniffed. She hadn't smelled so many bodies in a long time, and there was something odd about them, something that wasn't quite right. The tang of water was distant, yet under the scent of unwashed bodies and ale and animals she detected blood and misery.

Worrying her lower lip between her teeth, she tapped her fingers against her legs. That familiar hunger was back, making her want to reach out and inhale. A ball of anger coiled in her belly, like a snake waiting to pounce. "How will we know if the water nymph is here?"

"There are inns in town. We should get a room and listen to the chatter."

"Chatter?"

"Listen to the people talk," Vero explained, shifting the bag on his good shoulder. "They might inadvertently tell us what we want to know."

Elmira gave Vero a sidelong look. He was hunched over, his face pale, and she imagined he longed for a meal, a warm bed, perhaps even a bath. Biting down on her cheek, she decided to follow his suggestion, wondering if the wizard had known how smart Vero was. "Take us to an inn," she agreed.

When they found one, Elmira had to resist the desire to kill everyone and eat their souls. Vero said it would be inappropriate, at least until they found the information they were looking for. As it turned out, Dustania was peopled by giants, strong and healthy, which led her to believe their souls would be delicious. A shiver of delight went up her spine at the thought of feasting, but Vero led her to a table where they were served food, and a drink called ale that made her fingers tingle.

Afterward, she was much too tired to listen to the boring banter the giants kept up, laughing loudly as they did. Most of their talk was about slaves, prices, wages, trade, and women. So, after their meal, the pair of them went to sleep, sheltered for the first time since they'd left the pyramid.

It wasn't until the sun streamed in that Elmira leaped up. "We have to go." She shook Vero awake. "We're wasting time sleeping here."

Vero grunted but agreed, and after gathering their bags

they left the inn. Neither had the stomach for breakfast, even when the innkeeper shouted after them. Elmira walked with purpose, drawn to the crowd gathering around a platform. A giant stood on top, bellowing, while people raised their hands and called out numbers.

Elmira's eyes narrowed. The creature standing beside the man, a gnome with limp pigtails who stared at her feet, looked pitiful. Her hands and feet were bound. Rage surged in Elmira's heart. Her vision went dizzy as she realized the people were calling out the amount of money they'd pay to buy the gnome.

She growled.

"Don't attack yet," Vero cautioned. "We need information first."

"The bodies will be easier to search when they're all dead," Elmira said, a fierceness twisting through her as the memory of chains and stone came fresh and raw. She recalled the knife ripping her skin open, the blood pouring out while she screamed for mercy. No one had come, no one had helped, and in the end she'd had to save herself.

She was the only one who could save the slaves. Their fear permeated the air, and she sensed their pain, a terror she knew very well—except she had progressed, transcended to another level.

"I'm not saying don't kill them," Vero cautioned, "just wait until we know where the water nymph is."

Elmira crossed her arms over her chest and pointed at the bellowing giant. "Fine, but I want to talk to him."

They waited until the auction ended, and Elmira's rage increased as each creature sold, all of them hunched, dirty, with hopelessness staring out of their wide eyes. Jaw set,

Elmira stomped through the crowd. They stared at her, some making comments about her lack of clothing. She climbed the platform, ignoring the giants who tried to grab her arms, and planted herself in front of the bellowing giant.

"I hear you're the person who can help me," she announced, hands on hips.

The giant glared at her, but his anger faded as his eyes dropped to her bare stomach, long legs, and slim hips. His expression turned to a leer. "I am. What is it you're seeking?" He gestured to his pants and laughed. The giants behind him laughed too.

Elmira held in her rage. She would take comfort in their deaths later. "I'm looking for a water nymph. I have reason to believe you kept one as a slave here?"

The giant's grin faded. Folding his arms across his broad chest, he frowned. "You're too late. A bounty hunter bought her about a week ago, and they took the road leading to the capital. Such a beautiful, magical creature is rare, and they are difficult to capture, but if you are willing, I'll send my scouts out to look for another one."

Elmira's heart skipped a beat. The wizard's projections had been right; the water nymph had come through here. "A week ago? And who did you say bought her?"

The giant rubbed his fingers together and scoured the sky for an answer. "Oh, it was that self-righteous one. He only deals with mythical creatures and never kills. Nurimil is what he calls himself. But you'll be hard-pressed to catch up with him. He's known for slipping into the wild, never to be seen again, and he left on horseback. I'd say you could use a charm to find him, but magic doesn't work on him, which makes him even harder to find."

Elmira raised her eyebrows. The name, Nurimil, was vaguely familiar, but she didn't have time to dwell on memories. "Where can I find horses?"

"I don't deal in horses, only slaves." The giant grunted. "There's a horse trader down the road, and if that's not good enough for you, the Gyin trading post is about two weeks away, on the road that leads to the capital."

"And you say the bounty hunter is headed toward the capital?"

"I can't be sure." The giant shrugged. "I didn't ask because it's none of my business. All I know is that the nymph left with him."

"The water nymph has magic. All I need to do is look for signs of that, and I can track them," she said.

"Who are you anyway?" the giant demanded. "I've never seen an elf like you in this realm, looking for a slave. We were told the guild was after the water nymph, and only to sell her to a bounty hunter. If you're new to the hunters' guild, come back to my quarters." He waggled his eyebrows. "We can discuss future trade that will benefit both of us."

Elmira glanced at the crowd, which was dispersing. The hunger twisted in her belly, and an overwhelming desire to eat their souls rose. Her breath hitched and her fingers trembled. She wanted to see the giant scream, to hear him beg, to let him experience the pain he'd inflicted on so many others. Her eyes dilated, and a purr rolled out of her throat. "Show me the slaves. Perhaps I can pick another one."

The giant's eyes narrowed, as if he didn't believe her request.

Elmira opened her eyes wider and splayed her hands in

innocence. "Perhaps you have another magical creature who will benefit me?"

He shrugged, then relented. "If you want to talk business, we don't have another water nymph, but we have a few I held back for tomorrow's auction." He winked, then nudged her arm. "Can't be selling all the goods in one day."

Elmira held her breath, just managing to keep her reflexes from going into overdrive at his touch. Vero knew she hated to be touched, especially after the wizard's unwelcome and inappropriate advances. Her immediate reaction was to slap him across the face, but she held herself back.

"Bring your men," she suggested. "In case the slaves are unruly, and perhaps, after the tour, we can go somewhere private."

The giant nodded and beckoned to his men. Their eyes brightened as he led the way across the platform, into the slave quarters. It was quiet in there, and tension hung like a rope on the edge of a knife. Elmira studied the area, the lack of light, the putrid smell, and the scent of fear. Soft whimpers and low moans hummed in the air, a constant reminder that she wasn't somewhere nice. It was better than the crypt, but anything was better than the crypt.

Cages were locked with keys, and out of them stared wide, frightened eyes. Grimy hands gripped bars, and more than anything, Elmira wanted to free them.

She turned to the giant, but couldn't bring herself to touch him. Nausea rolled through her belly. "Tell me, what do you do when they misbehave? Tell me every detail. I want to know."

"We whip them." The giant gestured to the wall where a few whips hung, but each giant had one on his belt, along with other weapons. "We tie them down so they can't move, bend them over a plank of wood where an audience can see their shame, and beat them until the blood runs. That is the only way to deal with slaves."

Elmira trembled. "May I see a whip? Perhaps I need a stronger one for my own slaves."

"Go ahead." The giant gestured.

Elmira went to the wall and lifted one down. It felt good in her hands, light and long. She curled a fist around the handle and spun around. "Do you know what slavery means to me? Do you know what punishment and blood do to me?"

Confused, the giant and his three friends took a step back.

"It brings up the darkness. Terrible memories haunt me, and people like you with your darkness and desire for foul deeds are the cause of them. I have come to rid the world of people like you."

She lashed out with the whip. It caught the unsuspecting giant across his cheek, and he reared back. Instead of howling in pain, a grin covered his face and his eyes flashed. He yanked his own whip back, cracking it in the air.

Elmira grinned. "Come on," she taunted him. "I'm ready for you."

All four giants struck at the same time, and Elmira laughed, dancing around their whips and striking out with hers. She slashed their arms and legs, drawing blood with every blow. Hate surged so thick in her throat, she tasted bile. An image of the wizard mocked her as she moved. She'd killed him far too quickly, crushing in his face, and if she had the chance, she'd do it again, slower, longer, drawing out the agony, making him feel every blade, every slice he gave her. But she'd never get the chance again. The best she could do was bring her wrath against those who caused harm to others.

Madness roared in her veins, and when the lash of the whip cut across her face, her anger let loose. She exploded, and it seemed as if she and the whip became one. She struck out again and again, lashing and slashing until the skin of all four giants was broken open, blood pouring out. Yet the pain did not stop them. If anything, their own wounds encouraged them. Whips hissed through the air, and Elmira was not strong enough to withstand them all. They cut into her arms, ripped the skin from her legs, and broke open her cheeks. She screamed, rolling away from the giants into the hay, while the slaves beat at the bars. Slaves.

Elmira dashed toward a cage and pressed her hand against the bars. Recalling the way the stone had crumbled beneath her, she closed her eyes, ignoring the sting of a whip as it bit into her.

Let go.

The lock released with a click, and she ripped the cage open. Sprinting down the row of cages, she screamed, using her connection with stone and iron to open them with her bare hands. The slaves poured out, shouting as they dashed toward the giants. Some got the brunt of the whips, but they were furious, led on by Elmira's madness.

It was then, and only then, that the giants relented. When the sound of the whips slowed, Elmira spun around, watching the slaves overcome their slave masters. Hunger swelled in her belly. She ran back through the mass of slaves shouting, "You're free! You're free! Go, run, take back your lives."

Some of them took her at her word, but there were others who launched themselves at the giants, shouting, screaming, and crying as they railed against them. Elmira joined them, and when she reached the first giant, even though he wasn't dead, or near death at all, she pressed her hand against his neck and breathed in. The giant shivered and shuddered, but the pull was too strong. He fell backward, eyes bulging as his hands waved, trying to fight her off. Elmira perched on his chest and breathed in, relishing the taste of his soul. Her body trembled, shaking with euphoria. It was the best soul she'd ever had, and she wanted more.

31

ELMIRA

Elmira rejoined Vero when she finished, stumbling, eyes bright, drunk on the souls of the giants. The slaves were free, escaping down the streets, although shouts in the marketplace told her it wasn't enough. More giants would hunt them down, chain them, and take them back to the cages.

"What should we do?" she asked Vero, grinning at him because she couldn't help it. She was pleased with her actions and the souls felt good, much better than the guards she'd eaten.

"What do you want?" Vero asked, levelheaded as usual.

"I want the slaves to be free without fear of returning to this dark place."

"Burn it down." Vero pointed to torches, unlit but ready for nightfall. "Burn it down and they will never be able to return."

Elmira laughed. It bubbled in her belly before bursting

out of her throat and making her limbs tremble. "Light the torches," she ordered.

Vero did so and Elmira, still laughing, took the torches and hurled them toward the buildings. Some landed on the ground, harmless, but others caught in hay and burned slowly. A slight wind stirred, then blew harder, fanning the flames. White smoke billowed in the air, turning black as the fire gained traction and spread.

Elmira took a sobering breath and stood back, watching as the flames shot into the air. It was a dance, magnificent, and if she controlled wind and fire, it would easily spread and engulf the city, burning down the homes of the giants, the inns, and other slave quarters.

"We should go," Vero said, his tone urgent. "Someone will discover what we did. I saw horses behind the inn. We should steal some and flee."

"I don't want to flee," Elmira disagreed. "We came here to find the water nymph, and we failed. But this is an example of what I want to do wherever there is suffering and slavery brought about by magic. We can't slink away like thieves in the night. We need others to know what we've done, and of our power here. They have to know a new power is rising, times are changing, and if we make enemies, so be it. It is only what I expected. So let's stand here and take responsibility for our actions."

Vero only hunched and pointed. Billows of dust rose on the road, and angry shouts drifted to their ears. The ground trembled as the slavers gathered, and Elmira watched out of lidded eyes. "Let them come. Let them try to stop us."

"We don't have weapons," Vero murmured.

Elmira glanced at him, his hunched shoulder, his

mangled hand, and the packs around his feet. "We don't need weapons when we have magic, and I will not let anything happen to you. Stand behind me while I unleash hell on these slavers."

The dust settled as the riders came to a halt and dismounted. It was a strange motley of elves, drow, a few humans, and a couple of giants. The giants weren't riding horses, but a bigger beast that looked like a cross between a lion and a bear. Elmira stared at those beasts, lips curling. They were ferocious and likely fast. She wanted them.

One of the elves stepped forward, a shock of brown hair falling over his angular face. His skin was purple, and his eyes were red as he glared at Elmira. He was dressed in gold with an emblem of a fiery arrow on his chest. "Under what authority are you burning this place down?" he demanded, fingers tightening around a scroll.

Behind him the others dismounted, hands straying to weapons, although they waited, their eyes on their commander.

Elmira counted ten in all. Easy. She turned her gaze back to the arrogant yet handsome elf. "Under my own authority. My name is Elmira. I was the child with golden tears, and now I've grown up to fulfill the prophecy. I've come to rid the world of magic."

The elf frowned, and his fingers tightened around the scroll again. "That is not possible. Spare me your lies and tell me, who sent you?"

Elmira sighed. "You wouldn't believe the truth if it were standing in front of you. Tell me, under what authority do you question me?"

Eyes narrowed, the elf unrolled the scroll. "I come on

behalf of the Guild of Bounty Hunters. A water nymph passed through not too long ago, and I've come in search of her. Your actions in burning this place down make it difficult for me to achieve my task."

To Elmira's surprise, Vero stepped forward, coughed, and spoke. His voice did not carry much power but grew stronger at the end. "I assume you've come on behalf of a wizard?"

The elf's lips curled. "How do you know this?"

Elmira rolled her shoulders back, a smug smile crossing her face. "The wizard is dead, but we have taken on the responsibility of completing his work. If you worked for the wizard, you now work for us. As it turns out, we are still in need of the water nymph. What can you tell us about her?"

"Impossible," the elf cried.

"Look, I'm growing tired of your attitude. Is there anyone else we can talk to?"

A female elf stepped forward, red hair pulled back from her heart-shaped face. Fitted armor covered her muscular body, and her hands closed around the handles of two daggers. "If you truly are who you claim to be, we need proof before we can discuss matters of the guild with you. The wizard did not respond to our last message, leading us to believe something is amiss."

"If I had known you needed proof, I would have brought the stinking head of the wizard with me," Elmira retorted. "Although it would not have been recognizable. I beat him to death and I would not hesitate to do the same to anyone who gets in my way."

"Fancy words from a half-naked elf," the male elf sneered.

"I will not listen to this," Elmira snapped. "You want proof? Here it is!"

She opened her mouth, and two of the souls she'd just eaten rolled out. A mist hung in the air as they reformed into vague shapes, while howls poured out of their mouths. As soon as they stopped forming, they rushed toward the male elf and disappeared into his body.

The elf hurled himself on the ground and thrashed, twisting and bucking, tearing at his clothes. His body arched, and his bones gave way with loud, sickening snaps as he beat his head on the ground. "Get it out! Get it out!" he shouted until his words twisted in his throat. He gurgled, arched his back one last time, and then his neck snapped.

He went limp, limbs contorted in the dusty ground, sightless eyes staring at the peaceful blue sky. Elmira raised an eyebrow. That was interesting. She felt a slight weariness, a twist of hunger, but the spirits she'd unleashed were useless now. They had done their work in destroying another soul, leaving nothing left for her to consume. Tucking away the knowledge, she faced the guild riders again.

Horror had transformed their faces, and they were backing away, reaching for their horses. A few of them had vomited, unused to such a gruesome death, and the female elf had tears in her eyes. She lifted her hands away from her daggers and held them up as she knelt. After a moment, the others followed her example and Elmira looked on, grim satisfaction rising as the wind blew harder, spreading the fire to other buildings.

Elmira's skin itched. She turned, seeing her audience. The giants who'd run out to fight the fire were staring at her, buckets of water in hand. They'd seen, they'd all seen what had just happened.

"It's sorcery," someone whispered.

"Magic, dark magic," another voice added.

"Spirit magic."

Standing tall, Elmira addressed the crowd. "I will say this one more time. My name is Elmira. I am the child with golden tears, grown up to fulfill the prophecy. I am your greatest fear, a walking nightmare, for I've come to rid the land of magic and kill all who force others to suffer under their hands. What you've seen here is spirit magic, for I control the spirit realm and can unleash horror on those who oppose me. Here and now, you can make your choice. Are you for me or against me?"

Elmira grinned at their stricken expressions, and in the distance a child began to cry. The low wailing continued, a moan heard over the crackling of fire. A roof caved in with a boom, making people jump as the fire leaped to new heights. Black smoke billowed in the air and stung Elmira's eyes, but she waited.

"We will help you," the female elf said, not daring to lift her eyes from the ground. "What do you need us to do?"

"I want messages sent to every corner of the empire. I want it known that I am coming and building an army to stand against magic. I want allies, true allies who will join me in the fight."

The female elf nodded, chin trembling. "It shall be done."

Elmira rubbed her hands together. "Good. I also need to track down the water nymph, so I'll be taking your mounts."

32

ARACELI

The air was sour as Araceli left the palace, crossing the cobblestone road and hurrying down a narrow alley in a shortcut to the water fountain where she usually met Shyrin. At last, she had a day off, and she was grateful to escape the library. A week had passed since her incident with Lord Elias, and now the humans seemed to have vanished overnight. Araceli was relieved, even more so because Kaiden hadn't asked her to steal the scroll again.

She slept in the bed with him now, on the edge, as far away as possible. It felt wrong, but since the night he'd given her a massage, she'd slept much better than ever before, though she still blushed at the reminder of his fingers dancing across her bare back. Secretly, she wanted him to do it again, but she was too shy to ask.

When she burst out of the alley, she saw Shyrin sitting on the edge of the water fountain, wearing her demure priestess robes. Her hood was back and droplets of water hung in her white hair, catching the light like crystals. She waved and stood as Araceli joined her. The two embraced, and Shyrin pulled back. "What are you wearing?" Her fingers stroked Araceli's dress. "It's lovely."

Araceli had chosen the blue dress again, her favorite. Shaking back her hair, she twirled to give Shyrin the full effect before sitting down again. "I've come into a bit of luck," she explained. "Can you keep a secret?"

Shyrin's eyes widened. "Of luck? Araceli, that's marvelous. Do tell what happened, I could use some good news."

Araceli carefully told her about the new room and clothes, omitting the most important detail, although she felt bad. But she could not endanger her friend by mentioning the book or the jinn. "I want to better myself," she finished. "I've learned to read and write, but I want to become more than just a librarian."

"That's wonderful Araceli, but what are you going to do?"

"I was hoping you could help me with ideas. I don't know. I have the opportunity to learn ink magic in secret, although it's forbidden."

Shyrin squeezed her arm. "Why do you assume it's forbidden?"

Araceli licked her lips. "There's all this talk about station and staying in my place and not asking for things that are . . . above me. And I haven't seen any blue fauns act as ink mages. The ones I've seen are all servants."

Shyrin stood, pulling Araceli up with her and linking their arms together. "Walk with me. I've been studying . . . don't laugh. I've actually paid attention this time."

"Why?" Araceli hugged her friend closer as they walked.

Broad pathways stretched out, allowing horses and riders

and carriages to pass, but Shyrin steered them toward the gardens. They were off-limits to civilians, but no one would question Shyrin, an elykin, and no one would question Araceli if she walked with an elykin.

"One of the sisters sat down with me and told me it's time for me to take up my responsibilities. While the capital is secure, there is word of sorcery in the wild lands."

Araceli shrugged. "But that's not new. There are usually uprisings, and the army is sent out to quash them."

"This is different." Shyrin shivered. "No one we've sent has returned, and there are concerns, whispered about in secret of course, that a new power is rising, that the time of prophecy is near."

Araceli came to a stop and suddenly it was cold, despite the warm sun and the flowers lifting their joyful faces to the light. "What did you say?"

"I'm not supposed to tell anyone this, but you're my best friend. I want you to be aware that things might change in the capital, and if you speak up, more opportunities might be granted to you. So do something; don't be left behind. Learn ink magic, and teach it if you can find nothing else to do. I doubt we'll need it here, for the greatest city in the world protects us, but if you aspire to leave, you will need magic in the wild lands. Now I'm more grateful for my position, and I'm going to learn to read the omens in the stars. I'm going to apply myself so I can help and instruct."

"No, not that," Araceli countered, even though Shyrin's words resonated with her, much like Kaiden's had. "What did you say about prophecies?"

"Oh." Shyrin gave a nervous laugh. "If you believe in such things, the sisters believe that certain prophecies are coming true. They study the stars, follow the events of the world, and seek truths and revelations others call conspiracies or brush aside. I admit, I didn't have faith or believe them until one told me that after the spring rites, I'd meet a fellow elykin on the bridge, and he would change my life."

Araceli raised an eyebrow. "Isn't that a rather vague prophecy? I could say that after leaving this garden, you'll stumble upon a small child asking for food. It doesn't take much imagination to come up with a story."

"I agree with you, which is why I scoffed at the words. During the rites we had fun, we were drunk and silly. It was not a time for danger and darkness, but the elykin caught my arm and told me he was sent to deliver a message to me, specifically. About my parents."

"But your parents are dead."

"That's why I thought it was silly. Who would come with word of my parents after all these years? Apparently they were part of a rebellion of sorts against the empire, and they left me something of worth, a map or some kind of scroll that leads to something of significance buried somewhere. The elykin came to tell me where the scroll is, but he didn't want to bring it into the capital lest if fall into the wrong hands."

"Are you going to search for it?"

"No, but it made me think, if my parents thought about rebelling, I want to understand why. The purpose of the sisters is to reveal the truth and guide Nomadia with wisdom. If my parents thought something was wrong, I need the knowledge and foresight to understand for myself instead of solely relying on their information. Anyone can be persuaded to any cause, but I think it is important to thoroughly understand the issues at hand and search for the truth myself. The sisters have good intentions, but the incident at the bridge opened my eyes to what could be. I've been hoping you would have a similar revelation."

Listening to Shyrin left Araceli feeling torn, for her journey was not as straightforward and simple. She was using magic, hiding a book, and doing what no blue faun had done before. It was easy for Shyrin, an elykin, to speak of making a change and moving up, yet she was still walking the path laid out for her, while Araceli was detouring.

"I think you're doing the right thing," she told Shyrin. "I still want to know about the prophecies. And I know you want to learn now, but will you eventually consider searching for the information left by your parents?"

"I've thought of it, and I think so. When that day comes, I hope you'll come with me." Shyrin grinned. "It will be an adventure, and it's not odd for a priestess to choose traveling companions and set off to bring light and knowledge to the hidden corners of the empire. However, there is much for me to learn here first. Araceli, I know it's hard for you too, and I don't want to ignore the issue. I think you can be the first blue faun to stand up for yourself, to do something about the way your people are treated. I want to, but it would have more of an impact coming from you."

Sudden tears rose to Araceli's eyes. "You're such a good friend. I admit, I don't know how to begin. Even learning ink magic in secret seems wrong."

"Well, I will support you in any way I can with what little influence I have now. Perhaps it is better you learn in secret and surprise the capital with your knowledge. You are smart and talented and beautiful. I'm proud to have a friend like you."

Araceli nudged her, laughing through her tears. "Now you're just resorting to flattery!"

"I do what I can," Shyrin giggled, then straightened up. "Life is changing, though I didn't notice during the spring rites. That was fun, wasn't it? We should have more fun, yet it hardly seems like there's time."

"Let's make it a point to enjoy the next festival," Araceli agreed. "Shyrin, will you promise to share what you learn about the prophecies with me? Things are happening in the library too. This week, humans came, and they were searching for something."

Shyrin started, her eyes going wide. "Humans? Here? Now that's rare and disturbing news. I wonder if the sisters read that in the stars. What were they looking for?"

Despite trying to keep the truth to herself, it rolled off Araceli's tongue. "They wanted a magical book, and I believe when they couldn't find it in the library, they left. Still, it was unsettling."

"I can imagine, but what did they look like? Were they odd? Did they look different from us? The story books have them with tiny ears and eyes and hair on their faces."

Araceli thought of Lord Elias and shuddered. "They weren't so different from us, but there's something frightening about them."

"I'd love to see one in the flesh. I used to dream I'd run away with a human, and venture into their lands."

"You still could! Hurry to the city gates and see if one is still near," Araceli teased.

"Well, as long as they know I'm only chasing after them because they make the finest wine in the empire. If I learned their secrets, I could be rich."

Araceli laughed. "What would you do with your wealth?"

"Drink, of course." Shyrin shook her head, and the joy faded from her face. "Wealth seems such a dream to aspire to, but in reality, I want to do something to help others. Once I know enough, I want to venture out to the wild lands, start an orphanage, and make sure children don't go hungry and protect them from the dangers out there. Maybe you can come with me and use your ink magic to keep us safe."

"I'd actually like that," Araceli agreed, and dreams sparked in her mind. Perhaps the jinn would know a way to make it possible.

They continued farther into the garden, talking of mundane things until Shyrin had to return for afternoon prayers. They parted ways and Araceli made her way back to the palace, her heart lighter as she walked the streets of Nomadia.

The water fountain trickled merrily, and a bard sang beside it, using the water to throw his voice further. Bystanders gathered, some tossing a coin to the hat he held out as he sang. Araceli smiled, her mind whirling with the conversation she'd had with Shyrin.

It was enlightening and gave her hope for a future, and she felt grateful that she wasn't the only one who wanted to see a change in Nomadia. One day, she'd rise above her station and perhaps venture to the wild lands, although she much preferred the sturdy walls and safety of the capital for now. As she passed under the glass bridge that led to the library, she noticed a small crowd gathering. The great library was beautiful from the street, but what were they staring at?

Changing directions, she walked toward the crowd, trying

to peer above them and see what was going on. "What is it?" she asked a nearby elf.

He raised his eyebrows, and she saw he was the same one who'd led her to her new room. "There's been a robbery, a theft," he said somberly.

Araceli shrugged. Thieving wasn't so unusual, especially in the marketplace and the streets of the capital city. Once the thief was caught, a public whipping or other punishment taught them never to steal again. However, most thieves got away with their crimes. "Why are people gathered here?"

"Someone stole a book from the library."

Araceli stumbled back as if she'd been punched in the gut. Her mouth went dry and her hands felt clammy. Spinning, she hurried away, although she could guess exactly what had happened.

33

NURIMIL

Nurimil kept his eyes trained on the road as they walked, not wanting to see every attractive movement of Darya. No. The nymph. He had to put space between them, and thinking of her as Darya would only make him want to stay with her. She was slow, but already moved faster than last night, and she hadn't complained once about how her feet must hurt her. *Walking on scales.* He shook his head. It had to be uncomfortable.

She was adapting easily, but the look of confusion and disgust that had covered her face when she bit into the dried meat still made his shoulders shake with merriment. But no matter how adaptable and willing she was, they still needed mounts to speed their journey. Nurimil wished he hadn't dumped his map in the river. Even though there were signposts at the next crossroads, he needed to find a place off the beaten track, away from the road.

He tugged at his shirt as he thought of the place. While he certainly didn't want to go there, if he was being hunted, and she was being hunted, they couldn't stay on foot, on the road. Anyone could find them, and if the wizard used magic to track them down, it would be worse.

Once they got to Gyin—a flourishing trade post—he could purchase another horse and send Darya on her way. From there, the roads were full of travelers, since the trading post was perched in a midway point between the capital and the northern lands. It was also the crossroads of east and west travel.

Darya gasped as a butterfly flitted across their path, landing on the white flowers that opened their blossoms on the side of the road. She smiled, and his gaze dropped to the curve of her full green lips.

Suddenly, an awareness struck him, knocking his breath away. Forcing his eyes back on the road, he turned the thought over in his mind. Fated mates. That's what was happening. He'd first heard the term while drinking in a tavern in Eloof, and had laughed along with others at the idea. How ridiculous was it that fate should choose for him, especially at his age? Fate was for the young, the dreamers, and yet, somehow, he'd been caught in a net he could not escape. The best thing to do was find the nearest stream that led to the capital and tell her to follow it southwest until she reached the city.

"What is that?" Darya jolted him from his thoughts as she pointed to movement on the road.

Nurimil's hand shot to his sword before he dropped it. "A squirrel," he told her, almost laughing at her ignorance. "A beast that collects nuts and likes to dig up gardens."

Darya raised her eyebrows. "A pest?"

"Yes, they are a nuisance, yet harmless."

"We have creatures like those in the sea, usually tiny fish that like to nip at flesh. Harmless, but annoying."

It was pleasant to hear her speak, and suddenly Nurimil wanted to hear more from her, about her life, her people. "Do you have family in the depths? Yesterday, I recall you mentioned them, but I know little about the people who live under the sea."

Darya's smile dropped away, her luminous eyes narrowing.

Nurimil had expected to see homesickness or longing instead of the flash of anger. Had he insulted her? He opened his mouth to take back his words when she spoke.

"Yes, I have family, back home in Trilantis." Her mouth went tight. "I'm one of four lesser nymphs. My sisters and I are in training in the Court of Nymphs so that one day we can rule over one of the many kingdoms under the sea. Not that I have a choice, but I had assumed being part of the Court of Nymphs would come with responsibilities I enjoy. Unfortunately, my sisters and I are nothing more than glorified guards, tasked with keeping watch over the kingdom of sirens, in case of an attack."

"Sirens," Nurimil repeated. "So they look to you as if you're their goddess?"

To her credit, Darya gave a half smile and tucked a loose strand of green hair behind her head. "I'm no goddess, but the sirens look to the nymphs for protection because of our water magic. It's a more peaceful way than bloodshed of solving disputes. My magic keeps away the predators, the great sharks and squids who prey on sirens. Nymphs also convey messages from one court to another, and between other political factions in the sea."

"Politics?" Nurimil didn't know why it surprised him, but he'd always assumed the creatures under the water spent their time singing songs and chasing fish. It was an adjustment to wrap his mind around the fact that they were people and had their own organizational and political norms.

Darya shrugged, but he couldn't miss the steely look in her eye. Something felt wrong. "Does it surprise you? I don't know much about Nomadia, aside from the stories brought back from river nymphs and mermaids. From what I've heard, I believe life in the sea is not so different from life on the land. We are simply under the water, our roads are invisible, and we fight with magic and water, but in the end, we are people with duties and hopes and dreams. The Court of Nymphs has a political agenda to bring peace to the sea and unite the kingdoms."

There was that dissatisfaction in her tone again. "You do not agree with this?"

"Yes. No!" Darya's response was sharp. "I want peace. I agree with the move toward less bloodshed and more unity. But what is the use of water magic in a time of peace?"

"I've hunted many magical creatures," Nurimil told her, suddenly wanting to share. "They use their magic in many ways: to hunt food, protect their young, fight off predators, find a mate, and, most importantly, to celebrate."

"I'd like to see that," Darya admitted. "In the Court of Nymphs, magic is only used for protection. Any other uses are frowned upon. Having all this power without the permission to use it is frustrating, which is why I'm here."

Nurimil frowned. "Because of magic?"

"Yes. The day that everything went wrong was a day of celebration, of unity. The mermaids and sirens had come to a mutually beneficial agreement, a marriage in exchange for protection. You see, the sirens are warriors. They live deep under the sea in the twilight zone, and are rarely seen by landwalkers. Mermaids tend to dwell near the surface, in what is called the sunlight zone. They prefer to stay close to land, for there are many islands and reefs in the sea. However, the nymph who protected them recently lay down in eternal slumber, leaving them exposed. I assumed the council would appoint one of my sisters to rise to the role of their guardian nymph. Instead, the sirens and mermaids formed an alliance."

"Were you hoping to be given the promotion to guardianship?"

Darya paused, as if the thought had never crossed her mind. She grimaced. "No, the council would never agree to grant me such a high honor."

She sounded sad, and Nurimil's heart squeezed before he reminded himself he wasn't supposed to care, especially not about political affairs under the sea. Although fascinating, he had his own problems.

Pressing a hand to her mouth, Darya closed her eyes for a moment, and tripped. Nurimil reached out a hand to steady her, bringing them both to a stop.

"I'm sorry," he said gently, reluctantly dropping his fingers from her arm.

Darya pressed her lips together, her expression pensive. "I'm both sorry, and I'm not. I don't want to be a guardian,

watching the seas in case something happens. I want more . . .
more than the life meant for me there, and I want to prove
myself to the Court of Nymphs."

"Is that why you're here?" He took a step, and she fell in
stride with him.

"I'm here in part because I had no choice. A sea witch
cursed the sirens and the remedy for the fever lies in the great
library. Ironic as it is, I need the magic of the landwalkers to
help my people. I care about the sirens and I will do whatever
it takes to help them. I admit, it wasn't going well until I met
you."

She gave him a seductive look that made him want to
hide.

Frowning, he hurried to keep the conversation going.
"Why did they send you alone? If the Court of Nymphs
wanted this quest to succeed, they should have sent two,
three, or maybe more."

Darya looked stricken, making Nurimil wonder if the
thought had occurred to her. Her walking through Nomadia
alone would draw attention—had already drawn attention.
Plus, how did the wizard know exactly where she'd be?
Perhaps he employed a seer and had received a vision of the
future. With the magic that spread through Nomadia, it was
possible, but Nurimil wondered if something more sinister
was at work. He couldn't deny that Darya's evocative beauty
drew him in, but would a wizard want her just to sate his lust?
He doubted it.

"Because I'm the only one who can do this!" Darya spoke
in a rush, her voice higher than usual. "The Court of Nymphs
chose me for this task, to prove myself. I am a guardian, I have

water magic. Only one of us is needed. The rest stayed to explore alternative solutions to save the sirens. No one else could be spared."

Raising his hands, Nurimil tried to calm her down. "I did not mean to offend. Clearly, the Court of Nymphs works in different ways."

But Darya kept walking as if she hadn't heard him. "They wouldn't have sent me here in vain, as if they were trying to get rid of me. I know I made a terrible mistake, but this is my chance at fixing it. If I want things to change, I have to complete this task. I can't go back only to become a guard again."

Nurimil wondered if the Court of Nymphs were cold and callous and did, in fact, want to get rid of her for her mistake. He shook himself, knowing he had a tendency to consider those with power corrupt. Had the Court of Nymphs tricked her? Memories took him back to the moment when his father had chanted the spell and the sickness lifted from Jasmine's body, the dark pallor gone. It hadn't been enough. She was healthy for a while, and then it came back, as though the magic desired her life. It came and claimed her, and no spell could undo what had been done.

He remembered those dark days, his sister crying and his father staring out at nothing, waiting for her to rise again. Everything had changed then. Magic gave and it took away, and those who dallied with it wanted more and more until they forgot themselves and forgot what mattered. Nurimil was thankful he hadn't been tempted by fate or given the ability to perform magic of his own.

"What about you?" Darya asked.

He glanced at her and saw the misery written across her face. His conscience chided him, for it was his questions that had stirred up darker thoughts in her mind. "What about me?"

"Do you have a family?"

Nurimil stiffened. He didn't want to talk about himself or his family. Everything that happened had taken place years ago, yet it still had power over him, leaving him raw. But he wanted to give her something, anything, so she would not speak of family again.

"My mother died when I was too young to remember her, and my father remarried when I was five, I think. Her name was Jasmine, and she brought love and joy to every corner of the house. We were happy. Blessed. As the years passed, she discovered she couldn't have children, and so my father searched for a magical remedy." Nurimil paused. That magic was how everything went wrong.

"Did he find one?" Darya prompted.

"He was successful, and soon I had a sister." He'd loved the tiny child, despite her demanding cries, and he still cursed himself for what had happened to her. If only . . . but there was no going back in time, no way to remedy the mistakes of the past. He could only look to the future and strive to be a better person, although his past left him bitter. Especially when it came to relationships. It was why he preferred to work alone and why he walked the road. "But then Jasmine grew ill, and once again my father went out and came back with a spell to save her. But it did not last. A year later, she died."

"Oh, Nurimil."

He barely heard Darya and wished he hadn't begun. The rest of the tale tasted bitter on his tongue. "My father began to search again for the impossible, but nobody can bring the dead back. Eventually, my sister and I went to live at the Court of Healers, cared for by the sisters there. As soon as I turned sixteen, I left to seek my fortune and look for my father."

"Did you ever find him?"

"Never." Nurimil's throat tightened. He was almost forty and assumed he was done with that misery, yet it still ached, the not knowing. Had his father died in his quest? Or was he out there somewhere, still looking?

"What happened to your sister?"

Nurimil didn't miss the catch in her voice, the growing empathy for him. Why had he told her such a dark tale? But he knew why: to keep her mind off what the Court of Nymphs had done to her. He hated himself for caring.

After a long pause, he found the words to admit his failure. "I lost her too. When I returned to the Court of Healers, she'd already moved on, taken in by another family. I shouldn't have let her go; I should have gone back for her sooner. I imagine she's grown up now, and I hope, wherever she is, she's happy."

"How long ago was it?"

"Officially, I stopped looking ten years ago. Every now and then I hear of someone with the same name, but when I've gone to investigate, it's never either of them. The empire of Nomadia is vast, and I'm always on the move. We could pass each other like shadows in the night, and I'd never know."

Darya pressed her hand to her mouth, tears glimmering in her eyes.

"Don't feel sorry for me," he said roughly. "I made my own choices. Save your breath for the road ahead."

He quickened his pace, putting a gap between them, although he heard her pant as she tried to keep up. He didn't know what had come over him, for he'd never told another soul the tale of his family.

34

DARYA

Darya felt closer to Nurimil after their discussion, although his questions had stirred up anxiety about her quest. She was relieved when he'd shared about his past, although the haunted notes in his tone told her it wasn't something he'd forgiven himself for. She hoped he'd share more as the sunlight dimmed and a hint of the two moons came into view. A cool wind blew, sending the scent of water to her nose. Nurimil paused in front of a thicket. "Here we are," he announced, moving into what looked like a bush.

Darya hesitated, then followed, ducking her head to avoid the thick foliage. It smelled sweet, a blend of flowers and perhaps wood. She hoped they weren't going far, and he'd find a place for them to sleep soon. She desperately wanted to find a body of water and lie down under the waves. After walking all day, her strength was sapped, and she needed energy. How did the landwalkers thrive without the life force provided by water?

As if he could read her mind, Nurimil did not go far before he stopped. "Rest here. No one can see us from the road. We're still too close to the road for comfort, but I need daylight to find the hidden path."

Darya collapsed and pressed her fingers against the ground, searching for any moisture she could pull from it. Closing her eyes, she waited.

"What's wrong?"

In the shadows, she could just make out the lines of worry on Nurimil's face.

"I need water soon. Without it, I feel my strength drying up inside."

He sat down, near and yet far enough away that she could not reach out and touch him. "It's your life source, isn't it? The water? You can't live long without it."

Darya's heart warmed. She didn't have to tell him. He understood. "The longest was back in Dustania." A shudder wracked her body, and she shut her mind against it, determined to forget how the giants had abused her. "I'm not sure how long I can go without water, but I don't want to find out."

"Then it is fortunate we have to make a detour on our way to the trading post. I need to visit someone who happens to live by the lakes."

Darya sat up, anticipation swelling. She tampered it down. She shouldn't desire to spend more time with the man; in fact, she should focus on reaching the capital as soon as possible. "A detour? Will it take long?"

"No." His tone was reassuring, as if he were thinking the same thing she was. "In fact, it should speed up our journey. We need mounts, and although this isn't my first choice, it will have to do. While I bargain, you can enjoy the lake."

Water. Closing her eyes, she allowed peace to enfold her. Even as darkness closed around them, she sensed Nurimil's presence as though a spell had been cast over her. What was it about him that drew her in? It was more than the fact he'd saved her from doom and generously offered to guide her as far as the trading post. Pressing her lips together, she weighed her choices. Forgetting about him and focusing on her quest would be the wise choice, but desire was intoxicating. She'd have to persuade him, sate her lust with him and then, perhaps, it would be enough. The intoxication would fade, and she'd be free to continue to the great library. Yet even as she fell asleep, unease lingered inside her at the thought of seducing the human.

FOR THREE DAYS, they followed a rutted dirt path deeper into the mire. Moisture lay thick and anticipation shivered through Darya. Water was near. She'd pulled enough from the air to allow her to go on, but each day that passed without submersion drained her strength away.

Nurimil pressed forward relentlessly, taking them through gray trees. Ropy vines hung over their heads and furry moss covered the ground. If she didn't trust him, she would have thought he was leading her to her death. The landscape was beautiful though, dotted with red and orange flowers. Trees hung their broad leaves down, some green as moss, others blue like the sky, and still others purple. Each morning, the dew hung like jewels, and when the light reached them, they glittered like crystals. Darya licked them up when Nurimil wasn't looking.

When at last they came to a clearing, Darya's eyes widened.

The trees gave way to a circular opening. In the clearing, a mossy house rose, covered in vines and leaves as though it were trying to blend in to the wood. Beyond it, a shimmering lake glistened and continued south as far as the eye could see. Darya's fingers went to the clasp of the cloak, ready to yank it off and dash into the lake.

Nurimil held up his hand, his eyes somber. "Wait. We have to ensure the master is home. Once he grants permission, you may go to the lake."

"He owns this land?" Darya asked. It was the same way in the sea; there were certain trenches owned by sea monsters, and to trespass meant to risk death.

"If he's in a good mood today, he will help us."

Darya crept behind Nurimil as he approached the door, unable to tear her eyes away from the lake. Water lilies floated on it, and a great bird stood by the wild grass. After spreading its broad wings, it lifted into the air, giving Darya a flash of red feathers. Her pulse quickened. This wasn't so bad at all. Klarya would be spitting with anger to know that Darya was actually enjoying her task. Then the memory of Nurimil's words clouded her thoughts. She recalled the dark eyes of the council, jaws tight with anger. They disliked her and didn't believe she'd amount to anything other than a lesser guardian. If she wanted more, this was her chance to prove herself.

Nurimil knocked on the door, the vibrations shaking loose a pile of leaves that flew away. Silence followed, broken only by a splash in the water and the chirping of birds. Darya shifted from one foot to the other, itching to hurl herself into the lake. It was only for Nurimil's sake she held back.

A shuffling sound came and then the door moved back with a long creak, opening to reveal a gaping hole of darkness. A wrinkled face appeared and a pair of sharp blue eyes peered out from under thick white eyebrows. The man was bald and leaned on a walking stick, but when he saw them he grinned. When he straightened up, the years of age seemed to fall away from him like a shroud.

"Ah, thought you were a pair of no-good thieves. The woods been thick with 'em for the last couple of months. Spring weather brings both the good and bad out of hiding. Forgive my old ramblings. Nurimil, good to see you again, my boy." He gave Nurimil's hand a hearty shake, then peered at Darya.

Unsure of the mannerisms of landwalkers, she nodded at him.

His grin widened. "My lady, you must be from the waters. Do come in." He gestured to the dark opening and called, "They're friends, it's okay to come out!"

Little lights glowed from within, and although Darya was curious, her eyes were drawn back to the lake.

Nurimil touched the small of her back. Even through the cloak, a jolt of anticipation shot through her. "My friend here wishes to make use of the lake. She will join us when she is ready."

"Go on then." The man waved her away. "Watch out for the crocodiles."

Relief surged through Darya. She gave the odd man a smile of appreciation and strode toward the waters, her fingers pulling at the clasp of the cloak. It came loose and flowed from her shoulders, settling in the marshy ground. Her skin tingled, free from the covering, and soon she was running. With a bold leap, she dove into the waters and sank under the surface.

35

ARACELI

Araceli dashed through the halls, pulse racing, terrible thoughts twirling through her mind. The door to her room was innocent enough, but when she turned the knob, intending to burst in and demand answers from Kaiden, it was locked. She rattled it again. How dare he lock her out!

She knocked softly at first, then harder when there was no immediate answer. Her chest constricted as she backed away. Should she even go into her room, when she was sure the stolen book was there? What if Kaiden had been found out and was arrested? What if she was next?

Frantically, she searched the hall, but it was empty and quiet, with only the soft glow of daylight filtering out from under the doors. Eventually, the door to her room swung open, and Kaiden's intense stare sent a shock of relief through her. His shirt was open, his hair was ruffled, and his chest rose and fell quickly. "I did not expect you back so early," he said, holding the door open for her.

Araceli marched inside, scanning the room for the stolen books. Piled on the table was a collection of scrolls and books. Not just one, but ten. A knot twisted in her belly, and Araceli bent at the waist, trying to keep from vomiting. "It was you, wasn't it?" she hissed when she was able to speak again. "Why did you steal from the great library? They'll find you, and we'll both be arrested for this!"

Kaiden locked the door and strode past her. "Relax, no one saw me. We won't get into trouble. If we do, you can wish your way out of it. What good is a jinn if you don't take advantage of the wishes?"

His voice rang with bitterness, and there was an edge of anger and darkness to his movements she'd never seen. As though earlier he'd resigned himself to his fate, but now he wanted to fight her. All the happy, encouraging feelings from her conversation with Shyrin fizzled away, replaced with anger, frustration, guilt, and raw fear.

Now, she desperately needed Kaiden to go away, to undo what he had done, to fix the insurmountable problem he had willfully created for her. "Go back in time," she ordered, "and don't steal from the library."

Kaiden had already returned to the table and now he paused, his hands on a page. "Is that your wish? Because I cannot change the course of time; no one can. You're panicking. When I get done with these books, I will return them to the library as silently as I took them. Aren't you curious? Don't you want to read the books? To gain knowledge? To discover what I discovered? Or are you so frightened of being arrested?"

Araceli's fists clenched, but she didn't move, because part of what he said was right. She was curious, and she wanted to know. Without Kaiden, she'd never know what was written in the *Prophecies of Nomadia*. She closed her eyes, recalling Shyrin's words. Summoning her courage, she faced Kaiden. "I want to know, but after we find the truth, you have to return these stolen books."

"So one stolen book is okay, but these?" He waved his hands, those long, slender fingers catching the air. "This is too much?"

"A crowd has gathered in front of the library because no one has ever before stolen from the Great Library of Zandria. If they find you, they will be ruthless."

"No one will find me," Kaiden disagreed. "No one saw me."

"Why, because you have such great magic?"

His jaw tightened, and he rose, glaring down at her. "Yes, I have great magic. I'd think you'd know that since you summoned me, and I have the power to grant all of your wishes. If you dream it, I can make it happen. I am Kaiden the Great, Kaiden the Magician, Kaiden the Sorcerer, the Prince of Sand, the Time Walker, the Blade Bringer. I am all of these things and more. The tales of my life you can't possibly fathom. I have lived more years than you could dare to imagine. I have seen kingdoms rise and fall, I have helped rulers take their places and throttle others. When I am summoned, it is often on the brink of change brought about by someone powerful, ready to do anything and everything to achieve their heart's desire. And then there's you."

With each word he took a step, and Araceli backed away until her hands were pressed against the wall and he towered over her. His dark eyes gleamed and his nostrils flared. "You!" He stopped short of jabbing a finger into her shoulder. "You want magic that you don't understand, you want to rise above your station, and yet you're hindering yourself with every step you take. Where is your courage? Where is your desire for change? You're so confused you don't even know what to wish for, and then you tell me, the immortal servant, that I should be concerned about a petty theft. In your eyes I'm selfish and dismissive, which is true, but at least I know who I am. The world has jaded me by making me its prisoner, but if I had three wishes, I would not hesitate. If you can't bear my presence, then wish me away. Say it. Just speak the words and set me free." His eyes flashed with anger.

Araceli shrank back, words stuck in her throat. She wanted him to leave, but not without returning the books. But did she truly want him to go? If he left, everything would go back to how it had been, and while it wasn't a terrible existence—she had food, shelter, and a job—she wanted more. If this was the only way to get it, to put herself in danger, should she proceed? It wasn't all Kaiden's fault. It had all started with the mage. If he kept his word, he'd return in a couple of months and all of this would go away. Did she want it all to go away?

"I wish," the words tripped out of her mouth.

"Say it," Kaiden demanded, leaning so close his intoxicating scent filled her nose, his face mere inches away from hers.

"I wish..."

But the wish wouldn't come out, because she didn't know what she was wishing for, and conflict made her mute.

With a groan, he hurled his body away from her. "This is exactly why I'm leaving, of my own accord."

He couldn't! He was her jinn, and yet she did nothing to

stop him as he opened the door. Leaving it ajar, he slipped down the hall, leaving Araceli alone with the stolen books.

Anger fizzled, and she slammed the door shut. One of the books fell off the table and thudded onto the rug, pages crushed under its own weight. Muttering under her breath about the foul attitudes of jinns, she picked it up. The pages fell open, displaying words, verses as if it were a book of poetry. Frowning, she flipped it over and read the title. *Proverbs of Zandria.*

Why would Kaiden want a book of proverbs? She'd assumed he was looking at prophecies.

Brow furrowed, she picked up another book. *Rebellion of the Blue Fauns.*

Her heart sank. Who would write a book on the blue fauns? Especially on the rebellion.

Feeling sick, she picked up another title, and another.

An Introduction to Nomadian Politics.

The Advanced Guide to Reading Rune Stones for Nonmagical Creatures.

The Fall of Mages.

The Life and Times of King Horus.

Curses, Crushes, and Other Spell Breakers.

Seducing your Enemy.

Nowhere in the stack was there a book or scroll about the prophecies of Nomadia. With a pang, Araceli realized the books on the table weren't forbidden magical books. It was likely she'd pulled them from the shelves once, for they were available for anyone to read. Why was Kaiden reading them? What did he seek to find hidden in those pages?

Burying her face in her hands, she slumped on a chair, her mind spinning.

When her panic abated, she sat up, staring at the books. Kaiden was gone, but she hoped it was just momentary. When he returned, she'd ask him what he planned to do with the books he'd borrowed. In the meantime, she'd take another look at the magical tome. It lay on the table with the others, and when she picked it up, the runes glowed as if coming alive when she touched the book. This time, the book was warm under her fingers.

She opened it and began reading. Eventually, she came to a diagram. It was a circle divided into five sections. On each section runes were written; she guessed they were instructions, based on her rudimentary knowledge. She stroked her finger over the runes, for the ink was raised to form ridges on the paper. The page felt vaguely familiar. Was it the one she'd flipped to when she summoned the jinn?

Flipping to another page, she gasped when the words transformed into runes she could read. Running her fingers over the smooth parchment, she realized it was a spell, or instructions for using ink magic. Excitement thrummed, and forgetting about her spat with Kaiden, Araceli began to read.

36

ARACELI

Spellbound, Araceli read, spell after spell. Some she understood, some she didn't. She read until the words hovered before her mind, whether her eyes were open or closed, as if imprinting themselves in her memory.

The room darkening made her pause. Jerking up, she realized that she'd read for much longer than intended, and weariness pulled at her. Kaiden wasn't there to rub her shoulders or make her a meal. Eyes heavy, she closed the book and sighed, anxiously wondering if Kaiden would return that evening. Regardless, if someone came to her room, she couldn't have the borrowed books lying obviously on the table. She stacked them one by one and hid them under the bed. Then, despite her exhaustion, she took up quill and ink and practiced runes until her eyes closed.

Two days passed without a word from Kaiden, and the uproar at the library ceased. Anxiety twisted in Araceli's belly each day as she set foot in the great library, but no one came to question her or clamp her in irons. Still, every evening when she walked across the glass bridge, she stared out into the city, wondering where Kaiden had gone and if he would ever return.

She recalled his words, his insistence on who he was and what he'd done. It must bore him to sit in her room trying to unravel the secrets of a book when his previous life had been so exciting. Mulling over his words, she recalled that he'd said he often came at the start of change. Did he mean a revolution? But Araceli wasn't sure she wanted change, especially if she didn't know if it would turn out well for her. Things were okay as they were, weren't they?

The moment she thought it, a wave of shame passed over her. Even Shyrin wanted things to change, despite her background and station as an elykin. Araceli should want the same thing. Perhaps that was why no other blue fauns had risen to the top, because they were content with the status quo or, like her, passive and afraid of standing up and forcing change. Afraid of the repercussions. Afraid that what happened before would happen again.

She couldn't let fear rule her life. If Kaiden gave her a second chance, she'd do what he said, better herself and find a new position. If not for herself, then for Shyrin and the blue fauns who would come after her.

Mind made up, Araceli returned to her room, and there he was.

He sat at the table, looking devilishly handsome as he read. As the door closed, he looked up at her. His eyes were deep pools of sorrow, so raw, so transparent that for a moment she believed she was seeing his soul. Knowledge unfolded like an unfurling bud under the warmth of a spring sun.

Shutting the door behind her, she locked it, surprised at her relief that he'd returned. Embarrassed by her earlier judgement of him, she shifted from hoof to hoof. "You didn't steal the books, did you?"

Kaiden closed the book he'd been reading and rested his hand on top. "How do you know?"

Araceli shrugged. "The library thief was human, that's what I learned. He stole a magical book full of forbidden spells, the dark spells that should be burned, not locked away in the library. He broke through several wards of protections and curses. The thief catchers are giving chase, but most assume he's long gone from the capital."

"Ah." Kaiden tapped his fingers on the book's cover. "So you are interested in the truth."

Araceli's face burned. She took a step forward, intending to apologize, but Kaiden waved for her to sit.

His dark eyes bored into hers as he continued, "I didn't tell you the truth about the magical book you have for a few reasons. First, I recognized the book because the spell to summon me was inked into it."

"Why didn't you say so?" Araceli asked, confused.

"Because it is a book of dark ink magic. But it isn't just any spell book."

Araceli nodded, recalling the spells she'd read. The memory of them still hung before her eyes.

"It's a magical tome, and should be a forbidden book, for if one learns these spells, they can control ink magic."

Araceli's brow furrowed. "What do you mean, control ink magic? I thought . . . I assumed the point of a spell book is to learn to use ink magic . . . ?"

She trailed off as Kaiden's mouth tightened. "It is, but this is more." He leaned back in the chair, crossing his arms over his chest. "It's more than knowledge."

Araceli shifted in the chair, her tail swishing back and forth at the ominous expression on Kaiden's face.

"Have you heard . . . no. You haven't," he mumbled to himself. "There are four magical properties that make up the core of magic. Spirit, ink, water, and teleporting. Mages learn how to use these powers and spell cast, just as you are learning ink magic now, but they do not *control* ink magic."

"I . . ." Araceli hesitated, not wanting to sound ignorant. "I don't understand."

"Using and controlling are two different things. Magic users don't actually control magic, they study and use spells, legally. There is also dark magic, which is illegal."

Araceli swallowed hard. "Like curses?"

"Yes." Kaiden stared at her, his eyes hard.

Biting her lip, Araceli ventured another guess. "Like . . . like you? Someone used dark magic to force you to become a jinn?"

"Yes."

The strange note in his voice made tears burn Araceli's throat. She should set him free; why hadn't she already?

Kaiden's fingers tapped against the book again. "I'm not aware that it has happened before, but it is possible for someone to learn how to control all magic across Nomadia, using a combination of the four core powers. If one can collect four powers without killing themselves, they can shape the fate of Nomadia. The magical book you have teaches one not only how to use ink magic, but how to bend it to your will."

"Oh." Araceli suddenly felt afraid.

"I recall another book, similar to this one, that teaches one how to control the spirit world, perhaps even raise the dead. The book should have been destroyed instead of kept in the great library, and now it has been stolen. If someone is searching for the book of ink magic, and the book of spirit magic, it leads me to believe someone is looking to control the magic of Nomadia."

"Oh . . ." Araceli breathed, waiting for more, unsure what else to say.

"I have a theory." Kaiden raised a finger. "So far you've met two people who wanted the book of ink magic. The mage who had it, and the human who desired it."

"Lord Elias," Araceli confirmed. "You believe he stole the other book from the library?"

"Makes sense. If he couldn't find this one, just take the second best book for his needs. Why, though? And why did the mage leave this book to you, unless he knew Lord Elias would track him here to steal the book, maybe go so far as to kill him? Perhaps Lord Elias is trying to raise the dead."

"Then why would there be a spell to summon you? Jinns can't wake the dead."

"No, death is a final act and cannot be undone by magic. Although there is a way to commune with the spirits. After summoning a jinn one has to request to be taken to a sacred location and perform a ritual. Some call this time travel, but I'm beginning to think Lord Elias wanted this book because he needed to summon me. I've never served a Lord Elias, though perhaps we shall become acquainted in the future."

Araceli's mind spun, unsure what to think or say. "What do we do?"

"I don't know that there is anything to do. You played your

part already. By hiding the book, you kept Lord Elias from getting what he wanted. According to rumor, he's left the capital with another book, off to do his dark deeds elsewhere. There is nothing left except to go on with life and put this incident behind us."

"Oh." A wave of disappointment crushed Araceli's spirits, and she stared. All that for nothing? She hadn't known she'd enjoyed it, that feel of having a secret, of knowing something no one else knew and sharing it with Kaiden. Although, she still had the book of ink magic, at least until the mage returned for it.

"However, I went to the library, and I entered the forbidden room to read the *Prophecies of Nomadia*."

Araceli's heart skipped a beat. "What did they say?"

"As prophecies go, there were several of them, but I found one particularly interesting. I did not memorize it, but it spoke of a child with golden tears who will have the power to rule the elements of the world and steal magic. If that prophecy ever comes true, Nomadia as you know it will cease to exist. All of Nomadia thrives on magic, so if you wish to become an ink mage, you better learn now, before this golden-eyed sorceress rises and takes it all for herself."

"Yes." Araceli snatched at his words as though they would save her. "I will learn ink magic. I will do whatever you say. But what about the other books? The ones I hid under the bed?"

"I spoke with Mistress Vina, head of the library. She did not mind me borrowing a few books to ease the passage of my dull days here. It has been a while since I was active in this century, and I have some catching up to do."

"It was an odd collection," Araceli prodded.

"I enjoy being well-read." He grinned, and the rawness evaporated from his eyes, replaced with a wicked glint. "Now, shall we begin your lessons?"

Araceli joined him as he cleared away the books, but she felt the slightest inkling of a quiet unrest. What if Kaiden wasn't telling her everything? What if his theory about her being safe was wrong? If it was indeed the time of prophecy, someone was coming to control all magic. Which meant as long as she held the book of ink magic, she could prevent that from happening, or become one of the most sought-after persons in Nomadia. She considered the thought, then shook it away. No, other than the mage, no one knew she had the book. No one would come for it.

37

NURIMIL

"Thanks, Zal." Nurimil forced his gaze away from Darya as she dashed to the lake.

Zal poked him in the ribs. "It's about time you found a woman, Nurimil. She's beautiful." He chuckled. "Only you would choose a relationship as impossible as one with a water nymph. Are you looking for difficulty? Your life hunting beasts isn't challenging enough?"

Stepping inside, Nurimil closed the door behind him and dropped his saddlebag on the floor. "Zal, I'm only here because of a serious matter I wish to discuss with you. She isn't mine. I'm only helping her. For now." He let the last two words drift away as he followed Zal farther into the house.

"Where did you find her?"

"Dustania."

Zal snorted. "What were you doing in that evil place?"

Nurimil ducked under the low-hanging rafters and took a seat at a round table. Every nook and cranny of the house was stuffed with clutter, buckets, leaves, fruits, nuts, vials, and bottles full of questionable substances. And books. Papers and scrolls were stacked high on the table, and the shelves were covered with a mixture of books and faerie dust. Vines hung from the ceiling and faeries crouched on them, staring down at Nurimil as they lit up the room.

"That's why I'm here."

"Do tell." Zal poked at the fire. "I'll put a kettle on."

"I had a falling out with the guild and I'm on my way to Maca to capture the singing ostrich and win favor with the empress. If I gain her mark, the guild can't touch me, and they'll be forced to remove the bounty on my head. There's more." Leaning forward, Nurimil told Zal about Darya and his suspicions about the wizard. "I don't know why a wizard is hunting her, but it's smart to get as far away as possible before they pick up the trail. The road is the fastest way to travel, but it's too dangerous. That's how the she-viper found us."

"Mmm," Zal grunted, pulling out two cups. "Tea or coffee?"

"Coffee," Nurimil said. He needed something bitter and sharp to wake him up, and perhaps it would quash the odd attraction he felt toward Darya. Even with her out of sight and knowing she could use magic should she run into trouble in the waters, he felt the strangest urge to peek out the window.

"You're in luck. I crushed some beans this morning." Zal poured the water and a bold, rich scent filled the room.

The faeries danced, sending more dust raining down. Nurimil brushed it off his head, remembering why he hated those pesky beasts. Once he'd spent the night, and they'd stolen his blanket and boots and would not give them back until Zal—recovering from a fit of laughter—forced them to.

"Well. What is it you want?" Zal sat the cups on the table and perched on a stool, leaning over the pile of papers. "You're in trouble, no doubt, and so is she. What did you say her name is?"

"Darya."

"Pretty name. I'll take my chances if you aren't interested." Zal winked, then his face changed. "I'm not surprised by your coming. The wind changed yesterday. It worries me, but I've been afraid to read the signs. What if the visions are dark? Woe to us to live in such days."

Nurimil took a sip of the coffee, letting Zal's mind work. The man was given over to ramblings because of the visions he saw. It was impossible to tell if and when they would happen, but his mind was often full of dark warnings. Which was why he lived hidden in the middle of nowhere, lest others should misuse his abilities.

"I'll read the waters, just for you, my boy. I don't like to see you in trouble."

"We also need mounts," Nurimil added. "She needs to go to the capital, unless you know a remedy that can drive poison out of the waters?"

Zal jerked. "Poison?"

"She said a sea witch cursed her people with fever. She's here to save them."

Zal walked his fingers over a pile of books and paper on the table. "I don't like this. I don't like this at all. Water nymphs have no business on land, much less going to the capital city. Can she even read? This is some dark business."

Nurimil hadn't considered the fact that she might not be able to read. But surely water nymphs had a way of reading under the water? There was still so much he didn't know about her. His mind grasped at a solution. "Is it worth her going all the way to the capital? Or can you help? Surely you have a remedy among your works."

Zal took a sip of tea and stood. "No, if it's a curse, she'll need a counter-curse to combat the magic. Such things can be found in the capital. Perhaps she doesn't have to go all the way there, although it's much closer than going clear across the empire to the Maldive Cliffs. Unless you meet a traveling mage on the road, the capital is the quickest way to gain the remedy she seeks. She'll have to use magic to cast it."

"She has plenty of that," Nurimil said, recalling the arrow that exploded in his face.

"Good." Zal picked up a boat-shaped bowl and placed it on the table. Going to the kettle, he filled the bowl until water brimmed at the edges.

Sitting down again, he raised his hands and snapped his fingers. A low strain of music began, followed by a high-pitched chant. Faeries landed on his shoulders, chanting and swaying to the music they created. One flew over the bowl, tossing in dust. Zal's face went still and his eyes glowed unnaturally as he stared into the water.

Nurimil looked away. Watching him read the visions in the water made him feel uncomfortable, even more so since he knew Zal despised the ability, which provided few answers and too many questions.

Moments passed. The chant stopped, and one by one the faeries flew away. One tried to toss dust in his coffee, but Nurimil covered his cup quickly, shaking his head at the little creatures. He'd once taken a job to collect faerie dust, assuming it would be easy. How hard could it be to shake dust from a creature the size of his thumb? He soon learned faeries didn't like to give and preferred to use their dust for mischief. The task had taken him far longer than expected, and the pay was terrible.

At last, Zal's eyes went dim, and he sagged in his chair. Nurimil rose and removed the bowl, setting it by the fire. He poured Zal a fresh cup of tea, set it before him, and waited.

For a while it looked like Zal had gone to sleep, but when he opened his eyes, they were tired. Running his finger over the rim of his mug, he finally looked at Nurimil. "For the first time it seems the waters speak clearly, yet I wish they wouldn't. Change is in the air, a new power rises from the desert, and you would be wise to take your nymph and flee."

"Flee and go where?" Nurimil begged.

"Have you ever heard the prophecy about the child with golden tears?"

Nurimil stilled. His throat went dry and his fingers trembled. He tightened them around the coffee mug, hoping to stop them, but he squeezed so hard the mug snapped. Pieces of it exploded, and coffee spilled over the table.

Zal raised a bushy white eyebrow. "Ah, so you know the tales."

"It's not possible," Nurimil protested, even though it was.

Now it was Zal's turn to look confused. "What's not possible, my boy?"

"Never mind. Go on," he said, shaking the shards of clay and coffee from his fingers.

"You know the prophecy. When she rises, the power of the empire will shift, and her actions will bring about the rise of the dark lord. According to the waters, she has risen."

Nurimil shook his head again, but his disbelief would not be swallowed. "From where? And where is she now?"

"From the desert, my boy, are you listening to a word I tell you? It leads me to believe there's a line of truth in the tales about the lost pyramids. It's likely she's on a quest, searching for power, and if she is to change magic, well, there is only one way to do it. If one wants to control magic, they need to have the power from which all magic stems. Spirit, water, ink, and teleporting."

Nurimil closed his eyes, recalling the tears drying and then hardening into gold. That's when he began to fear, and he'd held her, hushed her, and then she stopped. He'd been with her for years, watching over her, making sure she never cried in front of anyone. She'd known how to hide her tears, to swallow them down, and now it was his fault. He should have stayed, or after she disappeared, looked harder.

"Why then, would a wizard seek to gain the power of water?"

"Perhaps he's at war with the child of prophecy? Perhaps he seeks to control all magic? Either way, Darya is in grave danger."

Nurimil pressed his lips together. It was as he'd assumed; her coming to land was no coincidence.

38

DARYA

Water slicked off Darya's back and swirled around her. The lake wasn't deep. All too soon, she reached the bottom where weeds grew. They danced in the ripples she created, lifting hopeful faces for a glimpse of light. She settled near them, brushing her fingers over the plants. The taste of the lake differed from the sea, but it was pleasant. A peacefulness settled within as energy surged into her again.

A brown whiskered creature passed her, dragging wood to the surface. She watched it, especially its round flat tail. She'd listened to stories of the landwalkers, but didn't know about them as well as the mermaids did. They'd be able to tell her the name of the lake creature and regale her with stories of the landwalkers and their habits. Part of her had looked forward to the alliance between sirens and mermaids, if only to learn about the culture of the mermaids, although she doubted they'd be happy in the depths of the sea.

An orange fish the size of her forearm swam past her, its

frowning mouth moving up and down. A thrill shot through Darya and she pounced, sinking her teeth into the side of the fish. Her feral side came out as she ripped and tore, sending a pool of blood into the water. Within moments, she'd swallowed the sweet meat of the fish and her eyes widened as she sated her hunger. She'd never tasted anything like it before; even the fish in the sea were saltier with tough scales and chewy meat. Not this fish. What made this fish so tender and delicious? The fact that it was in a lake, the peacefulness of it?

She finished her meal and immediately wanted another, even though she was full. Leaving the mangled carnage of bones behind her, she swam deeper, taking the same trail the flat-tailed creature had taken.

When she broke the surface, elegant white birds sat on the bank, long necks arched over a nest. It was spring, and Darya was certain eggs were in there, a sweet delicacy she'd only had once or twice. To preserve the ecosystem of the waters, it was forbidden to steal eggs from the sea creatures. Her mouth watered, but she held back. There was no need to disturb them, especially when she'd just eaten. Although the idea of traveling away from the lake and eating more of the disgusting dried meat that Nurimil provided was even less enticing now.

Nurimil. She turned around to face the mossy hut in the distance. From the lake, it was almost invisible and blended into the greenery. It was easier to think about him in the waters, when he wasn't around to cloud her thoughts. He'd seemed so sad when he spoke of his family, losing his mother, sister, and father. Would she be able to help him find them?

Giving herself a shake, she turned around. Why was she

thinking about helping him when she had her own task to focus on?

She hadn't met anyone who tempted her like Nurimil, not that she could stay with him. No, she merely needed his help for now, and then they'd go their separate ways. As a water nymph, she had great potential, and she doubted there were water creatures in need of protection among the rivers and lakes of Nomadia.

The shadow of a winged bird made her duck back underwater. Lifting her eyes to the sky, she watched, silent, as two black birds flew over the lake. A cold shudder went through her as they whirled, wings spread. With an arc, they returned from whence they had come.

A thread of unease passed through her, but she also noticed her strength was back and she should return to the hut. Her heart raced as she moved out of the water. It shimmered reluctantly off her scales, as if sorry she were leaving. As she went to retrieve Nurimil's cloak, she recalled the look in his eyes the first time she'd walked out of the water, hoping to drive him mad with lust. She wanted him to look at her again, and this time appreciate both her body and mind.

Wind whistled over the lake as she put the cloak around her shoulders, fingers fumbling with the clasp. Making her way back to the hut, she knocked on the mossy door as she'd seen Nurimil do earlier. The door swung open at her touch, giving a long whine that made her jump. Peering at it to make sure it wouldn't do anything unexpected, she ducked under the archway and stepped inside.

Little lights winked in and out, drawing her eyes to a table where Nurimil and an old man sat, talking in low tones. It was Nurimil's stricken expression that made her heart sink. His fist was on the table, and his face spoke of unspeakable grief mixed with anger and a hint of fear.

The man finished speaking and waved his hand, although his back was to her. "Well, come in then."

Nurimil stood as she entered, and his hand went to his hilt. "Considering what you've told me, we should leave now. Our being here puts you in grave danger."

"Bah!" The man waved a hand. "I still have a few tricks up my sleeve, no matter who shows up first."

Still, Darya detected a weariness resting on the old man's shoulders. He reached for his staff and then waved them on. "Come, you can borrow Boxie—and I do mean borrow." He glared at Nurimil. "She'll take you as far as the river crossing. Once you're there, send her back upstream and take the road that leads to Gyin. Although I think it's foolhardy to go into civilization again, it might end up saving you."

"We have no choice," Nurimil said.

"True, true," the man muttered, leading them out the door and around the house.

"Darya." Nurimil's eyes were intent as he spoke. "Zal has helped us, but we need to leave now and travel swiftly. We are being hunted."

Darya tilted her head. He wasn't telling her anything new. "How is this different from before? What has changed?"

Nurimil hesitated. "I'll tell you as we travel."

"Boxie!" Zal called, following the call with a low whistle.

Darya took a step back as the ground shook. Out of the trees came a beast twice the size of a horse with horns on either side of its head. It lowered its head and snorted, pawed the ground, then walked toward them.

Sucking in a deep breath, Darya stepped back, taking in the beast's hairy sides. It was a monster!

"Don't be afraid." Nurimil lightly touched her arm. "Boxie is a yak. On her back we can move much faster than on our feet."

"Mind you, she's no war beast, and she enjoys grazing." Zal patted Boxie's head. "Most creatures are afraid of her, however, so they'll stay away. She also loves deep water and can swim, just keep the crocodiles away. They've tried to attack her, despite her size."

"We'll take good care of her, and send her back to you," Nurimil promised.

"If I doubted that, I would not let her out of my sight," Zal chuckled. Lowering his voice, he spoke directly to Darya. "I won her in a game of dice. Lucky I was that night, and she's been with me ever since. She's fearsome to look at but has a gentle heart. You'll like her."

Darya nodded at his attempt to be friendly, although she still felt terrified of riding on the monster's back. Perhaps it would be no different from capturing a sea lion and riding on its back, aside from the horns.

Zal tossed what looked like a braided rug on Boxie's back and patted her side. "The only trick is getting up, and I haven't figured that one out yet."

He shrugged, but Nurimil pulled himself up and sat astride the beast, a grin on his face. He held out a hand to Darya, who accepted. She was surprised by his strength as he pulled her up behind him. Her legs trembled as she sat astride the beast, but she was grateful to lean into Nurimil's warmth.

Zal clasped his hands together, and little lights twinkled

from his shoulders. "Go in peace," he blessed them. "May your enemies never catch you, and may love warm your hearts."

"Zal. Thank you," Nurimil said.

Boxie lumbered off, but Darya glanced back at the mossy house, wondering why Zal had mentioned love.

39

DARYA

At first, Darya clung to Nurimil as the yak took them toward the lake. The creature kept to the shore, only getting wet up to her ankles, and Darya considered whether she should climb down and enjoy time in the waters while she had it, but her desire to be near Nurimil stopped her.

He kept glancing at the sky, and from time to time his fingers slid to the hilt of his sword. Darya noticed he had an extra saddle bag and wondered if Zal had given him more supplies.

At last, unable to hold her tongue any longer, she spoke. "What did you learn?"

Nurimil shifted, making her wish she could see his expression. When he spoke, his gentle voice hovered over the water like the buzzing, sparkling creatures that flitted back and forth. "Zal reads visions in the waters, sometimes of the past but mostly of the future. He knows many things. I had hoped he would have an alternative solution to your quest.

You need magic to purify the waters, and there are many mages who can create a counter-spell for you. Unfortunately, mages mostly dwell in the capital or in the far west of Nomadia near the cliffs. If we are lucky, we might encounter a traveling mage at the Gyin trading post who can create a counter-spell for you. It would mean you could avoid going to the capital and return to your people as soon as possible. The alternative is to go to the great library of Nomadia and ask one of the librarians for a book on magic. Those with magic, like you have, can perform spells and rituals. All you need to know is the recipe to make it work, usually a gathering of herbs and tokens, and then you just need to stand in the right place at the right time, a full moon on the brink of summer or something like that. I mentioned it earlier, but now I know with certainty that you were lured here, to Nomadia, because someone is hunting you for your power."

Darya pressed her lips together, recalling Mother's words and the faces of the council. No, they couldn't be in on what happened; there was no way they'd take such drastic action. Who would make a deal with a sea witch just to get rid of one nymph?

Nurimil continued, "Zal believes the child with golden tears has risen from the desert and is coming to change the fate of Nomadia."

"What does that mean?" Darya asked.

"In the days of old, the ancient philosophers believed that the fate of the world lay in nature, and if one understood how to read nature, they could divine the future."

"We have oracles in the sea," Darya added. "They collect pearls, claiming they have visions of the future. If one wants to know their fate, they must exchange a precious token.

What they do is close to magic, though. Sometimes what they say comes true, sometimes it doesn't."

"That's the problem with prophecies; how can one trust the validity of them? Half the time they are so vague they can apply to anything, and other times they simply never come true. However, that is not the case here. The prophecy about the child with golden tears came from a reputable source, one who has given many prophecies that came true. It was written in the ancient scrolls that when the child with golden tears comes, she will cause the dark lord to rise."

Darya shivered. "Who is the dark lord?"

She felt Nurimil shrug before he said, "I don't know. If we are living in the years, nay, the days before the dark lord rises, it would be wise to build alliances, to unite the people, and to have a plan for how to face him."

"I thought the empire is united already? The seven kingdoms are no more and pay tribute to the capital. Is that not correct?"

"You know your history, but aside from paying tribute, the hearts and minds of people are not fully swayed by the elykin rule. True, they brought peace and innovation to Nomadia, and they understand magic on a deeper level than the other races and kingdoms. Yet, if the right moment presents itself, the most shrewd kingdoms will form alliances of their own and pull away from the empire. If that happens when the dark lord rises, it will allow him to take over while the empire descends into chaos."

Darya considered this, and her thoughts returned to the Court of Nymphs. "If the elykin are wise, they will foresee this."

"It is my hope, but I am not aware of the political focus of the empire, nor what goes on in the capital. It is ruled by Empress Kashari, but she was not the ruler who united the empire, and while her power holds, it's only a matter of time."

Darya drew in a sharp breath. "You believe the empire will fall before the dark lord rises?"

"If its weaknesses can be exploited. Right now, the empress holds absolute power, but I travel through the wild lands. I've heard the rumors stirring in the shadows, mainly words, but if magic is put behind them, an uprising might change things."

"Who ruled the seven kingdoms before they were united?"

"They ruled themselves and traded with each other as needed. Some warred for land or to get away from the monsters that sprang from the caves or mountains or underground tunnels. The core kingdoms were the mountain fae, also known as ice lords, mages, humans, fauns, gnomes, dwarves, and elves.

"The mages live in the Maldive Cliffs. They aren't a race, but people with magical abilities. They tend to have high opinions of themselves, and anyone who does not pass their magic tests are cast out. They also have a tendency to kidnap children who show the potential to have magic.

"There are also humans, like myself, although our numbers have always been fewer than the others because we are not native to Nomadia. Most humans came from other shores to colonize Nomadia and usually intermarry with other races."

Intermarrying, what a curious thing. In the waters, the nymphs kept to themselves, as did the sirens and mermaids, although the alliance between sirens and mermaids would have been a rare occurrence of intermarrying. "Are you a full-blooded human?"

"I can't be sure, and it never concerned me. My father remarried an elf, and she was one of the kindest people I ever met."

He fell silent, reminding Darya of his misfortune. She wanted to comfort him, but how?

"Elves and fauns tend to dwell in forested lands," he went on at last. "Fauns fought the hardest against the uprising of the elykin, and every move they make is watched carefully by the empire. The empire even takes their children as tribute and threatens them with death if their kin misbehave or entertain ideas of rebelling."

"That's terrible!" Darya said, thinking of the siren babies, their bubbles of laughter and curious eyes.

Nurimil nodded. "It is, as is slavery and oppression. The empire picks its battles and because it is so large, the powerful rule and grow more powerful while the weaker suffer under their laws."

Darya's brows knitted together. "What can the people do?"

"Against magic and power? Nothing, unless they wait, look for weaknesses, and form alliances. The problem is, once power is gained, it's difficult to look at what's wrong and seek to help; it's much easier to keep to oneself and stay out of other people's problems. That's what the gnomes and dwarves do, and they are largely left to themselves."

Darya listened to his words, and a question took form. Closing her eyes, she asked it before she lost her courage. "Why did you buy me and free me from the slaves? There were so many others . . ."

His fingertips grazed her hand. "I know, but I saw you, Darya, and I had to act."

A fluttering began in her heart at knowing he had simply looked at her and wanted to save her. But what about the others? She'd felt the burn of the whip and the fear of help-lessness after they took her power away from her. It was dizzying and terrifying to know that it was still happening to others. Was it right for her to walk away with her life when she had magic? If they turned back, she could return to the slave quarters, bring about a terrible storm, and strike down the giants with water magic. Pivoting, she half turned on the yak, her hands slipping from Nurimil's waist.

"What if we could go back and free them?"

Nurimil scratched the back of his head. "Many have tried, but it leads to bloodshed and death. Many powerful people, including wizards and mages, benefit from the slave trade. They provide incentives and pay hunters and warriors to keep it in check. It would take a mighty power to bring down the slavers."

Darya grew quiet. The empire was not what she had expected. True, there were quiet places, peaceful and beau-tiful like the lush lake land they traveled through, but she, a newcomer, had already seen a bit of the horror. What else lay in store for her in Nomadia?

40

NURIMIL

They pressed on into the night, and the yak seemed content to travel down the river. The trees moved back, allowing the light from the twin moons to shine down, guiding them onward.

After their conversation, Darya had grown quiet. Now she pressed against him, her arms around his waist, her head resting on his back. The closeness of her made him feel uncomfortable. Part of him wanted to push her away, while the other part of him relished the contact. What if he turned around, took her in his arms, and kissed her? She was a curious creature, and he wanted to make love to her before they parted ways so he'd have a pleasant memory to hold on to.

Already she was making him feel things he didn't want to feel, stirring up emotions he'd long kept pinned down. Her spirit had loosened his tongue, and he doubted it was sorcery. It was simply her. She wasn't ignorant like he'd assumed.

Although she knew little about the ways of Nomadia, she learned quickly, and her compassion for people was potent. Again, he wondered if she had suffered at the hands of the giants, and his jaw tightened.

Even though magic did not work on him, it would be foolish to go up against slavers, even with a water nymph on his side. Those in power would hunt him down for the price on his head. Darya was better off without him. As soon as they reached the trading post, they'd go their separate ways. There was only one problem.

The child with the golden tears.

He uttered an oath under his breath. He couldn't run away and turn a blind eye to what was happening in the world when he felt responsible.

HE WAS sixteen and standing in her room. The window was open, and the scent of lotus flowers drifted in. It was late spring and beautiful. The spring storms were gone, and the frost had vanished, allowing the healers to plant a garden and begin their travels to the neighboring farms, ensuring all was well in the surrounding areas. Most of the healers were humans, but some were elves, slender and beautiful with long hair. They all reminded him of Jasmine.

"I'm leaving to seek my fortune," he told his sister. "I'll find a trade, a way to make money, and when I return we can leave the Court of Healers and have our own place."

She was only eight, and threw her arms around him. "Don't leave yet, stay another year. Then I'll be older, and I can come with you."

She'd said the same thing the year before, and he'd given in, but not this time. He loosened her arms. "I'm too old to stay here, and the healers have been kind, but I'm a man. I want adventure, I need to travel. I promise I'll return when you're older."

"When I'm ten, can I come with you?"

"We'll see. I have to find money, enough to buy land, a horse, seed . . ." he trailed off, running a hand through his black curls.

She scrunched up her nose. "But we have money."

"No," he held up his hands as she went for the bag of gold, hidden in a hole in the ground. "Keep it for yourself; it belongs to you. And remember what I told you about your tears?"

"Never let anyone see me cry," she repeated.

He hugged her tight and then let go. She didn't cry when he went to the door. Instead, she smiled at him, hope brimming in her eyes. "Goodbye, Nurimil."

He grinned at her, itching to be off on his adventures. "Goodbye, Elmira."

TWO YEARS later he'd returned, exhilarated from his adventures, but the healers told him she'd gone off with a family. He'd been angry at them for letting her go, but realized it was selfish of him to deny her the rest of her childhood. He wasn't concerned when he found the bag of gold where they'd hidden it, realizing it was for the best that she'd left it behind.

It was unfortunate the healers could not tell him much about the family that took her away. He tracked her as far as the Guild of Seekers, and there her trail went cold. The seekers were obsessed with treasure and went on long quests, searching for what was lost and assumed never to be found again. They knew nothing about a child; either that, or they'd been lying. Now he wondered if, by some turn of fate, someone had discovered his sister's secret and taken her away. Then why was she suddenly appearing after all these years? She'd be thirty-two now, which left a wide gap of twenty-two years. Had she been in hiding all this time or had something much worse happened to her?

When he was young, he'd assumed her tears were unusual and exploitable, which is why he encouraged her to keep them secret. Years later, he learned about the prophecy, which had frightened him and made him wish he'd searched harder for Elmira. He also had to consider what link she had to the dark lord—or perhaps it was simply her actions that would bring about his reign. And who was the dark lord, exactly?

The trading post would be the ideal place to gather news from across the empire, but it was also full of people and the most likely place for him to fall into a trap.

He had to be cautious and careful if he hoped to reunite with his sister, protect Darya from the wizard, and keep from being captured by bounty hunters.

41

ELMIRA

Hunger bit into Elmira as she and Vero traveled down the road. The mounts she'd taken from the guild were fast, but they were also bloodthirsty, used to hunting and ripping through meat. Elmira had left the guild behind, for they were too slow and also too frightened after the destruction of Dustania. Besides, they had messages to send out for her, although Elmira had little faith in them. The wizard's cruelty had taught her not to trust anyone, and if she wanted to find the water nymph and rule Nomadia, she needed to do it herself. Vero was the only one she trusted, silently following her commands and offering his guidance as needed.

Since leaving the sand dunes, he'd changed, becoming more assertive. She knew he believed in their quest, but there had to be more. Narrowing her eyes, she examined him as he rode on the beast, his back still hunched, broken hand held to his chest. He kept their provisions, and the bags hung on either side of his short legs.

"Vero," she called to get his attention. "We're close to getting what I want, but what do you want?"

He startled and hunched over even further, keeping his eyes on the road. "Mistress, when you succeed it will be enough for me."

Elmira sighed and snapped her fingers. "No, it won't be. I'll have it all, and what will you have?"

"You," he whispered, so low she almost did not hear it.

Elmira opened her mouth to respond, and it all rushed past her, as that one word resonated in her soul. The thick cloud of hatred within loosened. Staring at Vero, she saw the brokenness, the pain, and something else. A deep loyalty and longing. No matter what she asked of him, he would follow her to the ends of Nomadia with his undying devotion. He would offer her his soul if he thought it would assist her. The powerful knowledge resonated within Elmira. Hardening her heart against it, she turned her eyes back to the road. She could not go soft because of Vero's devotion. "There has to be something."

Vero was quiet for so long, at first she thought he hadn't heard her. When he spoke, a wistfulness laced his words. "I've heard that in the land of humans, where the vineyards flourish and the land is ideal for farming, there is a Court of Healers. They know all the remedies of magic, and if they could straighten my back and regrow my fingers, I could serve you better."

His words sent a jolt racing through Elmira. Her pulse quickened as a memory rose. It gripped her, forcing her to look back and remember.

SUNBEAMS DANCED ACROSS HER FACE, warming her, and she giggled, running into a garden that smelled of lotus flowers. A boy chased after her, taller, darker, and leaner than her, but she loved him. They were shouting with glee, and she didn't see the rock until it was too late. Tripping, she crashed into it. The flesh on her knee broke open, and blood poured out. It was so bright, so vibrant, she felt as though it were draining her life away. Fear seized her, and she pressed her hands against the wound, tears streaming down her face. The boy was there then, curly black hair springing from his head, his dark eyes full of concern. He soothed her, saying comforting words and telling her not to cry as he picked up golden pieces and tucked them into his pocket.

ELMIRA'S MOUTH tightened as the memory left her. Her fingers dug into the fur on the beast's back so hard it growled. "The Court of Healers," she repeated.

She was ten when she left, but she recalled the healers, her older brother, the orchards and gardens, and knowing she had a secret that she had to hide. He'd told her never to cry, never to let anyone see her tears, or the gold. He'd warned her, but she was too young to realize the repercussions of her talent, and what might happen should others discover that her tears turned to gold.

Clearing her throat, she spoke louder. "I know this Court of Healers. We will go there after we catch the water nymph."

Deep inside, she knew she wasn't simply going to heal Vero. She wanted that for him, but she also wanted answers. Why had the healers allowed her to leave? Why hadn't they protected her? She'd only been a child. And what had happened to the boy, her brother? An uneasy sensation went down her back, so when the air shifted, she was thankful for a distraction.

"Look." Vero pointed. "There's a tiny track just off the road, almost impossible to see through the underbrush."

Elmira dismounted. "Good eye." She sniffed, closed her eyes, and pressed her hands against the ground. Flickers of light came to her vision, as though the stones in the ground wanted her to see what had passed that way. She didn't know much about stone magic, but she sensed water and caught a flicker of scaled feet. Kneeling in the mud, she decided to trust her instincts. "Let's follow the footpath. We'll have to leave our mounts behind, but if we catch the water nymph, it will be worth it."

Vero did not protest. Instead, he slid from the beast's back, threw a bag over one shoulder, and followed Elmira into the thicket.

They followed the footpath for three days until the forest spit them out into a clearing. Although Elmira enjoyed the walk through the shady forest, the scent of pine, and the chatter of woodland animals, she was growing impatient. She'd missed much of life, but the hunger was back to a level that left her almost nauseous. Eating souls was all she could think about, and the detour into the forest had been a terrible idea. The hunger made her wish she'd stayed on the road, which eventually would have led to a more populated area.

When she saw the house, her spirit leaped. Striding across the clearing, she banged on the door.

"Back so soon?" came a voice, and the door opened.

An old man peered out and his cloudy blue eyes cleared

as Elmira smiled. Pushing the door open, she strode inside, eager for the man's soul. "Expecting someone else?" She grinned.

The man's expression changed quickly, going from surprise to horror and then resignation. Elmira didn't like it, and hesitated as she lifted her hand to his neck. "Tell me what you know."

"You're her, aren't you?" The man's voice did not quaver with weakness or fear.

Elmira did not like that either, and her fingers closed around his neck, squeezing firmly. "I'm who? How do you know me? Never mind all that. Did the water nymph come this way?"

The man's gaze went to the hearth, where a bowl of water sat. Elmira recalled that the wizard used water for scrying, and an idea formed, just as a shower of dust flew into her nose. Letting go of the man, she sneezed, and a swarm attacked.

They were miniature people with wings on their backs. They buzzed around her, taking turns pinching and biting. Raised bumps appeared on her skin and Elmira waved her arms, for the first time wishing she wore more than her scant garb. After what she'd endured under the wizard's hand, the bites were a mere annoyance and caused little pain, but she spied the old man sneaking away, moving toward a back door.

With a shriek, Elmira opened her mouth, choking and gagging as a spirit came out of her. Its white mist surged around the creatures. While they fought it, Elmira chased after the man, following him through the house and out the door.

Water slapped into her face, followed by the jarring thud

of a wooden bowl. Elmira reeled backward, arms waving. The old man was stronger than she expected, and her vision went dizzy as water burned her flesh. Then, with a snarl, she was up and tackling him to the ground. He swung, his fist connecting with her jaw. Elmira brought her elbow down hard on his chest, followed by a blow to his head.

The man coughed and lay still, the wind knocked out of him. Sensing victory but still cautious, Elmira's fingers tightened around his throat, allowing him to take shallow, gasping breaths. Blue eyes bored into hers and he panted as he said, "You're the child with golden tears, all grown up now."

Elmira paused, then squeezed harder. "Have we met before? How do you know me?"

"I've seen your coming. In the waters."

"What about the water nymph?"

"I can't tell you." The man twitched and his hands came up, closing around hers.

"Can't, or won't?" Elmira challenged.

"There's a man. He's concerned. Wants to meet you."

Elmira stiffened.

"He's afraid, but he cares very deeply about you."

Elmira's brow furrowed. The hunger within begged her to kill the man and eat his soul, but now her mind was curious. "Who is this man?"

"Does the name Nurimil mean anything to you?"

There it was again, that name. She pressed harder.

"You don't have to do this," the man croaked, fingers hardening around hers as he struggled for breath.

"I do," she whispered, gazing into his eyes so he'd see she had no remorse. "I have to, because no one else will."

"Ask yourself: Who is the dark lord?"

His faint voice faded as the life left his blue eyes, and Elmira breathed in, shivering and shaking as the soul sank in and her cravings were fulfilled. When the last hints of euphoria faded, she stood, feeling the strength in her bones. The man's soul was unlike any other. Older, yes, but there was a purity, a wiseness to it. She tasted the essence again and again; it was delicious, strong. When she swallowed, she glimpsed a vision, perhaps a recent memory.

A man sat at the table across from her, wavy black hair around his shoulders, misery written across his face. She knew that face, at least the shape of it, and those eyes, that hair. It was much longer than she remembered, the face much older. A blur of words echoed around her.

"... take the yak ..."

"... river crossings ..."

"... trading post ..."

She felt as though she could walk for miles without growing weary, and she turned just as Vero walked out of the house. It appeared he'd taken the time to gather more supplies, and he carried a map in one hand. His eyes went to the dead body before he handed her the map. Elmira blew dust off it as she held it up, noting the marking of the house, the shape of the lake, and the crossing of the river.

"Vero, I have good news. I know where we are going and who has the water nymph."

"Who?"

"His name is Nurimil, and I think he's my brother."

42

DARYA

Nurimil seemed more thoughtful after they left Zal's cottage, although he was still kind to her, and didn't mind if she slept in the river. She used the opportunity to catch fish and ignore the dried meat Nurimil offered. Sometimes she caught a sly smile on his face, as if he knew what she did under the waters.

"Do you always travel like this?" she asked, fastening the cloak around her shoulders as they prepared to leave for the day.

Nurimil like to travel long into the night, and the yak didn't seem to mind. The land had turned into a marsh, and sometimes the air stunk of bog water. Mud was everywhere, and occasionally it rained, making the journey miserable, Darya assumed, for humans. She didn't mind at all.

"Always," Nurimil replied, tightening his belt and brushing wet hair out of his face.

Darya tucked her chin into her shoulder and watched him, thinking of how magnificent he looked standing there. He'd splashed water on his face earlier and his shirt was open at the top, giving her a glimpse of his broad chest. When he turned, his eyes locked on hers. She held his gaze, her breath catching as she tried to read his thoughts. Continuing to hold her gaze, he finished buttoning his shirt, then crossed over to her and extended a hand.

Darya took it, her fingers tingling at his touch. Her protective barrier of scales fell away. Even though he couldn't see her arousal under the cloak, she wondered if he sensed it. Angling his head, he brought his other hand up to cup her cheek, keeping her gaze pinned on him.

"I will not pretend to ignore this attraction between us," he admitted with a heavy sigh. "I felt it the moment I laid eyes on you, and while I don't know what draws me to you, I know our fates are bound together, somehow. I must make it clear, though: you are better off without me. There is an inescapable darkness in my past that is rising, and I must figure out a way to stop it."

Darya pressed her own hand against his cheek. Confusion rode through her, but stronger than all her thoughts was the warmth that flooded her body. Every inch of her tingled with desire, and she wanted him to lean closer and claim her with a kiss. The admission of his attraction to her was exciting, while his determination to separate was wildly disappointing. "What are you saying? Whatever darkness plagues you, we can face together."

"No." He shook his head, his thumb brushing her cheek, so near her lips she gave an involuntary shiver. "You are on a quest to save your people and I would not hinder it with my problems. I made a mistake long ago and I don't know what I can do to remedy it. But I would not drag you down with me."

Darya swallowed hard, moving her hand down to his chest. "Is there something you learned at Zal's that you're not sharing with me?"

Nurimil dropped his hand from her cheek and stared at the waters. He took a slow breath. They were so close.

"Yes, but not everything should be shared. You should focus on your quest and saving your people." He reached out, squeezed her hand, then tried to let go, but she held on tight.

"Nurimil," she breathed, squeezing her eyes shut and summoning the courage she needed for the words to come forth. "I'm not saying this because you saved me, or maybe I am. I don't know. This is my first time in the empire of the landwalkers, and for the first time I'm doing something that matters. While yes, I need to save my people, here I can finally use my powers as I was meant to use them, and I can help you too. Don't turn me away because I'm finally doing something that counts. And if you're right, and the darkness comes, you'll need me."

With a groan, Nurimil swept her into his arms, pressing his forehead against hers. Darya barely dared to breathe, feeling as though some spell had captured her. "I don't deserve your help," he said. "You've done enough. It's not that I don't appreciate your power, I do, and I know things would have gone much differently with the she-viper if you hadn't stepped in and used your abilities. I know what you can do, but the wizards and mages of Nomadia are not to be trifled with. They have powerful magic and spells. I've seen people lose their minds and betray their friends because of magic. I am unique, because magic doesn't work on me. I'm immune from them, but you aren't, and I don't know any magic that can protect you from what's coming. Darya, you were lured here because someone is searching for your power. They want to kill you for it. So it's best if you leave as quickly as you came, before they find you."

Disappointment swelled, and Darya closed her eyes, not wanting him to see how his words affected her. Of course he didn't want her to stay, and she couldn't. Once she found the remedy, she had to return to the Court of Nymphs, and everything that had happened in Nomadia would be naught but a pleasant dream. Stiffening in his arms, she pulled back. "Don't fear for me. I will go as quickly as I came."

He let her go and stepped away, although his voice was still gentle. "Don't misunderstand me."

"What is there to misunderstand?" Darya asked, unable to keep the bitterness out of her tone. "We are two individuals brought together by fate for a short time, a human and a water nymph. We will help each other then go our separate ways, nothing more, nothing less."

Instead of responding, Nurimil turned on his heel and marched toward Boxie. Darya stared at the waters, determined to calm down although she felt like crying. It only made sense. She was leaving, and he had to get the bounty off his head. How long could she travel with him before succumbing to her desires? She turned to ask Nurimil how much longer it would take when a bird swooped out of the air and dove toward him.

"Watch out," she shouted and swept her hand toward the

water. She made a fist and unleashed it, sending a spout of water into the bird's side. The impact knocked it away and Nurimil spun, drawing his sword as another bird dropped out of the air.

"There's more!" Darya called, glimpsing five or six birds circling them.

They were big creatures, about three feet tall with a wingspan of at least six feet. Black and red feathers covered their bodies, and Darya saw sharp beaks and curved claws as intelligent black eyes turned toward her. She sent another spout of water into the air, blasting another bird back as Nurimil's sword flashed. Crimson stained the ground, and black feathers drifted down to cover the stain.

One of the birds recovered from being struck by water and pecked at Nurimil. He slashed its neck and drove his sword into a third. It all happened so quickly. Within moments, all five birds lay on the ground in an array of blood, feathers, and slashed bones.

Darya stared, taking in the carnage before slowly lifting her gaze to Nurimil. He wasn't paying any attention to her and was squatting on the ground, picking up a red feather. He tucked it into his pocket and strode to Boxie, who was chewing grass by the stream and watching the commotion out of bored eyes.

"Those were vultures," Nurimil explained as he mounted Boxie. "They are passive birds and usually eat the dead. Why they are attacking the living, I don't know."

Something white flashed on the ground, something that wasn't a bone. Darya picked it up before joining Nurimil. "Here, what's this?"

Nurimil's rough fingers grazed hers as he took it, then pulled her up behind him. With a toss of her horns, Boxie strode further into the mire, leaving the dead vultures behind. Darya leaned against Nurimil for a moment before pulling back, not wanting him to know how using magic made her feel weary. It hadn't been too much, and she silently pulled moisture out of the air, using it to refuel herself. When they stopped for a rest, she'd submerge herself and regain her full strength.

"It's a note," Nurimil said, unrolling it. "A scroll."

"What does it say?"

Nurimil was quiet, and Darya imagined he was scanning it. "It's not meant for us, but it's from the Guild of Bounty Hunters. Odd, not that I spent much time there, but I don't recall vultures being used as messengers. This is a note detailing the destruction of Dustania. Shortly after we left, the village was attacked, the slaves set free, and the slave quarters burned down."

Darya's heart leaped. "Set free," she repeated, thinking of the giants, their whips, and how someone had finally given them what they deserved. Their trade was destroyed and the slave quarters burned down. She wished she'd been there when it happened, been a part of the attack that ruined the livelihood of those wicked giants.

Nurimil, though, was thoughtful, not excited.

"Isn't that good news?"

"The scroll mentions a she. The child with golden tears has risen. She's coming."

Hope evaporated, and suddenly the spring air seemed cold. Darya felt Nurimil's spirit wilt as if she could see it with her naked eyes. Every time he mentioned gold tears, a darkness passed over him, and she did not understand it. She felt small and alone, as if they stood on opposite ends of a bridge over a deep gorge.

"How much longer until we reach the trading post?"

"Two weeks, maybe less," he said, and fell silent.

43

DARYA

Late one afternoon, Nurimil clucked to Boxie, bringing them to a stop. Immediately, Boxie dropped her head and began to graze, chewing at the long grass that hid the water from view. The marshy country had turned back into a river, and white butterflies danced in the air and the trees were farther back from the water, leaving the plain open. It was quiet, and the summer sunlight warmed Darya's skin.

Nurimil slid off Boxie's back, leaving Darya to perch uncomfortably on top. She squinted at the sun. "Why are we stopping?"

"We need to break for a bit." Nurimil reached up to guide her down, and Darya allowed him to do so. "I also thought you'd appreciate more time in the waters." He nodded to the lake.

Darya wiggled her toes in the damp grass, still perplexed by why they'd stopped so early. "What will you be doing?"

Nurimil hesitated. "Can I ask you a favor?"

Darya widened her eyes. "Me?"

"My supplies are running low. I need more dried fish to sustain the journey, and I thought we could stop here . . ."

He trailed off while Darya laughed. The idea that he needed more fish was absurd, and yet . . . "All you have to do is ask."

A muscle in his jaw twitched, reminding her how he'd admitted to their attraction and his resolute desire to do nothing about it.

"What will you do while I catch fish?"

"Build a fire. The ground is wet, but if luck holds I'll find dry wood near the trees. If the smoke gives away our location, I think we can handle it. These woods are rumored to have poachers, nothing more. If anyone comes and tries to take Boxie, you know what to do."

Darya curved her fingers. "Yes, use water magic."

Nurimil nodded, then spun on his heel and marched away.

Darya watched him for a moment before diving into the lake. There were plenty of fish, some the size of her forearm, others larger. She chased after them, using water magic to catch them, then tossed them ashore. Once she caught three, she floated lazily in the lake, keeping an eye on Boxie while allowing her body to rejuvenate from the brief use of magic.

Creatures swam around her, some with long tails and snouts—crocodiles, she recalled. They hovered at the surface of the water, only snapping with their powerful jaws when an unsuspecting fish or frog went by. They were the same size she was and left her alone, passing by with bulbous eyes that stuck out of their scaled heads. Darya watched, amused, and realized that she hadn't appreciated life in the sea. The creatures there were colorful and varied, swimming by as though they did not have a care, keeping together in groups to protect against predators. The lake was smaller, calm, with interesting creatures within it, but it was nothing compared to the sea.

Swimming farther down, Darya ran her fingers along the bottom, disrupting mud and the tiny fish that swam away from her. It had been so long since she'd been able to do anything personal that didn't require approval from the Court of Nymphs. When she was younger and without duties, she would frolic in the waves, chasing after precious stones and jewels. She had enjoyed working with them, stringing them together into necklaces and bracelets.

All nymphs wore jewelry, gifts of the sea that were unique to each location and used for trade. Darya still remembered Mother's delight when she'd discovered Darya's collection. Back then, Darya was proud and eager to show the court her talent. She hadn't known they would take them away from her, selecting the more precious jewels to send as gifts to another court. Then they divided up the best jewelry and wore it themselves: pearl necklaces, diamond earrings, coral rings, and stone bracelets.

Darya still recalled her stunned silence, and then anger when they took what she'd spent years collecting. When she protested, Mother rebuked her, saying the court knew what was best for the nymphs and she needed to share her gifts. She'd been so ignorant back then and was loudly bitter about how unfair she thought the court was. Since then, she'd only collected stones and jewels in secret, though she made sure to have something to share in case Mother asked.

Now, she wanted a token of her time spent in Nomadia, if

nothing else than to remember it by. After scooping up a handful of dirt and mud, she made her way to the surface to sift through her findings.

The scent of fire stung her nostrils as she emerged. A long trail of smoke rose into the air, and beyond the waving grass Nurimil was perched over a fire, feeding it.

Cupping her hands in the water, Darya sifted through her findings, smiling as she revealed two stones, one small and squat, the other oblong. If she collected a few each day, she'd have enough to make a necklace, a reminder of her time in Nomadia.

A snapping made her jump. Glancing across the meadow, she spied Nurimil breaking sticks and feeding them into the fire. Desire coiled in her lower belly. Lifting herself out of the water, she tucked the stones into the cloak before fastening it around her shoulders and joining him.

"I caught three fish," she told him. "I'm curious to see what you do with them."

A half smile came to Nurimil's lips, and then his eyes widened when she presented him with the fish.

"This is more than I was expecting," he said. Taking one by the tail, he pulled out his knife.

"Will it be enough?" Darya asked, squatting by the fire. She'd heard of fire, had seen the torches blazing in the slave quarter and the pale candlelight that seemed utterly insignificant in comparison. But this fire was different. It gave off heat. The flames moved and danced as if they could hear the song of the wood and were possessed to answer the call. Fascinated, she stared, unable to take her eyes away from the way the wood charred, turning to ash.

"More than enough," Nurimil said.

The strange note in his voice made her tilt her head up. He was staring at her, eyes dark, a look of desire on his face. Darya drew in a sharp breath, pulse thudding in her ears. Would he take a step, make a move? Did she want him to? Her legs quivered, and suddenly the fire was too hot, the smoke choking her. Tears overwhelmed her eyes, forcing her to use the cloak to wipe them away. When she lifted her head back to Nurimil, he'd turned away and started to scale the fish.

A well of emptiness rose in Darya, so thick she could not have spoken if she wanted to. Taking deep breaths to calm herself, she watched Nurimil work. He'd rolled up his sleeves, and his powerful arm moved back and forth, shedding the protective armor of the fish until white flesh showed through. It wasn't as gruesome as her way of eating, yet it was disturbing, and time-consuming. It was a wonder the landwalkers got anything done if they had to spend so much time preparing to eat.

Darya watched while Nurimil wrapped the fish in leaves, using the grass to secure the small packages. He made a shallow hole in the ground, put them inside, then used a stick to cover the hole with glowing coals and rocks.

"That is how you cook?" Darya asked from where she perched on a rock, rubbing the lake stones between her fingers. She didn't have her whalebone knife to whittle holes in them, nor string to put them together. She'd have to wait.

"You've never seen food cooked before, have you?" He patted dirt over the hole and sat down on the other side of the fire.

Darya shook her head. "I've heard of it, but never seen or tasted cooked food before." Wrinkling her nose, she recalled the dried meat Nurimil had given her. "It does not smell or look appetizing."

Nurimil chuckled. "If we had more time, I'd take you to the places where the food they serve would change your mind."

"I doubt that," Darya smiled, feeling lighter because of his amusement.

"You would, but I can be very persuasive when I need to be," Nurimil countered. "What do you drink in the sea?"

"Drink? Like you drink from your waterskins?"

"Yes, but there's more to drink than just water."

Darya furrowed her brows. "Like milk? Fermented juice?"

"You know about fermented juice?"

Darya shrugged. "That's what the mermaids call it, at least in stories. They'd go ashore and drink the fiery, fermented juice provided by the landwalkers."

Much to Darya's surprise, Nurimil threw back his head and laughed.

Darya's smiled at his amusement. "What's so funny?"

Shaking his head, he stood, dusting off his pants. "When I was just a boy, my father owned a vineyard. We grew grapes and when the time came for harvest, we'd press them and store them away. He was a well-known winemaker in the valley, and I always thought I'd follow in his steps."

Darya's heart warmed as Nurimil shared more of his past. It made her feel closer to him, when he was open and honest about his lost dreams. "Why did you become a hunter instead? Surely you still have time to go back and become a winemaker."

The light faded from Nurimil's eyes, replaced by a hardness. "No, it's too late for that. I've always been searching, looking for someone or something. It seemed natural to turn my life into an unending hunt. I enjoy the challenge, and I've gotten to see beautiful lands and meet people I'd never have met if I hadn't gone out into the world, searching. People such as yourself."

His gaze lingered on her, and Darya opened her mouth, at a loss for words, enchanted by his gaze. Dropping her eyes to the fire, she waited for him to speak, to say something else. But the silence stretched, broken only by the flames licking up wood, a hushed crackle and pop. When Darya dared to meet Nurimil's gaze again, she saw something new there.

Giving himself a shake, Nurimil cleared his throat. "We should go," he said roughly, standing. "The fish can dry as we continue."

Feeling as though she'd lost something, Darya rose as well, watching as he uncovered the fish. A mouthwatering scent rose, and even though she'd protested against cooked food, she wanted to taste it. Unwrapping a leaf, Nurimil scooped up flesh and placed it on his tongue. "Ah," he breathed. "With some roasted potatoes, carrots, and onion, this would be the perfect meal. Would you like a taste?"

"I ... no ..."

"Open your mouth," Nurimil coaxed, scooping up more fish with his fingers.

Licking her lips, Darya opened. The flaky flesh hit her tongue, so moist and soft it seemed to melt. She chewed, and the flavor surged through her senses. She tasted the moisture from the lake, the smoke from the fire, the char from the wood, and salt. Opening her eyes, she stared. "That was delicious."

Nurimil gave her a triumphant smile, a teasing glint in his eyes. "See, I'm already converting you."

His knuckles grazed her cheek as he brushed a drop of water from her lips. Darya shuddered, eyes flickering to his lips. For a long heated moment, they froze, as though suspended in time. "Darya," he whispered.

She tilted her head up, ready to take the kiss that hovered on his lips, a kiss that never came. Dropping his hand, he stepped away, leaving Darya gasping with disappointment.

Neither of them spoke as they prepared to leave, and it wasn't until they were on Boxie's back, trotting away from the smothered fire, that Darya realized she'd forgotten all about her quest.

44

ARACELI

Spring deepened into summer, and Araceli grew used to Kaiden's constant presence. Her ink magic progressed as her knowledge of runes and the language of magic deepened. The flowers were in bloom and the trees in the palace gardens were covered with green and blue leaves. Within another month, the midsummer festival would take place, and Araceli was looking forward to another evening with Shyrin, whose duties had seemed to expand, taking over more and more of her days.

During the summer it was difficult to concentrate on her tasks; the warm weather beckoned her to forget about duty and enjoy the outdoors. As Araceli walked the glass bridge to the library, she caught sight of one of the water towers, a rooftop attraction for the royals. Magic was used to create a pool that fell over the edge of a tower, creating waterfalls that led into more pools. They were a sight to behold. Araceli wondered what it would be like to stand on top of the world and dive into cool, clear water. Perhaps she'd never know.

When she walked into the library, Mistress Vina was waiting. "Araceli, come. I'd like a word."

Daydreams fled as she followed the elf into her study. Mistress Vina shut the door behind her, gestured for Araceli to sit, and sat herself behind the desk.

Araceli's stomach sank as she took a seat, racking her mind for what she'd done wrong and trying to think of whether any false rumors were being spread about her. "Araceli," Mistress Vina began firmly. "It has come to my attention that you are learning ink magic, and from what I've heard, you are doing a very good job."

Araceli opened her mouth to respond, but Mistress Vina held up a hand. "I don't know who your instructor is, nor do I need to know how you've learned. Being self-taught is an accomplishment, particularly in the ways of magic. I don't know anyone in your station who would have taken the initiative upon themselves to learn something new, to do what none other has done before, and I commend you for it."

Araceli's heart warmed with the praise and she clasped her fingers together, hardly believing what she was hearing.

"Now, being summer, a new class of scribes has come to the library to learn magic and a teaching vacancy has opened up. I'd like to recommend you for the position of teaching rune magic. It is a beginner course, nothing too hard, and covers the basics you already know. Should you be accepted for the task, you'll split your time between your duties here and teaching." Leaning forward, she smiled. "I believe the position pays a small stipend. What do you think?"

Araceli clasped her hands together, eyes shining. "Think?

Mistress Vina, this sounds wonderful. I accept. Thank you for putting my name forward for this!"

Mistress Vina smiled and picked up a piece of paper. "I've always been interested in your well-being, Araceli. Your work is a credit to the library. I am hopeful, for your sake, that this is only the beginning of advancement for you."

"Thank you," Araceli gushed. She wanted to laugh, to shout, to hug Mistress Vina and then burst into tears.

"Your work speaks for itself." Mistress Vina signed the paper. "I'll turn in this recommendation and provide details by the end of the week. In the meantime, take half a day. You deserve it, and the library is quiet right now."

Araceli hugged herself as she left the office, eager to tell Shyrin and Kaiden. They'd both be proud of her. Her workday passed in a blur, and when the sun was bright in the sky, Mistress Vina waved her away.

Araceli practically danced as she returned to her room, opening it to find Kaiden half dressed, as though he'd gotten distracted during the act. He stood by the window, staring out at the city below them.

A shyness came over Araceli as she shut the door. "What are you doing?"

Kaiden glanced over his shoulder, brushing his hair back from his face. "The people look happy out there. I've watched them come and go, hand in hand, running, laughing. The city is full of warmth and joy."

"It's summer." Araceli joined him by the window, looking down into the expanse. "No one wants to stay indoors in the summer. The weather is perfect, the best foods are available, and for a time, I think they forget their woes and just enjoy."

"That sounds nice."

The lonely, wistful note in his voice made Araceli want to comfort him. She hadn't considered the oddity of his situation in a while, trapped in her room all day, reading, eating, drinking, and waiting for her to make another wish.

"I have good news and the rest of the afternoon off. Would you like to go out into the city with me?"

"You want me to come with you?" He seemed perplexed.

Araceli shrugged. "I don't want to stay inside for the rest of the day. I know a spot, the only meadow there is in the city. We'll go there."

He grinned. "I'll pack a picnic, but first, tell me, what is this good news?"

Araceli beamed. "Mistress Vina is recommending me for a position to teach rune magic. It's just beginner level, everything I already know, but it's the first step in progressing from a librarian into an ink mage."

Kaiden's face did something funny, and then he moved so quickly Araceli didn't have time to react. His arms came around her and he squeezed, embracing her until her cheek was tucked into his bare shoulder. Her skin tingled as their skin touched, and a wave of heat passed over her. For a moment she enjoyed it, and then she pulled back, flustered and embarrassed.

This time, Kaiden's expression had changed to proud satisfaction. "I told you. Did I not tell you? And now, see, you're moving up in Nomadia. This is cause to celebrate. I had a feeling I needed to save the wine for something special."

Kaiden packed a basket of goods while Araceli changed into a light dress. They left the palace and strode out into bright sunlight, the rays heating their skin and dancing on their heads.

Kaiden breathed deeply and sighed. "I've missed this. Lead on, Araceli."

A lush summer breeze blew as they reached the park, a series of green hills and a stretch of meadow that led to the walls of the capital city. Broad trees with green and purple leaves grew around the entrance, giving the park the illusion of being a forest. Araceli and Kaiden entered, following the paved path down the center.

Around them, people swayed in hammocks or lay under the shade of the trees. Children chased each other in the grass while bold red butterflies flittered around the flowers. This was the common park, where anyone could enter. It also connected to the gardens in the palace, which only the elykin had access to.

Araceli led them to the shade, and they rested their backs against a tree while Kaiden pulled out the spread he'd packed for them. A board, followed by white cheese, red grapes, crackers, dried meats and fish, figs, tiny melons, and a bottle of wine. Kaiden spread the meal out, taking his time to arrange it on the board. Araceli watched him with amusement. "Were you a chef?"

"No, but if you're going to eat, a meal should please the eyes and the tongue. Food is meant to be savored, and a well-made meal should go on for hours."

Araceli picked up a bit of cheese, a cracker, and a fig. "Who has time to eat for hours?"

Kaiden poured the wine and took a sip. "Clearly you've never been to a court dinner, or a political meal. The key is to first make your guest hungry, tempt them with the delights you have and then, as they eat and drink, their guard will come down. They will be more amicable to your plight and at the right moment, when they are full, happy, giddy on drink, ask for what you want. If you have done your job well, an alliance will be made and the meal will turn to one of celebration. If not, it could erupt into bloodshed. What one serves during the dinner is crucial. Some meals make one irritable while others inspire more amicable feelings."

"What kind of meal is this?"

"A celebratory meal, of course. There is no need to seduce you with food and wine." Kaiden smiled and handed Araceli a glass of wine. "To your success."

Their glasses clinked, and Araceli took a sip, eyes shining over her cup at Kaiden. He stretched out, placing the board between them. When the sunlight caught his eyes, they appeared amber, and the glint made her heart ache. The moment stretched until Araceli blushed and picked up a fig to distract herself. "You have many stories, I'm sure. Will you tell me one?"

"Many, but they all end the same way."

Araceli detected a note of sadness in his tone, even though he tried to jest. "Who were you before the curse?"

His eyes misted. "That was a long, long time ago."

Araceli took another sip of wine as his voice mellowed, sending her on a journey to a time she could not imagine.

"I was born in the dunes of Iscaria. The land there is hot and sandy with frequent windstorms. My people lived in tribes, fighting for land, food, shelter, all the necessities for life. Our greatest enemies were the lizard people. They were more adept to living off the land, and they were fast and quick. They attacked our tribe mercilessly until my father discovered a solution. We dug holes to hide from the lizard people and guard ourselves in the sand. One night my father dug so far, he found stone, and that was the beginning of the pyramids."

Araceli gasped in surprise, but Kaiden did not hear.

"When the tribes of Iscaria discovered that safety from the lizard people was possible, they came to join us, and my father oversaw the construction of the great pyramids. But it did not stop there. The people rallied around him as a leader, and his aspirations grew. He was never content, always pushing for more land, more wealth. The people called him blessed, for the spirit of the desert spoke to him. He was called many things, but those who have great power will always be targeted, and because I was his only son, the sole heir to the kingdom, I became the target. A spirit cursed me to come at the beck and call of every lord and use my magic to grant wishes. Three wishes. For a while I escaped such a fate. I hid the lamp that called me forth and life went on with only the shadow of foreboding. And then it happened." His mouth tightened and his face changed, a glaring, furious look contorting his handsome features.

"You don't have to talk about it," Araceli said.

"It wasn't all bad." He shrugged.

"What do you do when the wishes have been fulfilled? Does your life become your own again?"

"No, far from it. I've found it tough to live my life when, at any moment, I can be whisked away at the beck and call of another. After every wish was fulfilled, I returned to the lamp to sleep."

"How long has it been since you were cursed?"

"After two hundred years, I stopped keeping track."

Araceli could not imagine being at the beck and call of others for so long. Maybe she should set him free, since he was helping her. What was one more wish when she didn't know what she wanted? But with him around, everything was different. She was bolder, braver, and her life had changed because of him. Yes, because of his magic, but also because of how he'd encouraged her to forget about limitations. One more wish, and then she'd let him go, free at last to go where he wanted to.

45

DARYA

E ach day she and Nurimil traveled together was harder than the last. He knew much about the land and how to navigate it, and she admired that knowledge. Yet tension hung between them, a tension Darya could not hope to overcome. Despite acknowledging their fledgling attraction, Nurimil continued to treat her with respect, and nothing more. Darya yearned for more and had to satisfy herself with his words and the softness in his eyes that told her he struggled just as much as she did.

The water moved, slowly at first, then picked up speed, rushing on to some unknown destination. The afternoon sun was hot on Darya's face when she heard the faint sound of thunder.

"What is that?" she asked, although her heart leaped at the sound of it, and she thought she knew what it was before Nurimil confirmed it.

"We are nearing the crossings. Two rivers converge and

pour into a great basin. Here is where we let Boxie go and figure out a way to get down the falls without killing ourselves."

A waterfall. Darya's cheeks flushed in anticipation. The mermaids dwelled near waterfalls, but aside from stories, Darya had never seen one with her own eyes. "I can take us down," she volunteered.

Nurimil turned as the yak came to a stop. His hand landed on her thigh, sending a pleasant hum up her body. Darya's breath caught, and she squirmed, forcing herself to meet his gaze.

Warm eyes studied hers with an intensity that left her feeling unsure about what was going on in his mind. After a moment, he removed his hand. "I'm going to trust you."

His words thrilled her, and she didn't take her eyes from him as he dismounted and pulled off the saddlebags. "I'll tie everything down so we don't lose it in the water. I assume there's not a way you can keep everything from getting wet?"

"I'll try," she smiled at him, although her heart thudded in her chest.

He reached up to help her down. "It doesn't matter. We're almost to the trading post, and we'll restock there."

Right. Darya refused to let that knowledge dampen her spirits. Although she'd be leaving Nurimil, she'd be much closer to the capital city and the completion of her quest.

Nurimil tied a bag around his waist while Darya faced the waters, fingers on the clasp of the cloak. With a twitch of her fingers, her scale armor covered the smooth skin of her body, and she dropped the cloak.

Behind her, Nurimil gave a sharp intake of breath and stilled. "Darya—"

A whistling sound cut him off.

His arms came around her, pulling her down as an arrow sank into the mud, inches from her feet.

Darya scrambled for footing as Nurimil yanked the cloak off the ground. "We have to go!"

A moment later, they were in the water as arrows whistled around them, pinging the water as they surged in. Wide-eyed, Darya watched them, a rain of malice from the trees. Where had they come from?

Nurimil had let go of her the moment they entered the waters, and he was swimming downstream, away from the volley of arrows.

Darya peeked her head above water, catching movement in the trees. A person darted out and began running toward the yak, and then shouts erupted as someone pointed at her. Ducking back under, Darya swam to catch up with Nurimil.

His hand closed around her wrist, and he pulled her to the surface, gasping for breath.

"It's likely poachers," he whispered, his breath warm against her ears. "They've come for Boxie. Zal will never forgive me, but we're outnumbered. The current is strong here. Can you take us down safely?"

Darya felt the pull in the water as another arrow sang past them. "Hold your breath," she said, wrapping her arms around Nurimil.

They dove, and her feet fused together. She smacked her tail in the waters, sending a spray up on the bank. Hopefully, the water would distract them while she and Nurimil escaped.

He was right though; the current was strong, and it dragged at her, similar to the sea currents. She fought to keep near the surface for Nurimil's sake, rising to allow them to breathe, suppressing her gills so she could breathe like him and know when to rise. Although she suspected that, from her life under the water, she still had an edge over the human and could hold her breath much longer.

When they rose to the surface again, gray boulders rose on either side of the river, and people ran alongside them, shouting and waving their arms, occasionally sending arrows into the river at them. One had a net and cast it, leaving no doubt in Darya's mind that the poachers were also after her.

With a scowl, she swam faster, keeping one arm tight around Nurimil.

The roar of the falls filled her ears, drowning out the shouts. Suddenly, the water churned, spinning her. Mist rose, making it impossible to see over the edge, and Darya's heart dropped as they were yanked toward the precipice.

It was a great cliff, much bigger than she imagined, and for the first time, she doubted her powers. Nurimil's arms tightened around her waist, reminding her that he was relying on her to see them safely down the falls. Tightening her jaw, she closed her eyes, chanting against the slew of water that surged around her, hoping Nurimil could hold on. It was almost impossible to lift him to take a breath. And these were not her waters. Would they listen to her and obey?

She pulled the waters around her, asking them to bear them gently over the edge and avoid any rocks that might dash them to pieces at the bottom. The falls thundered and groaned, like a great beast unwilling to obey.

"Breathe!" Darya cried as they reached the edge and the realization of what was about to happen struck her.

Nurimil gasped but when she caught sight of his face, his

eyes were sparkling, as if he were looking forward to going over the edge and being sucked into the void. Adventure. That's what he lived for: impossible feats and the wild adventures that he came out of alive. How ironic that he, the human, should look forward to such a drop when she, a creature of water, was frightened of the strength and power of the falls.

Summoning her power, she wrapped them in a wave as the water spit them over the edge. It was like falling through a downpour of tiny pellets of rock. Darya twisted, using her body to protect Nurimil from the stinging spray. Water rained on her head, drumming against her body. White mist flew past her, followed by a flash of colors: bright green, shimmering yellow, rich purple, and an azure blue, darker and brighter than the sky. A flicker of orange captured her vision as she fell into a rainbow of colors and shot out the other side.

And then they weren't in the falls at all but beside them, streaking down like a fallen star shooting out of the heavens. Darya took deep breaths, willing Nurimil to do the same as she saw their destination. A pool spread out in front of them, and a moment later she and Nurimil dove into the watery arms of the pool beneath the falls.

46

NURIMIL

Nurimil laughed as they shot over the edge of the falls and then they were soaring, free of Nomadia, free of the icy waters. The cold spray soaked his clothes to the skin, and he lost hold of his cloak. He could only hope his money bags were still tied securely to his belt. The water was rough and forceful, but Darya held on to him. Still, once they went over the edge, exhilaration pumped through his body and for a few moments he was weightless, hanging between the slim threads of life and death. They might crash on rocks, breaking every bone in their bodies, or drown in the waters.

Vaguely, he was aware of Darya's honey-colored gaze on him as they fell, although he could not read her expression. The scales on her tail caught and reflected the shimmer of light from the rainbow. Water droplets hung like blue diamonds as a wave surged out of the falls, wrapping around them. The momentum of their headlong fall slowed, and then they crashed.

Nurimil's vision dimmed as they went down into the depths, almost into blackness. The impact knocked the breath out of his body, and when he tried to draw air there was nothing but water, filling him, constricting his heart until it burned.

He tried to hold back, but his body shook violently, trying to breathe, to live. Pressure tightened around him as though heavy rocks were rolling over his chest. Arms spinning, legs kicking, he struggled for something to push off of and take him back up to the light. Bubbles escaped from his mouth, taunting him as they danced over his head, lazily making their way back to the surface.

Suddenly, two powerful hands tugged at him and he broke the surface, treading water, coughing, and spitting. Spinning, he regained his balance as he sucked in a deep breath of pure air. The water hung sweet on his lips, refreshingly cool, and he tilted his head back, gazing at the mist and thunder far above him.

He should be dead. The fall was much too high, and the rocks should have killed them, but they were already downstream, and the river continued to pull them, easing them to another pool.

Hints of cedar wood and spice drifted from the shore, and birds shrieked at each other as they flew overhead.

"Nurimil?" Darya called, concern making her voice high.

She was beside him, a hand squeezing his shoulder as if her touch could keep him afloat. He realized she was steering them to the bank, into shallow waters. Within moments, he felt the firm riverbank beneath his feet.

Admiration for her flooded him, and he stood, waist deep, his hands going to ensure his belt and sword and coins were still with him. They were, and he sighed with relief, raking a hand through his wet hair. The shore was visible, with giant trees hiding the path. It would take a moment for him to gather his senses and figure out where they were, but he didn't care.

"We're alive," Darya said, glancing from him to the falls and back again.

A bubble of relief and desire expanded in his chest. He laughed and tugged her closer. She was beautiful, and the waters were crystal clear, allowing him to see the shift as her tail gave way to two legs. She smiled, but her eyes were anxious as he laughed.

"Have you done anything like that before?" he asked, angling his face until her green lips were just below his. Water droplets hovered on them like jewels, and he wanted to do nothing more than kiss them away.

"No." She shook her head, and her scale armor disappeared. "I've never seen a waterfall before. I didn't realize they would be so gigantic."

"I have a confession." Nurimil lowered his voice, running his hands down her back, feeling the scales melt away into smooth skin until she stood naked before him, her nipples grazing his chest.

Her eyes had turned into liquid pools of desire, enticing, compelling him. Resistance faded. Who was he to turn his back on destiny and say no to his fate? The days he'd pent up his desire, tried to hide it from her, gave way.

"What?" Darya gave his belt a tug, a gentle nudge showing him what she wanted.

"For a moment there, I thought we'd either fly or die."

A teasing smile lit up her face. "You did not trust me?"

"Trust?" His gaze flickered to her mouth. "The way I saw it, if we lived or died, at least we'd do it together."

"I kept my word," she purred. "I brought you down safely, and here we are."

He pulled her hips against his, sensations firing through him as her breasts pushed up against his chest. He could feel her hard nipples through his wet shirt, and need pulsed through him. Bringing his hand up to cup her cheek, he pressed his lips against hers. The kiss was wet, sweet, and then turned hot and urgent.

The days of wanting and waiting merged into that moment and he could not have pulled away even if he wanted to, and he most certainly did not want to. She moaned, and the sound was so satisfying he wanted to hear it again.

Darya opened her lips, and their tongues twisted together as his hand moved down her wet back. In that moment he knew he'd crossed a threshold and gone where he shouldn't have gone. There was no turning back now, no denying the desire that coursed through him like a current pulling him to the edge of all reason.

Ignoring his hesitations, he kissed her urgently, as if kissing her would drive out the voice of reason and remind him he had other duties to attend to. He was sealing his fate, twisting his destiny with hers, and now he'd care what happened to her and where she went. He'd think about her as he fled to the jungles and then on to Maca, and every night when he slept under the stars, he'd want her beside him.

Forcing himself to the present, he ignored all those warnings and kissed her, as he'd wanted to the moment he laid eyes on her.

47

DARYA

Darya leaned into the kiss, pressing against his hard body as the waters around them seemed to fade. The thunder of the falls in the distance matched her heartbeat, the rhythmic beat increasing as Nurimil kissed her. His fingers traced a path down her backbone, ending just above her hips, and there his touch lingered, as if he dared not go further. Spreading her legs, she pressed against him, and suddenly she wanted to be out of the water and on the land where the remnants of who she was could not interfere with the way he made her feel when he touched her.

Their heads moved back and forth, trading kisses. He smelled like Nomadia, rich and dark with hints of spice and cedar. Even the lake couldn't wash away the essence of him and Darya breathed him in, gasping for breath, dizzy from his heated kisses.

She opened her mouth, hoping for more. His arm tightened a moment before his lips moved, nipping her lower lip and then trailing down her jaw. Tilting her head, she allowed him to kiss her neck, unable to keep the throaty moans from escaping her mouth. As if encouraged by them, he continued, pressing fervent kisses to her collarbone and pausing on the swell of her breasts.

She took the momentary pause to reach for his clothes, unsure how they worked but longing to rip them off his body so he would stand like her, naked.

"Wait," he paused, his hand covering hers as he let go. "I want to admire you."

Darya caught the lust in his eyes and stepped back, knowing exactly what he wanted. This time he wouldn't turn her away; this time he would look on her with a worshipful look in his eyes and take her, making her his own.

He undressed as she moved an arm's length away and submerged herself. Moss-green hair floated around her as she rose slowly out of the water, inch by inch, taking in the intense desire written across his face. He studied her from head to toe, and she appreciated the silent praise, the look of pure hunger that darkened his eyes. It felt like power, the strongest kind, as if he would do anything to look at her, to kneel before her, to sample her powers. In that moment, she knew she could ask him for anything, and despite magic not working on him, he would give in to her every whim. She wondered if the intoxication of desire was a kind of magic. All she had to do was open her mouth, command him, and he'd respond.

But she didn't. Because she wanted him to keep looking at her like that, and she wanted more than just his eyes on her.

"Darya," he breathed as she walked across the shallow water to him.

He tossed his shirt, leaving it floating in the water. Moving farther back, he flung his belt. It almost reached the shore, then lay half submerged in water. His pants followed, and Darya quickened her pace. He was perfection. His arms and chest were muscular, and a few scars crossed his body. Boldly, Dara stared at his hardening length, and her nostrils flared. She wanted him more than she wanted recognition in the Court of Nymphs, more than the praise for saving the sirens.

The knowledge burst in her mind like bubbles popping, and she knew with a certainty she'd never felt before that even though her adventure with Nurimil was coming to a close, she wanted it to continue. She wanted to be with him, to help him, to use her powers. Had she come to Nomadia to save her people, or, somehow, was her future twisted into the fate of Nomadia?

Nurimil knelt in the waters as she drew nearer, water dripping off his toned body, hastened by the heat in the sun; or perhaps it was the heat in his body. When she was close enough to touch him, she drew her fingertips across his cheek. He lifted his head and closed his eyes, like a man saved from darkness, drinking in fresh air and beauty again.

"Nurimil, what if I came back?"

His gaze met hers, full of confusion. Still, he reached for her, and she gasped as his hand touched her thigh, holding her still in front of him.

"Came back?"

"After I save my people. You were right; they sent me here because they wanted to be rid of me. When I return, I'm not sure what will happen, but even should they decide to promote me, I feel more alive here, with you, using my water magic as it was meant to be used. I can help you fight the coming darkness."

"Darya," he murmured, his breath against her navel, "you don't have to make such a life-changing choice right now, I would not demand that of you. There is time . . ."

He trailed off, pressing his lips against her skin, taking his time. The ache in Darya's heart wanted to ask more, to hear confirmation from his lips. But each kiss, each touch, made her skin tingle, taking away that need to know and leaving her to savor each sensation. Spreading her legs, she held onto his muscled shoulders as he kissed her inner thigh, then moved up, touching her at the apex between her legs. She squeezed, fingers digging into his shoulders as a cry escaped her mouth. He nuzzled her with his lips, adding his tongue, licking her there until a sharp hiss came out of her mouth. Knees weak, she trembled, unsure if she could remain standing. And then he stopped.

Darya panted, eyes dilated as he pulled her down into the waters beside him. Turning her, so her back pressed against his chest, he continued to brush his fingers up and down her body. His hand cupped and squeezed her buttocks, then parted her legs until she felt him slip inside.

Time froze, and she arched her back, waiting for him to take her, but he didn't. Instead he waited, fingers trailing up her belly, squeezing her nipples until she thought she would burst. She pushed her hips back, squeezing, taking him, and only then did he move, thrusting back into her. A frenzy took over, and heat surged through her body as waves of pleasure swept her away.

Nurimil took her hard and fast. Distantly, she heard his answering groans, felt his lips like fire on her skin and her need for him grew with an intensity she'd never known until she lost control. Pleasure burst through every nerve ending, and she screamed as she came so hard lights danced before her eyes. For several moments, she couldn't catch her breath and lay panting in the water while Nurimil held her tight against his chest as if he'd never let go.

Darya had no idea how long they lay in the water, Nurimil holding her against him. A thrill of pleasure hovered in her belly and she smiled, unable to restrain herself. She wanted him again and again. Did he feel the same way? She was sorry when he unwrapped himself from around her, tugging her up with him. When she faced him, a wry grin covered his face, giving him a youthful appearance.

"Darya," he scolded playfully, "we have to find you some clothes. I can't drag you around Nomadia naked."

Then he kissed her on the mouth, as if sealing what had taken place below the falls.

48

ARACELI

"How was class?" Kaiden's lazy voice drawled as Araceli shut the door.

Her heart skipped a beat as she stared at him, sleeves rolled up, curls tight around his neck as he chopped vegetables. What was he doing? The room smelled delicious, as if he'd turned it into the castle's kitchen. Sniffing, she took another step. "It went well, I think. A few of the students might be troublesome, but nothing I can't handle. What are you doing?"

"Cooking, isn't it obvious? You must be famished after your day of teaching. Magic is wearying."

He continued to chop bright red tomatoes. The tang of onion hung in the air and Araceli peered over at the bubbling pot, seeing chunks of orange carrots and cubed meat. As Kaiden mentioned, she did feel tired, but it was a good exhaustion. She was also exhilarated, because she'd done what no blue faun had done before, and he had made it possible. Ever since the day at the park where they'd celebrated her promotion, a shift had taken place. Now, when she looked at Kaiden, she yearned for more than their friendship and the odd bond of jinn and mistress.

Putting down her books, she moved behind the screen to change and refresh herself, while Kaiden continued talking. "A suggestion for you," he said. "Remove the word 'think' from your vocabulary. You're an instructor now, you don't 'think,' you either know or you don't know. Your students will respond to your confidence and knowledge."

"I will," Araceli agreed, peeking at herself in the mirror. Rubbing her horns until they were shiny again, she brushed her hair and stepped back out.

Kaiden pointed to a seat at the table where a glass of bubbling liquid sat, along with ink and parchment. "Sit."

Araceli did, studying his graceful movements. He was so beautiful it made her heart squeeze, with his dark curls, bronze skin, and the sharp curves of his chiseled face. How had she not noticed before? Well she had, but he'd been rude back then. Now? She pinched the bridge of her nose. It was foolish to fall in love with a jinn. He was ageless, and so old and scarred by the many lives he'd lived. She had nothing to give, nothing to offer him except freedom. It pricked at her conscience, and a lump swelled in her throat because she was afraid. If she uttered the words to set him free, he'd disappear and never come back, and she didn't know if she could handle him disappearing from her life. Eventually he'd resent the bondage to her, but not yet; she still had time for a second wish.

"You're pensive." Kaiden's voice cut through her thoughts. "Drink."

Wrapping her fingers around the stem of the glass, Araceli caught a whiff of peaches. "What is it?"

"Peach wine. It's a sweet dessert wine and goes well with chocolate. Perfect for a celebration."

Araceli took a sip and allowed the flavor to wash through her. A pleasant hum began in her lower belly. "What are we celebrating?"

"You, of course," Kaiden said. He ceased chopping and lifted his head, catching her eye.

Araceli swallowed hard, enchanted by the amber flakes in his gaze. She took another sip. "None of this would have been possible without you."

The words, although true, felt gaudy and lame the moment they left her lips.

Kaiden's eyes narrowed just a bit, and then a slow smirk formed on his lips. "It's my nature to be generous with my gifts," he quipped.

Those words also rang false, as though he were attempting to make light of his curse.

"Kaiden." Her voice caught, but the wine helped her be brave. "Thank you."

Picking up a bottle, he refilled her glass, leaning so close she tasted the mint on his breath. When her glass was full again, he dropped his hand, touching hers, so soft and gentle that Araceli's lips parted. Her heart thudded as though it were racing away from her, and her gaze fell to his lips.

His jaw worked, sending a shudder of desire up her spine. "If you keep studying, you will become a great ink mage." Leaning closer, his voice dropped lower. "Besides, you have the book, which will make you the greatest ink mage in all of Nomadia."

Araceli tried to steady her breathing. "Is that what you want me to become?"

"If it's your heart's desire." Pulling back, he strode across the room to the fire. He stirred the stew, leaning over the hearth as though considering. "You have the book of ink magic, and as long as you avoid the dark spells, you will become more than an instructor. I believe the next path for you will be to procure a wand. From there, you can truly begin spell work."

Araceli sucked in a breath, her mind racing. Yes, she wanted that, but . . . "What else do you know about magic?"

"It would be arrogant of me to claim I know more than I do." Kaiden sat a bowl of stew before her, then sat across from her. Lifting a spoon, he blew on the steaming meal.

Araceli's mouth watered just watching him, for reasons aside from the stew.

"I watch, I listen, and I read, but I rarely use my own magic, aside from granting wishes." He spoke matter-of-factly. "If used unwisely, magic can turn the most innocent hearts dark; it can cause obsession and greed and betrayal. If one drinks too freely from the cup of magic, it will destroy them."

"But not you?" Araceli asked, the broth from the soup warming her body.

Kaiden's dark eyes held hers, his spoon hovering over his bowl. "Me? Araceli, don't misunderstand. I'm the worst of them all."

Araceli's brow furrowed. "Surely not, you've been . . ." she fumbled for the words, "a bit sharp-tongued, but you're not evil."

His eyes clouded. "There was a time when I tricked each

new master or mistress with magic, but no, never you. You've done nothing to incur my wrath."

Unsure how to respond to that, Araceli took another bite of soup, but she couldn't miss the pleasant hum in her lower belly that had nothing to do with the peach wine or the warm soup.

"When you're like this, it's hard to believe you could do anything evil," she whispered, a blush forming on her cheeks.

"Believe what you wish, but trust your instincts. They are often right. You're young still, and you haven't seen the madness of the world, the lust for power, the desire for magic, and the mania that fuels dark passions."

Standing, he picked up the bottle. "Now, no more talk of dark things. More wine?"

Araceli lifted her half-full glass, smiling across the table at him and thinking she wouldn't mind desire and passion as long as he was involved.

49

DARYA

Time passed far too quickly as Darya and Nurimil left the river behind and found the road. Miraculously, the cloak had survived the fall, so Darya dressed in it again while Nurimil promised that, once they reached the trading post, he'd purchase clothes and shoes for her.

"How come going to the trading post is safe, yet you are concerned about being on the road? What is to stop the bounty hunters from finding you in the trading post? You said it's a popular place, and crowded."

Nurimil scrubbed a hand over his face, eyeing her.

Darya turned her gaze back to the road, wishing the burning within would go away. Ever since the waterfall, she and Nurimil had been more friendly and familiar. But aside from embraces and stolen kisses, he wouldn't let them go any further, and Darya found it frustrating. Why was it okay once, and suddenly not anymore?

She could tell he was having a hard time keeping his

hands off her, and yet he held himself back. She could only assume it was because they were nearing the trading post and would part ways soon. If he was trying to make it easier on her, he was only making it worse, but she acknowledged his restraint and let it go.

"I will disguise myself, and I'm hoping I still have friends in the village who will not turn me in," Nurimil admitted. "It is dangerous, but we have no choice but to take a risk. If all is well, I'll buy a new horse and provisions for my journey to Maca while securing passage to the capital for you. If we're in luck, my friend Gavin will be making his way to the capital for the summer festival. He travels with bodyguards to protect his goods, and if you are being hunted, they will help."

Darya fingered the cloak and said nothing, because Nurimil was determined to leave. What he didn't understand was that she did not need protection when she had water magic. Still, he seemed to think others would prove stronger than her, despite the fact that she'd overcome every single obstacle that stood in their path. "What happens after the capital?" she asked instead, keeping her voice low.

"Gavin knows the capital. He spends months there each year and can guide you to the great library, then send you on your way. I would caution you against traveling alone to the coast, though."

"Are there any direct bodies of water that lead from the capital city straight to the great sea? If I can travel by water, it will be much faster than walking across land."

"I'd imagine so. When we are in Gyin, I'll find a map and plot out a way for you to return to the great sea. Still, I don't want you to travel alone. It's dangerous."

Darya bit back her frustration, holding her tongue to keep

from reminding him that if he came with her, she wouldn't have to travel alone. She did not want him to stride into the capital and be taken by those hunting him.

The trading post was actually a tiny village complete with a wall, a gate, and a few crisscrossing roads. Darya's heart sank as they approached it, reluctant to leave the road and the comfort of traveling alone with Nurimil. Instead of heading toward the gate, which was open but crowded, Nurimil turned to the side, moving along the wall, head down.

Darya followed, eyes round. She'd never heard so much noise before, and the smell! The bleating of sheep and goats filled the air, although many grazed outside the walls in the open land. Wagons lumbered toward the gate and away from it, laden with goods. A boisterous laugh or a rough shout occasionally broke through the constant babble of voices. The life and energy in the village reminded her of the kingdom of sirens during a festival, fraught with merriment, but out here she was an outsider, not a great nymph watching over the celebration and ensuring none would come to harm.

Nurimil paused in front of a gate, pushed at it, then slipped inside. "No one is supposed to know about this entrance. Keep your head down and walk quickly behind me."

Darya followed him into the fray. The path was dusty as bystanders lingered, but no one approached them or gave them a second glance. Darya was just beginning to relax when Nurimil pulled open the door of a building and stepped inside. The light inside was dim, and after walking in daylight it took a few moments for her eyes to adjust. By the time they did, Nurimil was already speaking, and she heard the jingle of coins as he passed a small bag to the man on the other side of the counter.

She couldn't hear what was being said, but suddenly the memory of standing on the auction block while coins jingled around her came back. She stiffened, fingers gathering around her cloak as the worst thoughts invaded her mind. Was Nurimil selling her to the man?

When Nurimil turned back to her, her fears faded, and she felt foolish. Taking her arm, he guided her down a dark hall. "The innkeeper gave us a room for the night. He's an old friend and will ask around for us for a bit. His wife also has some old clothes that may fit you. Someone will bring them up."

Darya nodded, feeling out of her element as she followed Nurimil up a flight of stairs and into the room. There was a bed, to the side of which was a bucket of water and a basin.

Nurimil latched the door behind them, strode across the room, and pulled back the curtains. Light flooded the space, showing off the old wood, the sagging beams of the roof, and the dust gathering in the corners.

"It's not much," he said, "but the window provides an escape should things go wrong."

When Nurimil faced her, his expression was guarded. "Darya, I hate to leave you here, but I'll return before nightfall. I need to make inquiries, find a horse, and find out if Gavin is in town. I'll need my cloak to move through the village. I'll return as soon as I can."

"And you want me to wait. Here?" Darya's mouth wobbled as she spoke, suddenly feeling like an unwanted inconvenience to him. Part of her wanted to lash out and tell him she'd find her own way, but she still needed his help.

Tugging free the cloak, she tossed it to him, not bothering to cover her smooth green skin with her scale armor.

His mouth tightened but his eyes went soft, then he took the cloak and swept out of the room.

Darya was alone. She turned, but the room was barren. There was nothing to do. She paced for a moment, then went to the window, which had a view of the village, somewhat blocked by other buildings. Since there was nothing else to do, she sat and watched the people.

50

NURIMIL

The cloak smelled like her, giving Nurimil pause as he shut the door behind him. What were the odds that a wizard would sweep in and steal her away while he bartered in the street? His hand went to his sword hilt, but he couldn't detect magic in the air. No, he simply had to hurry and trust she'd be there when he returned.

The frown on her face told him she hadn't liked the idea of staying alone, and he didn't blame her, but it was relatively safe and, more importantly, out of sight. He couldn't walk the village with her trailing after him.

Preoccupied by his thoughts, he slipped down an alleyway between two buildings, heading to the stables where horses and other mounts were sold. The trading post served as both a place to find goods, relax, and enjoy some much-needed entertainment for travelers. It also presented a danger. Any moment, a bag could drop over his head and he'd be yanked into an alley, knocked out, and delivered back to the guild. Aware of his surroundings, he pulled his hood low over his face, hoping no one would recognize him as he approached the horse stalls.

A male elykin stood outside of the stables bellowing instructions as his wagon was loaded. He was fair-headed with the large, furry ears most elykin had, making them look something like a cross between an elf and human with the ears of a giraffe. Blond hair stuck up straight from the male's head, almost as long as his ears.

"Gavin!" Nurimil called, relieved at finding his friend so quickly.

The elykin, Gavin, spun, then a broad grin stretched over his face. He strode across the road, pale eyes wide. "Nurimil? By the gods, what are you doing here? Last I saw there was a rather nice bounty on your head. Every hunter from here to the capital is probably looking for you. Are you trying to get caught?"

"I know." Nurimil kept his head down and turned his back on the buildings. "Gavin, I'm in a bit of a pinch. The guild has kicked me out and is hunting me, but I have a friend who needs safe passage to the capital."

"A friend, aye." Gavin nudged him and winked.

"Something like that," Nurimil grumbled. "She's unfamiliar with the land and will need a guide to take her to the great library. I'll pay for passage if you're up for the task."

Gavin slapped his back. "Keep your money, Nurimil. You'll need it wherever you flee to. As it turns out, you're in luck. My caravan is leaving for the capital this afternoon. We hope to get a good start toward the city before night falls. Will she be ready by then?"

Nurimil ran a hand through his hair. So quickly. He'd

expected they'd have to stay at least one night, maybe more in the village. Instead, they'd barely arrived in time. "I'll ensure she is. I need to buy a horse and supplies for my own journey."

Gavin raised an eyebrow, then jerked a thumb toward the stables. "I'm sure you noticed by now, but soldiers are everywhere. You can't go in there without getting caught."

Stunned, Nurimil raised his head and stared back at the stables. "Soldiers? Why?"

"The news is all over." Gavin's face turned serious. "Surely you've heard? The slave quarters in Dustania were burned to the ground, the trade destroyed, and rumor is there's an elf sorceress on the loose, eating souls and calling herself the child with golden tears."

Nurimil swallowed hard and kicked a loose rock on the ground.

Gavin continued, "The soldiers are searching for the elf sorceress. Detachments are moving up and down the roads, securing each trading post. It is assumed she is searching for something powerful, and they hope to stop her before she reaches the capital."

"They believe she's that much of a threat? One person alone cannot take over the city."

"True, but there were powerful people who kept the slave trade running. They are upset about what happened, and I believe this effort from the capital is largely because those people are spearheading this campaign, and the capital is benefitting from it."

Nurimil made a fist, punching it into his palm. "They're concerned about the fall of slave trade when they should be more concerned with protecting their borders and their people!"

"Ridiculous, I know." Gavin's sandy blond hair waved as a sudden breeze whipped up. "But it's no surprise the empire has the wrong motives for taking action."

"How many have you seen?"

"Small detachments, groups of no more than twenty."

"Twenty? Is that a joke?"

"Come, Nurimil. I know you can take on twenty by yourself, but I think the empire wants it to look like they care when they are just appeasing the wealthy. Only time will tell."

"True," Nurimil agreed. "I am more concerned about the coming of the dark lord and what it means for Nomadia."

"Aye. Times are changing. You'll need to be careful out there," Gavin cautioned.

"I always am." Nurimil straightened. "The day is wasting, Gavin. I wish we could prolong this discussion over a mug of ale or two, but if soldiers are here, I need to go before they start guarding the gates."

"Wait." Gavin raised his hand. "You've done me a few good turns, and now it's my chance to return the favor."

Gavin crossed the street again, and after more bellowing and waving, returned with a loaded horse. "Here. We can spare this beauty. She's packed and ready for a long trip."

Nurimil took the reins and glared at his friend. "I can't accept this."

"Nurimil."

"Gavin."

Gavin took a step back. "You're in a bad spot, besides, I'm not giving you the horse. Return her to me the next time we see each other."

Nurimil pulled a sack of coins free and tossed it at Gavin. "Agreed, but only if you hold on to my money until we meet again."

Gavin smirked, tucking the money into his belt, then pointed at Nurimil. "Go, find your friend, and I'll meet you outside the gates at half past noon."

Nurimil stroked the horse's velvety nose, and she nudged him, encouraging him to mount up. Her bags were packed, and he flipped open a saddle bag, noting the food and water. Shaking his head at the generosity of his friend, he guided the mare back to the inn.

Darya started when he opened the door, eyes round. "I didn't expect you back so quickly."

Locking the door, he faced her. Apparently, someone had come by because she was dressed now, a barrier to the temptation to take her one last time before they parted ways. The dress was a simple plain brown one that swept to her feet. It did nothing to complement her beauty, but it was probably for the best. Aside from her moss-green hair and emerald skin, if she wore a cloak and pulled the hood up, she'd be completely unremarkable.

"Business went well, but we have to go."

His heart twisted at the expression that crossed her face, leaving him on the verge of caving in. If she begged him, he'd put his life at risk and go with her to the capital. If only she'd ask. He couldn't say no, not to her.

Darya did not beg. Instead, her brow furrowed, and she nodded. "I'm ready."

Nurimil retrieved his horse from the stable and led them through the village.

Now that Gavin had mentioned it, he saw soldiers moving

through the throngs of people, wearing the white livery of Nomadia and the empire's emblem, two moons surrounded by stars. It was a symbol of peace and unity, but Nurimil felt anything but that as he moved to the gate, keeping his head low, one hand on the horse's reins and the other on Darya.

She also wore a cloak, but she kept her head up, her inquisitive eyes taking in the activity on the streets. He wondered if similar trading posts existed under the sea, where he could not fathom life taking place. How did they talk? How did they trade without their relics floating away?

Each step he took to the gates was a step away from her and felt like a noose tightening around his neck. He continued forward until they reached a line just outside the gates. Nurimil's heart sank as he peered over the shoulders of the man in front of him.

"What's wrong?" Darya whispered.

"The soldiers are at the gate inspecting everyone who goes in and out."

Darya's eyes went round. "Do you believe they will stop us?"

"I'm a wanted man," he told her. But he couldn't be stopped, not now. Nor did he want to tell Darya that they were looking for the child—now a woman—with golden tears.

Darya's finger slid around his wrist, and she squeezed. "Trust me."

He glanced at her, but she pulled him forward, leading him into the line of people impatiently waiting to be let through. Nurimil thought of the side entrance he'd come through earlier. If not for the horse, he would have gone through it again, but it was just large enough for a person, and no beast could get through it.

Five soldiers stood in front of the gates in two lines, two of them letting travelers in, and two letting them out. One stood over the process occasionally demanding further inspections, especially of the loaded wagons.

Nurimil kept his head down as they neared the front of the line. A wagon was in front of them and the soldiers gathered around, inspecting it.

Darya's fingers twitched, and a bucket of water splashed over, upsetting the horses. One of them reared up, hooves kicking the air. The soldiers shouted, but Darya kept moving, leading Nurimil through the chaos at the gate and out to the road.

Nurimil kept his head down, shoulders tense, waiting for someone to shout or call after them. But there was nothing. The chaos grew distant, and then they were out on the road, a meadow running on either side. A bard played in one of the meadows while dancers swayed to his music. A crowd grew, tossing coins or drinking ale as they relaxed, enjoying a bit of merriment before moving on with their journeys.

Darya was watching the bard, a wistful look on her face. "Before I left the sea, there was to be a celebration, a union between sirens and mermaids. It was a rare occasion where the Court of Nymphs were invited to take place in the festivities."

"You enjoyed those festivals?"

Darya smiled, but he had the sense it wasn't a genuine smile. "It was a change from the boredom of routine; a chance to be free spirited."

Nurimil looked at her, wondering what her life truly had been like with the Court of Nymphs. While she was determined to save them, there was something else, another sensation he couldn't put his finger on. Was it duty, not desire, that drove her actions?

He meant to respond to her, but caught sight of Gavin. Taking Darya's arm, he escorted her to the wagon.

Gavin finished tying a rope and glanced over. "You made it out of the gate," he remarked, his eyes lingering on Darya.

On instinct, Nurimil wanted to step in front of her to protect her from Gavin. It was an irrational thought, because Darya wasn't his, and Gavin was his friend. He'd made it clear they both had to go their own ways, yet he couldn't help the protectiveness that overwhelmed him.

"Gavin, this is Darya. Darya, my friend Gavin will escort you to the capital and help you find the great library."

Gavin grinned. "A pleasure to meet you, Darya." Then he stepped back. "Take a moment, I need to ensure the crew is ready to go."

Nurimil appreciated his friend's instincts, swallowing hard as he faced Darya. Letting her go was harder than he expected, even though he knew it was the only way she'd be safe.

"Nurimil." There was no smile on her face when she spoke his name. "Thank you."

"It's been an honor," he told her, stupid words, but nothing else would come out.

"Be safe," she said, and then she opened her hand.

In her palm lay a pale, oblong stone woven onto a leather thong.

"What is this?"

"A gift." She stepped closer, her fingers brushing his chest as she lifted it higher. "It is a sea stone. I hope it brings you good luck wherever your travels take you."

"I can't accept this."

"You can. You helped me and I have nothing to give, except this."

A shadow crossed her eyes as he took the sea stone. Cupping her cheek, he kissed her. A slow and tender good-bye. When he pulled away, her eyes were shining, but she was the one who stepped back, breaking contact. It hurt to see her go, and she did not say another word as she joined Gavin and his crew.

Nurimil raised a hand, and she waved back. Before he lost his courage, Nurimil swung up into the saddle and urged the horse into a gallop.

51

ARACELI

O n Araceli's next day off, she went to meet Shyrin on the glass bridge that separated the temple from the palace. It was much bigger than the bridge that connected the palace to the library, wide enough for ten people to pass in a row, with viewing rooms overlooking the city set off from the bridge. Araceli had visited a few times, but the bridge was usually crowded, and once a guard had even chased her away.

Now she walked tall and proud, wearing the dark garb that marked her as an instructor. A few turned and stared, blatantly shocked at her status, but she paid them no mind. Instead, she held her head high, hooves clopping over the bridge, tail swinging behind her until she reached the midpoint. She went down a few steps, and there was Shyrin, dressed in a white robe that offset her short hair. When she saw Araceli, she stretched out her arms and the two embraced. "Congratulations," Shyrin whispered, her eyes shining with tears. "I'm so proud of you. How is it?"

347

Araceli pulled back, still holding her friend's hands. "To be honest, the first few days were rough. Some of the students heckled me, but when I made their books fly, they decided to pay attention and listen. It's busier than I thought it would be, helping them learn and grading assignments."

"But you like it?" Shyrin asked, her voice all breathy and whispery.

"I do," Araceli agreed, willing herself not to be ungrateful. "It presents more of a challenge than stacking books, and the students ask brilliant questions. I have to go back and research some things, which means long hours at the library and fewer days off."

She thought of Kaiden each time she had to stay later, and conflict twisted through her. He still demanded she keep up her lessons from him, and in the first few weeks of teaching, she'd gotten little sleep. Now, though, she thought she had a handle on balancing her schedule.

"How old are your students?"

"Most of them are between twelve and fifteen, children of lords and ladies who sent them to the library to learn something over the summer. Some of them are genuinely interested in ink magic and apply themselves, while others do the bare minimum. I'm not sure how their other schooling is, although I've heard most go to academies or boarding schools where the coursework is rigorous and passing or failing is unforgiving. They will have one test at the end where they must perform the rudimentary skills of ink magic in order to progress to the next level."

"That is marvelous. I'm happy for you." Shyrin squeezed Araceli's hand. "Has it gotten easier, or do you want to talk about it?"

Araceli bit her lip. It was always difficult talking about the differences between how they were treated because of their races. It was odd, given that the capital of Nomadia was so diverse and distinct, how something as simple as becoming the first blue faun to teach ink magic could cause such a stir. "People talk and stare, because it is unusual. At first I felt uncomfortable, like everyone was watching to see what I'll do next and if I mess up."

"Like being on stage?"

"Yes, like being a performer. And you know me, Shyrin, I don't like to call attention to myself. I'm still learning to navigate the discomfort, but knowing I have friends to cheer me on helps."

"Good. If you want to talk or if I can help with anything, let me know. I'm always happy to help a friend."

"I truly appreciate that. What about you? How is training?"

Shyrin gave a shaky laugh. "Sometimes I just wish everything could go back to before. The priestesses are so serious and full of doom and gloom. The head priestess keeps telling me she read in the stars that the world will change soon, and I need to be prepared. I can't tell if it's her way of encouraging me or if she's deadly serious. I don't like it. They talk too much about the prophecy regarding the child with golden tears coming to ruin Nomadia. I don't see how though; the capital is so strong."

Araceli chewed her lower lip as a memory came into her mind. Kaiden had mentioned the very same prophecy, following it up with the fact that it was nothing to worry about. "What is the prophecy about the child with golden tears?"

"I don't like to repeat it." Shyrin scrunched up her nose. "It's so dark, but the words I recall are:

Beware the child with golden tears
Trapped by sand throughout the years,
Furious from the pain endured
Woe to those whose fate insured
When her power comes to pass,
The empire will fall into her hands
For none has power to withstand
The rule of golden-teared hands

Araceli took a slow breath and let it out. "It sounds gruesome. When does the head priestess believe this will come to pass?"

"Soon." Shyrin shrugged miserably. "Whatever soon means. Today, tomorrow, in five hundred years, she did not say. Only soon. It is one of the most miserable, vague words. To be honest, I hate it there, with their somber prophecies. Don't hate me, but, Araceli, if it continues like this, I'm going to find the elykin and take him up on his offer to find out what my parents left for me. I know I said I wanted to study the wisdom and knowledge of Nomadia so that I could instruct and help others, but I'm unhappy. I don't believe marrying a wealthy lord would lead to happiness either. I just want to get away from the city. It's crowded and full of voices. Sometimes I think we were meant for something more than the endless rhythm of work Nomadia gives us, each according to their station. But I can't find out what it is; I can't read the stars here among all the noise."

Araceli's heart sank. She turned away, staring at the people milling in the streets. A wagon had turned over, spilling fruit across the cobblestones. The man driving the wagon was shouting while children rushed in, scooping up handfuls and darting into the shadows and alleyways. A few were helping to reload the wagon, and the horses pulling it were receiving a thrashing. They snorted and bucked, eyes white and round as they tried to get away from the merciless whip. Closing her eyes against such cruelty, Araceli turned back to her friend, wondering how many times she'd closed her eyes to wrongdoing because she felt helpless to make a difference. "When will you leave?"

"I'm not sure if I'll even go." Shyrin sighed. "It feels like a betrayal to leave Nomadia and all I love. But I've always wondered, what's out there? Is there more than just this, and will I find the answers if I leave? My heart is drawn to the idea. And Araceli . . . I have another confession."

Araceli stiffened, preparing her mind because she should be happy for her friend. "What is it?"

"I've been seeing the elykin regularly," Shyrin admitted, drumming her fingers on the railing. "At first I just wanted to know more about my parents. I was curious why they left something for me after all this time. I've been sneaking out after dark to meet him. He's leaving the city at the end of this month. Three weeks is all I have to decide whether or not to go with him."

Dreams spiraled and collided like a half-built tower crashing to its doom. "Do you like him?"

"Like, love, I don't know? But I want to find out. I kissed him twice, don't tell." Her eyes lit up. "It was like . . . how do I explain it? When we drink and there's that blissful, pleasant hum in our bellies, it felt like that except stronger. I want to know more, but is it worth leaving everything to find out?"

Araceli thought of Kaiden, and she wondered what he'd

say about love and leaving and following your heart and dreams. Should she tell Shyrin about the jinn or let it go? It felt as though she were lying to her best friend by not sharing that life-changing secret.

52

NURIMIL

The road east was quiet, and Nurimil rode hard for days through lush countryside toward the humid mists of the jungles. He felt torn and sorry that he'd left Darya as his speed increased, although he had no business being with a water nymph. Again, he reminded himself that she was the one with magic, and the knowledge that she'd saved him, not once, but at least thrice, was not lost on him. Still, he couldn't stop the warring in his heart as he fled.

Wasn't that what he always did? Fled when he had the chance to stay? He'd left his sister, believing her to be safe in the Court of Healers, and look how that had turned out. His sister. He should find her and stop the madness and chaos she was creating. He should turn around and follow the trail of chaos that led directly to her instead of pushing toward Maca to save his own neck.

He knew he was being followed, felt the eyes on him. But it wasn't until one misty evening as he dismounted that he caught the flash of red. Shaking his head, he drew a dagger and his sword. If there was just one person after him, he could take them out before they got more help. He flung his dagger into the thicket, right where he imagined the person would be standing. There was a clang of steel against steel and then a shout. "Wait! I don't want to fight!"

There was more movement in the foliage and then, out of the bushes stepped Tyrina, the redheaded elf. Dirt streaked her normally clean face. She held his dagger in one hand, hers in the other.

His mouth tightened, recalling the last time he saw her. "If you're after the water nymph, I don't have her anymore."

"I'm not." She sheathed her dagger and tossed his on the ground between them. "Nurimil, I came to talk, to warn you."

He grunted. "Why?"

She sighed and crossed her arms. "I was in Dustania when it was attacked."

Now that he had a moment, he detected the stark fear in her eyes and the tremble in her fingers as she held onto the hilt of her sheath. Whatever had happened there had unnerved her. Beyond the dirt on her face, her eyes were red-rimmed, and dried blood coated one of her legs. Was it hers? She didn't seem to favor one leg over the other as she stepped closer.

"Surely you've heard what happened?"

Nurimil frowned. "I did."

Tyrina pressed a hand over her mouth, staring into the trees. When she spoke, her voice came out choked. "She's mad, Nurimil, raving mad, and she's looking for the water nymph to drain her power. I watched her suck the life out of two of my companions. It was horrible. Shortly after, we learned the Guild of Bounty Hunters has fallen. I doubt anyone is searching for you, and if they are, there's no way to redeem the bounty."

Nurimil went still. He'd hoped Darya would complete her mission and return to the ocean before his sister heard of her. Should he go back? Keep pressing forward? And how had the Guild of Bounty Hunters fallen? It was nigh impossible. He wasn't sure if he should trust Tyrina's words, even though she looked lost and terrified. "Fallen? What happened?"

"Remember when Hector sent you out to get the nymph on orders of the wizard? He double-crossed you after the hunters from Maldive complained and put a bounty on your head. Whoever hunted you down was meant to bring back both you and the nymph. Five hundred gold coins was the reward, but the wizard was paying three times the amount for safe delivery. Shortly after, we received a vulture stating the wizard was dead, but that the nymph was still needed and we should hold her at the guild. That was the last we heard before the guild was attacked. I'm not sure who led the attack or why, but I heard it from a reliable source. Since then, I've been tracking the sorceress, who calls herself Elmira. We were nearing the trading post, and that's when I picked up your trail."

Nurimil had to give it to her, Tyrina was an excellent tracker. Still, her story did not add up. He retrieved his dagger from the path and sheathed it. "But why are you following me now? What do you want?"

Tyrina bristled, then her shoulders sagged. "You were one of the best bounty hunters the guild had because magic doesn't work on you. You're the only one who can go up against her without being killed."

Nurimil's mouth tightened.

"Hear me out before you decide," Tyrina begged. "As long as I've known about you, you only hunt magical creatures, but you don't kill them. You never bring in the bounty if it's on a person, and you're picky with your tasks. You also work best alone. I don't know why you choose not to kill, but this is different. If the prophecies are true, she's the child with golden tears who will bring about the rise of the dark lord. She has control over the spirit world, and she's coming to destroy Nomadia. If you don't do something, anything to stop her, or at least try, we will all perish."

Tyrina's words slammed through Nurimil like a punch to the gut. He physically backed away, his hands tightening around the reins. As much as he hated the fact that she'd tracked him down to beg for his help, he also knew she was right. But how could he get back on the horse and face the road, knowing she wanted him to kill his sister? Yes, he wanted to stop Elmira, but not like this. Did he even have a choice?

"Please, Nurimil." Tyrina clasped her hands together. "I would ask others, but you know what it's like to be a bounty hunter. We don't have friends and everyone hates us for what we do to them. With you, it's different. You've never killed or dragged someone back to slavery or made them pay for their crimes. You have a chance. All you have to do is find the water nymph, and the sorceress won't be far behind."

53

DARYA

The road to the capital of Nomadia arced and curved, taking them on a winding journey that would lead to the southern entrance of the great city. Darya rode on the lip of a wagon, clenching and unclenching her fingers, body tense as wheels caught in ruts, bouncing her on the seat. Her new clothes were rough against her skin and itched, even against her protective layer of scales. She didn't know how the landwalkers did it, wearing clothes all day every day. Her throat was constantly dry from the dust the wagon kicked up, and she longed to flee and hurl herself into a body of water.

Twisting her fingers together, she reminded herself that her people needed her. The sirens were counting on her. She should forget about her momentary discomfort and relax, because she was nearing the capital. So she sat quietly and nodded politely at Gavin and endured the conversation of his crew of traders, both male and female, all of whom had sharp tongues, lively stories, and hands that were quick to draw a blade. No one, though, bothered her, just asked sly questions and eyed her with curiosity.

At last, one day, the road widened, and Darya's breath caught in her throat. Beyond the grove of trees that grew on either side of the path, she caught a bluish shimmer, a river winding alongside the road. Gasping, she half stood from her seat. The wagon jolted, and she fell, tumbling into the dirt. It wasn't a hard fall, but Gavin waved a hand all the same. "Are you alright?" he asked, his voice gentle as he made his way toward her.

She nodded, dusting off her hands. "The river distracted me."

Putting a hand over his eyes to shade them from the sunlight, he peered between the trees and grinned. "Go ahead," he encouraged her. "We'll reach the city by nightfall. I'm sure the crew would like a brief respite. We'll start again at high noon."

"Thank you," she breathed, her relief so strong she almost hugged him.

Gavin chuckled and called to his crew, "Let's take a brief break!"

A cheer met her ears as Darya stepped off the road into the cool blades of grass. The air smelled like summer and something else, a vague stink. Glancing over her shoulder, she noticed the road dipped down, and in the distance was a smudge on the horizon. Was that the capital? If so, her quest was almost at an end. Undressing, she waited for excitement to swirl through her, and relief to ease the tight ball of anxiety that sat low in her belly. But all she felt was numbness, and an eerie discontent that had lingered since the trading post.

After tossing the dress on the ground, she dove into the

water, sinking down as her legs fused together, forming back into a tail. The waterproof covering over her eyelids flickered into place, as did the webbing on her hands. Taking a breath, she let water filter through her gills, and the giddy sensation of being back where she belonged almost hurt.

Except they weren't her waters.

Sinking to the bottom of the river, she lay among the waving reeds, watching the fish swim mindlessly back and forth and trying not to think about him. The way his kisses had sent a blaze through her body, his lingering gazes, their open discussions, and the fact that instead of curing her desire, their stolen tryst had only left her wanting more.

Nurimil had left her because he was right; they didn't belong together and they had nothing in common. She needed to put him out of her mind. Wherever he was, she hoped he was finding a solution to get the bounty off his head. She hoped he hadn't encountered another hunter or some other evil. Nomadia was wild and she could not imagine walking through the land without power, as he did.

Stretching her fingers, she realized she was procrastinating, even as water magic surged around her. Instead of lying in the river, she should be on the road, headed to the capital, determined to help her people. What would the Court of Nymphs say if they could see her now?

Yanking herself out of her thoughts, she propelled herself toward the shore. Now that she'd rejuvenated, her resolve was back. By nightfall they'd reach the city, she'd go to the great library, find the cure, and swim back. Despite Nurimil's warning, she intended to go alone. She was a water nymph with magic. The waters were her domain. She could handle any water beast that attacked her.

A wave of blue caught her eye as a shimmer of scales glided through the water. A tail, similar to her own, undulated in the waves, and Darya hovered, spinning. Was it a mermaid? Or another water nymph who dwelled in the river? She caught a glimmer of green and a surge of familiarity came over her. Her mouth gaped open as her name was called. "Darya?"

Darya stared, and a volley of questions raced through her mind. "Klarya? What are you doing here?"

Klarya paused, tail still swishing as she crossed her arms over her chest. A smirk grew over her face. "Darya, are you just now getting to the capital?"

Darya's mouth opened and closed as Klarya swam around her, taunting.

"You are slow, aren't you? Did you honestly believe the Court of Nymphs would trust such an important task to you? You're a failure. You've messed up everything, and this was their one chance to get rid of you. So I came, I have the remedy, and I'm returning."

A swift and sudden anger almost choked Darya. She sputtered, staring at Klarya in disgust. "You lie! They sent me here. This is my task, my duty. You couldn't handle the fact that I might succeed, which is why you came after me, to try to show me up. Not this time, Klarya."

Klarya's smirk dissolved into a frown. Eyes flashing, she raised a hand. "That's enough, Darya. You know I speak the truth. Think about it. Think long and hard about what was said, and what wasn't said."

Darya thought back, recalling Mother's words as she escorted her to the surface. She remembered the bits of conversation she'd overheard before she faced the court, and the terrible thoughts that had run through her mind. A trembling began. She knew she was being tested, that they wished her gone. She'd never considered that they might not want her to come back, might not welcome her back at all.

"You see the truth now," Klarya went on. "The court had to get rid of you, had to pin the mistake on someone, which is why you were chosen to guard the realm. That way, when the sea witch came, it would be your fault."

Darya's head snapped up. "What do you mean when the sea witch came?"

Klarya shrugged.

"No!" Darya cried. "No. You wouldn't. They *wouldn't*! Why would they endanger the lives of the sirens and destroy an alliance on purpose? It's not true, it can't be true."

Klarya's eyes darkened. "Oh but it is, and it's not all about you, Darya. This plot has been planned for a long time. All we needed was the right opportunity. You know this is true because you've felt it, the tedious boredom the Court of Nymphs has sunk to. We watch, we guard, and there is nothing else. But we have something the sirens and mermaids don't have: we have water magic, magic that wasn't meant to lay unused at the bottom of the sea. And now we have something else: the magic of the landwalkers. Now we can truly rule the seas and use our magic to take whatever we want. And you, Darya—you were a liability, which is why you are now an outcast. Mother did not want you to die, though. She believed you should have a chance to choose another life, so that's why you were chosen."

A terrible scream roared out of Darya. She was angry, furious even, but she also knew, deep down, that Klarya's words were true. She'd seen the signs, had suspected, but in her concern for herself, she'd done nothing. Now she didn't know what the Court of Nymphs was going to do with their might and power, but regardless, she was powerless to stop them.

Her ball of magic slammed into Klarya's chest. Darya reared back, preparing for another when a whirlpool swept around her, yanking her down. Still screaming, she launched herself at Klarya, breaking free and spinning into her. Together, the sisters whirled in the spray, trading blow for blow. Darya chanted, her fingers moving as a wave flipped her, head over tail. She slapped the water hard, knocking the breath out of her body. With a groan, she threw another ball of water at Klarya, only to have it punted away by Klarya's tail.

Gritting her teeth, Darya formed another ball, and this time it hit hard, slamming into Klarya's head and knocking her backward. Klarya retaliated with a wave, which sent Darya spinning. She didn't have time to recover before a whirlpool caught her. Dizziness made it impossible to see straight, and then a rain of water pounded down on her head, the pressure so intense she cried out from the pain.

Somewhere in the distance she heard Klarya shouting, "This is it, Darya! You're on your own. Don't chase me, and don't come back if you want to live."

The pressure increased until Darya felt like her head was being crushed between two stones and would explode. She shrieked, fingers ripping at the riverbed. Then, suddenly, it was gone.

Darya let go and allowed her body to float as she struggled to breathe. Slowly, the pain ebbed away, leaving her with the raw realization that she was alone in Nomadia, without a duty, without a quest. A bottomless pit of blackness settled in her stomach, and she waited for the tears that never came.

An overwhelming sense of aloneness swallowed her, and she drifted for a time. The Court of Nymphs had done something terrible, and she wasn't sure what kind of magic they'd used or who they'd made a deal with. Part of her wanted to go back, to understand, but she also knew nothing was left for her there, because Klarya was right. Darya wasn't strong enough to take on the entire Court of Nymphs; even now, a weariness surged through her after her battle with Klarya. She'd spent too much energy.

When her head poked above water, it was odd to see the sun shining and hear the deep-throated croak of frogs, as if nothing at all had happened. Darya peered through the trees, but she couldn't see Gavin and his crew. She needed to tell them to go on without her, then she'd return to the river, regain her strength, and form a plan.

Heavily, Darya pulled herself to shore. Ignoring the clothes on the riverbank, she let her scales cover her again as she walked through the trees. The air smelled thick, heavy with the tang of blood and bowels. She was almost back to the wagon when she saw them. She recognized Gavin first. He lay on his back with blood dripping out of a slice in his throat. Dead eyes stared upward, and his fingers gripped a curved knife.

Horror seized Darya, and she backed away as a whimper escaped her lips. The rest of the group lay on the ground in a mangle of broken bones, blood, and smashed faces. Whoever had done this hadn't just killed them—they'd mutilated them.

Bile rose in Darya's throat. She whirled around to run and

came face to face with a female elf. At least, she looked as though she'd once been an elf. Wild black hair stuck out from her head, her pointed ears looked like horns, and she was unnaturally skinny, as if bones had risen from the ground and been covered with skin. The elf grinned, showing off a tiny row of sharp teeth. Black, bloodshot eyes lit up as she said, "So. You must be the water nymph."

54

ELMIRA

Elmira rolled back her shoulders, smirking at the stricken look on the water nymph's face. The nymph backed away, but Elmira shook her head. "Don't run. It's futile."

Then she laughed; she couldn't help it. The giggle burst up out of her, because she was full and happy. The souls she'd eaten mere minutes ago had left a comfortable buzz inside her belly. It was odd, but she could see the nymph's spirit, and also her magic, shrouding her like a cloak. It glimmered and shined, so beautiful, and Elmira advanced, hand outstretched.

"Don't come near me!" the nymph hissed, twisting her fingers.

Elmira heard a roar and ducked as a wave washed over her, soaking her rags. Spitting, she turned her head to the river and then back to the nymph. "Did you do that? With your magic?"

"Yes." The nymph's golden eyes narrowed. "I did that with my magic, and I can do more. All you need to know is that I'm going to stop you."

Elmira licked her lips. Water magic would taste so delicious, and soon she'd be able to do the same thing.

The nymph held up a hand, palm out, and began to chant.

The bubbling sensation within Elmira grew stronger, and she laughed again. "You. Stop me? You don't know who I am, do you?"

The nymph continued to chant.

"I'm Elmira, the one who was prophesied about. When I cry, my tears turn to gold. I was safe, I was hidden, until my brother left me. Then they found me, took me to the lost pyramids, and tortured me. They used my blood, my pain, to satisfy their need for power. They used magic to destroy me. So I'm going to destroy magic."

The nymph kept chanting.

Elmira opened her mouth just as something tightened within, as if all the moisture was being pulled out of her body. A soul rolled out of her mouth, and the nymph wavered. Her tongue tripped over her words, and her limbs visibly trembled.

The soul hovered in front of the nymph, and the tightening sensation left Elmira's body. She pounced, knocking over the nymph and throwing her to the ground. The nymph squirmed beneath her, eyes wild, hissing and clawing like a wild beast as Elmira settled on her chest.

"There's no need for that," Elmira purred.

But the nymph wouldn't listen. She kept fighting.

Elmira made a fist and struck her hard across the jaw.

The nymph stilled, and then a high, piercing cry came out of her mouth.

It hurt Elmira's head and made her ears ring. She just wanted it to stop, had to make it end. Raising a fist, she struck the nymph again, bone smacking flesh and bone over and over. The cry turned into a wail. It wouldn't end, would never end, so Elmira leaned forward and breathed in.

The tendrils of magic tasted like sugar on her tongue. She took another deep breath, sucking in the nymph's essence. It was delicious, even better than the souls already humming through her body.

Beneath her, the nymph arched and shrieked, almost bucking her off, but Elmira did not care. She was in the throes of pleasure and nothing could stop her. Magic sank into her, molding to her skin, her very being. Her body trembled with it as she writhed on the peak of unspeakable pleasure.

Starlight danced in her eyes, and the scent of water was stronger than before. For the first time, she noticed how every living thing, even the plants, used water as an energy source. They all took it in, absorbed it, and she could use that energy. The power of water was hers, all hers.

She was so far gone it took her a while to realize a voice was shouting her name. At first, she thought it was Vero, whom she'd told to hide in the trees, lest he get killed by an arrow or blade. But then she realized the voice wasn't his at all.

Elmira stood up, legs shaking, staring down at the nymph's still body. She'd never taken magic from another before, and wasn't sure if the nymph was dead or alive.

"Elmira," the voice came again. "Stop!"

She turned as a man carrying a sword ran out of the trees.

He was familiar, yet not familiar. A bubble rose in her throat, this time not a giggle, but a small sob. A memory came back to her, not so much as a memory but a scent. The smell of lotus flowers while running barefoot through the mud in the orchard, laughing in the summer breeze as he chased her, calling her name.

It faded just as quickly as it had come and she eyed the man, taking in his sword, his garb, the wild look in his eyes as he stared from her to the nymph. The pain behind his gaze. Before she asked the question, she already knew the answer. "Who are you?"

55

NURIMIL

Nurimil couldn't breathe as he stared at her. She was petite, with high cheekbones, short black hair that barely touched her shoulders, and she was thin—far too thin. Her fine bone structure was just like her mother's, but she had their father's dark hair and eyes. Just like him. Splashes of blood covered her legs and arms, and the look in her glazed eyes was pure madness.

Tyrina was right, and Nurimil's heart broke just looking at her. When he saw his friend, dead by the side of the road, the wagon turned over, the horses gone, he knew something terrible had happened. And now, Darya was lying there, likely dead, at Elmira's feet. He didn't know whether to cry in rage or guilt or sorrow, but he had to do something. He'd left his sister at the Court of Healers, and now she was a monster.

"It's me," he said. "Your brother. I'm Nurimil."

Her gaze went vacant. She bit her lower lip and raised a

ANGELA J. FORD

thin hand. "Nurimil. Yes. I remember. I had a brother who promised to return, but he didn't."

Instead of being accusatory, her words were nothing more than fact, yet each one felt like a dagger sinking into his skin.

"I waited for you. I waited and then I got tired, and I decided to go on my own adventure. It didn't turn out well." Her voice rang with bitterness. "At first it did, until that accursed Kymeria took me to the pyramids. She lost control of her people and then the wizard came, and my life was hell."

"I looked for you," he whispered, voice thick with unsaid words, with grief at what had happened to her. In the sunlight he saw the faint marks on her arms, the rawness around her ankles and wrists.

Elmira tilted her head. "The wizard did unspeakable things in the name of magic, and I killed him." Venom laced her words. "I'll kill anyone who gets in my way. So run, Nurimil. Run, Brother. Because I will destroy the magic of Nomadia."

His heart stilled. He knew what he had to do. Tears burned his throat, and he tightened his hands around the hilt of his sword. "I can't let you do that, Elmira. People will die. Enough innocents have already died. You can't have that blood on your hands."

"I can!" she snapped. "I want that blood. I need it. I want people to look at me and fear, and know that I have come to make their lives hell, to take away everything they thought they had, to bring fear and hopelessness, to be their biggest nightmare. I've come to kill, and if innocents die, so be it."

She lifted her hands into the air and screamed.

A sharp wind blew, and gray clouds rolled across the sky.

Elmira laughed, a wild, mad laugh. Taking a step, she wobbled as though she might fall.

It was now or never.

Nurimil dashed toward her, blade lifted as rain pellets struck his face. Elmira was fast, and she sidestepped the blow. Shaking, he spun around to face her as the rain poured down. Could he do this? Could he kill his own sister? His eyes were drawn to Darya's body on the ground, and a swift fury rose within. With a yell, he swung at Elmira, again and again.

She danced around him, laughing and spinning as if they were children again, playing a game of chase and it was all an elaborate joke.

At last, Nurimil sank to his knees in the mud while the rain poured down around him. Lightning flashed in the distance, and the air shivered with the faint hint of thunder. Tears rolled down his cheeks, and his chest hurt as if Elmira had plunged a blade of her own into his heart.

"I'm not going to kill you," he heard her faint whisper. "Because you're my brother, and my quarrel is not with you. But get out of my sight, lest I change my mind."

Nurimil hung his head, wondering how close she was. If he could reach out, give one thrust, she'd be on the ground, and he'd drown them both in the river. She'd killed Gavin and his crew; she'd killed Darya and perhaps countless others.

But when he looked up, Elmira wasn't there. He thought he heard her laughter by the riverbank, but he couldn't see her and didn't want to. He didn't want to have to kill her. Crawling forward, he scooped up Darya and rocked her back and forth, holding her body on the bank as tears shook him.

A trembling hand touched his face. He opened his eyes, staring straight into hers although there was a dullness there, a sort of hopelessness. Her face was bruised, and blood welled from her bottom lip, but her hand pressing against his cheek gave him strength. "Darya," he groaned, squeezing her tightly.

"You saved me," she whispered.

Her voice was so tiny, so frail, a fierce need to protect her rose. He cursed himself for leaving her, for letting everything that had happened take place. Holding her in his arms, he staggered to his feet as she moaned. She felt so light. Too light, as though the wind would blow her away. Her fingers curled around his shirt as he made his way to the trees, back to where he'd left his horse.

"I came back, Darya, and I'm not leaving you again. You're going to get better, and then we are going to make a plan."

He felt her nod, but her body trembled as he lifted her onto the horse's back. He swung up behind her and gave the horse its head, galloping through the rain.

56

ARACELI

R ain poured, pounding on the cobblestones as if it would drown Nomadia. Gray clouds rolled across the sky, and in the distance, even darker ones loomed.

Araceli pressed her hand against the cool windowpane, fear stirring in her heart as she watched it. "We don't get storms like this in the capital," she said to Kaiden.

He rose from the table and came to stand beside her. "I heard the magicians in the capital control the weather."

"It's true. They observe the four seasons, but the weather stays mild. Winters are cold, but never bitter cold. Summers are hot, but always pleasant, and a light rain is all that happens, enough to enjoy, but never hard enough to frighten. They have other methods of bringing water to the capital, and the underground water systems keep the soil fertile. I've never seen a storm like this, and it makes me think they've lost control. Something is happening."

Saying it out loud made it seem real, and her anxiety rose, thoughts going to Shyrin and the omens the priestesses had read in the stars.

"It frightens you, doesn't it?"

She glanced at him as a lightning bolt shot across the sky, pulling her eyes back to the window. Thunder boomed, rattling the glass. The raindrops danced, then poured down harder, limiting their view of the road below them.

Araceli's heart skipped a beat, and she moved closer to Kaiden, aware of his presence, his scent, and his eyes studying her. It was there, had been there for a long time, that shift in the air, the change between them. She'd tried to ignore it, focusing on her studies, but every time she looked at Kaiden, a yearning made her body tremble. Each touch made her skin tingle and her body ache for more. Sleeping beside him at night was agony, for she wanted to bridge the gap, roll over, and find herself in his arms. When he dressed, uncaring whether she saw him without a shirt, her eyes lingered on his hard muscles. Sometimes she bit her lip, longing to run her hands down his chest, to see more of his sculpted, magnificent body.

The truth kept her from taking a step and making a move. She tried to forget about it, avoid it because he was a jinn, hundreds of years old, and she was holding him against his will. If she truly cared, she'd release him and see if he stayed. But she was afraid that the moment she spoke the words he'd disappear, teleporting far away from her, and she could not bear the thought. If he was gone, everything would change. She was already losing Shyrin; she couldn't lose him too.

The simple words lay unsaid on her tongue, but when he

looked at her like that, she thought she'd do anything to make him happy.

"I am afraid," she admitted. "I don't know what is going to happen."

"It is natural to fear the unknown, but you are an ink mage now."

"An ink mage in need of a wand," she corrected him, her eyes straying to the book's hiding place.

The mage who had given it to her hadn't returned, and she wondered when he'd come, and whether she'd have enough time to learn all the secrets of the book before then. "Teaching has helped me advance my knowledge, but I want more."

"Such is the life of a mage: always searching, always desiring more power, to increase their magic, to lead, and to rule."

Araceli smiled, but another boom of thunder shook the room, making her jump. "Do you think I am like the other mages?"

Kaiden's eyes softened. When he spoke, his voice held a strange note. "No. Compared to them, you are extraordinary. These months I've watched you mature and take your place in the world. No matter what happens"—he gestured to the window—"you know enough now to stand on your own two feet and survive. You don't need me or anyone else to tell you what to do, or where to go, or how to speak. I've lent you but a tiny bit of my magic; the rest you've done on your own."

His beautiful words made her chest hurt. "Why are you kind to me, when I haven't set you free?"

Kaiden smiled, but his eyes were set with determination

as he moved closer, forcing Araceli to look up to study the haunted expression on his face. Her breath caught in her throat. The very air hummed with tension, and she felt that if she reached out, an invisible barrier would stop her. She should move, look away, but she was trapped under his gaze.

"Do you want to know?"

"Yes," she whispered.

Lightning flashed again, and rain streaked the window. Araceli twisted her fingers together as he closed the distance between them, sliding his warm hands around her neck and cupping her face. Soulful brown eyes studied hers, brimming with unsaid words. Araceli's body trembled at his touch, and she bit back a moan. The ache in her body increased as her gaze flickered to the curve of his mouth and its tantalizing proximity. Heat blazed within her as he angled his head and pressed his lips against hers.

Araceli's eyes closed, and suddenly her hands were around his waist, pressing her body against his. She felt dizzy, breathless as he kissed her. It was heady, delicious, and her mouth opened, desperate, begging for more. He tasted like potent wine and dark chocolate. This kiss was anything but chaste, and he didn't stop.

His fingers traveled into her hair, twisting to angle her closer to him. The warmth in her belly increased, and she had the sudden urge to rub the space between her legs to make the aching stop. Something grew there, as though she were on the brink, and kissing him would not save her, but it was all she had. His teeth nipped at her lips, and suddenly he pulled back with a groan.

Disappointment clouded Araceli's vision, but he still held

her, a hand on her back. A sob came out of her throat. "Please." She laid a hand flat on his chest, feeling the muscles shift. His heart was beating just as hard as hers. "Please don't do this unless you mean it. I can't take it. I don't want your pity, and I don't want you to kiss me just to pass the time."

His eyes widened. "Araceli, you wound me. Do you think so little of me that I'd trick you, toy with your feelings this way? If I wanted to play with you, if I did not mean any of this and only sought amusement, I would have kissed you the day you opened the book and summoned me. We've spent time together, talking and learning. We've shared meals." A wicked glint came to his eyes. "We've even shared a bed."

Araceli's cheeks burned.

"I admit, I did not relish the prospect of working for you at first, in your tiny room with no bed or light." He chuckled. "Much has happened since then, and I've come to admire your resilience and strength. I've never served a blue faun before, but it has been a pleasure. You aren't like my former masters and mistresses, hungry for power, tossing down three wishes without regard for anyone else. You take your time, and at first I found it frustrating, but now I appreciate it."

Kaiden's eyes misted over, and he stroked her cheek with one hand.

Araceli leaned into his touch, heart throbbing at his words. Was it real? He cared for her? A whisper of doubt crept into her mind, but he continued.

"I've lived many lifetimes, some of them pleasant, others painful, full of wishing for it all to end. I grew arrogant and callous toward life, because nothing has been my choice—until now. Kissing you, caring for you, is my choice. The years rubbed away my resolve, and I grew weary. But you . . . you're a breath of fresh air to a long-buried soul. You've brought hope to my black, hopeless heart. Will you have me?"

Araceli nodded, tears slipping down her cheeks. "Yes. Kaiden. I am yours."

The wind howled outside, and the sky turned black, ignored as Araceli lifted her lips to Kaiden's. He kissed her hard, as though he were a lost soul and kissing her would bring him back to life. She opened her mouth, breath ragged as his hands ran down her back and squeezed her bottom.

Liquid heat spiked. A low moan burst from her lips.

"I want you," he whispered, teeth nipping at her ear. "All of you."

She could not have responded if she wanted to because he kissed her again. Each kiss was a brand, burning through her skin, fanning the flames within. Turning, he guided her to the bed and pushed her down, breaking the kiss to run his fingers down her neck, ending at the top of her dress.

"I want to see you without any of these garments that hide your beauty from me."

Earlier those words would have embarrassed her, but now she sat up, reaching for the buttons on her dress.

"You do mine, and I'll do yours," he suggested.

"Kaiden," she whispered, fingers going to his chest.

"Don't speak. I want you to feel this, to experience."

Her fingers snagged on a button, but his hands were on her chest, opening up her dress, exposing her to his touch. She was only halfway done with his shirt when he bent his dark head, cupped one of her breasts, and took it in his mouth. When his tongue lashed her nipple, her head rolled back. She took a sharp breath as a flood of pleasure rolled through her. Arching her back, she cried out, wordlessly begging for more.

The ache grew, and she pressed her hands against his bare chest, almost ripping off his shirt in her haste. Her hands moved down, brushing over his pants and he paused, a groan turning to a growl. He moved to her other breast, biting, nipping, then pushed her flat on the bed, moving the dress down her hips. It slid off her legs and pooled on the ground, leaving her naked to his eyes for the first time.

Pausing, he took his time, his gaze running the length of her body. Araceli lay back, waiting for hints of shyness and embarrassment, but they never came. The look on Kaiden's face was worshipful. He lay down beside her, gathering her in his arms. Turning on her side, Araceli kissed him hard, then pulled back. "I didn't think you'd ever feel this way about me."

He smiled, although his eyes were nothing but dark pools of desire. Kissing her shoulder, he traced the slope of her curves. "That's the beauty of it; it's surprising."

"I'm glad you changed," she admitted. "It was so small, and yet I felt it. I've cared about you for a long time, but I wasn't sure if it was because you were the first to see me for more than a librarian or a blue faun."

"I still see you." His caress was tender, and he kissed her again.

"Kaiden," she gasped for breath, but he wouldn't let her. His kisses continued and the ache inside, that fever, that burning, increased.

"Say it again," he encouraged, his hand over her belly, resting on her thigh. At first, it was a light touch, just grazing her.

His fingers pressed, pulling her legs open. Araceli felt

faint as he stroked her inner thigh, fingers rising higher with each move. Moisture pooled as he arrived at that spot between her legs where the ache was strongest. With a gasp, she closed her eyes and spread her legs farther apart, welcoming the sensation.

He stroked her there, bringing her to another level with only his fingers. Pools of heat gathered. She panted against his neck while he kissed her. The world danced and faded until it was only him and her and his fingers, bringing her higher, to the peak of pleasure. Her body bucked, her back arched, but he held her, unwilling to let her legs close or increase the movement. His kisses drove her mad, and she didn't know what she wanted, but she was so close to being there, to the apex of everything. As cries burst out of her mouth, they were kissed away by his warm lips.

"Say my name," he whispered, urging her on with his lips, his tongue, his hand.

"Kaiden."

"I wish." The pace of his finger increased, stroking her, driving her mad. "Say it."

"I wish," she gasped, pushing herself against him.

"For you,"

"For you."

"To be free," his voice purred, dipping in the final word.

"To be free." She gasped as she reached that peak and an orgasm flooded her senses.

Quaking and trembling, she let bliss wash over her. It took a few moments to realize what he'd made her say. She'd just given him freedom. Her mind was fuzzy as waves of pleasure rolled through her, but Kaiden was still there, holding her. His hand left her body, and he kissed her, long and hard.

Suddenly, a crack of thunder boomed across the room, shattering her euphoric feelings. Lightning flared, three intense flashes, white and hot, streaking through the black sky.

Araceli's eyes widened.

She reached for Kaiden, but one moment he was there, lying on the bed, holding her, and the next he was gone, leaving a cloud of mist in his place.

Araceli leaped off the bed, almost falling over as her legs trembled. A wildness took over as she spun around, eyes darting to every corner, but the room was empty.

"No," she whispered, horror dawning on her. "No! Kaiden!"

All those words, all those things he'd said. Were they true? Or had he grown weary of waiting for wishes that would never come and seduced her to gain his freedom? Stunned, Araceli turned back to the bed, which still held an imprint of him. But he was gone.

Pressing her hands to her mouth, she slumped to the floor. The shaking began, starting with her hands and going all the way to her hooves. Her heart hurt, hurt so badly she thought her chest would cave in. She rocked back and forth, holding herself, but she couldn't stop the tears. They leaked out of her eyes, covered her cheeks, and dripped off her chin. A cry rose in her throat and suddenly it was a scream of sorrow and pain and frustration and hopelessness. She choked on her tears, still rocking back and forth as she sobbed, shoulders shaking.

She'd come so far, gained so much, but it didn't matter because he'd lied to her, tricked her, pretended to love her with his flowery words. The moment he gained his freedom, he'd left her alone. His last kiss still burned on her lips; his touch still warmed her skin. She wept, her heart breaking in two, because he was gone.

57

ELMIRA

Elmira dropped her hands to her side and laughed, her chest heaving from the effort it took to create the wild storm. The black clouds twisted above her and rain soaked through her thin clothes, sending droplets running down her skin. It felt good, so good! No wonder those with power always sought more. It filled her body, burning away the odd feelings she'd had when she saw her brother again. It sent waves tingling up and down her spine. A pleasant hum inside made her eyes water, and she swayed, drunk on power. It was so much, so filling, that it spilled out of her; she could not have kept it inside if she wished.

Vero watched her, hunched under a broad leaf that sheltered him from the worst of the storm. When she glanced in his direction, at first it seemed there were two, maybe three of him, his eyes shining, his body hunched. She liked him like that, weaker, smaller than her, yet now that she'd gotten what she wanted, it was time for him. She'd take him to the Court of Healers and help him stand straight and fix his hand. After that, she and her loyal companion would be invincible.

She grinned, and when her vision cleared she realized Vero wasn't looking at her at all, but rather at the river. Pivoting, she followed his gaze. The bank overflowed, waves splashing up on the bank as the rain beat down. A glint of gold was in the waters, moving back and forth. Likely a piece of refuse. At least, that's what she thought until she saw a sparkle. It was hard to tell from her vantage point, but it looked like a vessel.

Stretching out her hand, she curled her fingers. The water churned around the vessel and she drew it up. Water shot up and out, hurling the object onto the muddy bank.

"Mistress!" Vero shouted, anticipation in his voice. "It's a lamp!"

Elmira's heart skipped a beat, and her eyes went wide. How could it be? Had the river sent her a blessing? Had the fates smiled down on her quest at last?

She lunged, picking up the object and wiping mud off it. Water slicked around her so hard it was difficult to see, but she wasn't quite sure how to stop the storm she'd started, so she stumbled away from the river and joined Vero, huddled under the leaf.

Elmira balanced the object in her palm, and all the fight went out of her. The euphoria from stealing the nymph's magic faded into awe as she and Vero stared first at each other, and then at the lamp.

It was ancient and oblong, chipped, and made from a pure gold with scratches and runes covering the base. At one end was a handle, arched and so fragile she was surprised it hadn't broken off in the river. In the middle was an opening for a candle, and on the other end was a long stem to pour out the candle wax or oil.

Vibrations came from it, and Elmira knew she'd found the jinn's lamp. "This is it, isn't it?" she whispered.

Vero opened his mouth, his eyes wide. "It's just like the drawings the wizard had."

Emotion threatened to overwhelm her. "How does one summon the jinn?"

"It's simple. Rub the lamp, and he will appear and be required to grant three wishes."

"Three wishes," Elmira repeated, already knowing exactly what she'd wish.

She only needed two wishes; the third she'd use for Vero.

Lifting the lamp, she held it up to the streams of light that were beginning to peek from behind the black clouds. It was an omen, a sign. Victory was so close.

Lifting two fingers, she stroked them lovingly across the swell of the lamp, the way one might stroke their lover's skin.

She repeated the motion once, twice, thrice.

And waited.

To be continued in Book Two: *Treachery of Water*. Visit: angelajford.com/lore-of-nomadia

EXCLUSIVE SHORT STORY

Don't miss this exclusive short story.

He's an immortal fae knight, she's a cursed warrior. To save their people from annihilation, they must go where the living have never gone before.

Every few years, the swarm comes, a terrifying pestilence that consumes the living. One sting from the deadly creatures brings not death but something much worse. . .

Every few years, Rainer, a fae knight sworn to protect the mountains, prepares his people to lose everything.

No one knows why the swarm comes, and no one can stop it.

Except for her.

Zelma is a warrior, sent to find the legendary firedrakes in the mountain. Instead, she's attacked by the swarm and left to die.

When she awakens in the hall of the fae knight, she's determined to continue her quest.

However, the sting has changed her, and new, frightening abilities awaken.

Afraid of becoming the target of the fae knight's wrath, she fights to control her magic as they travel into the heart of the mountains.

Will Rainer and Zelma save their people? Or will her magic kill them first?

Of Fae and Flame **is a complete, stand-alone short story set in the Nomadian universe.**

Only available at: https://angelajford.com/product/of-fae-and-flames/

ALSO BY ANGELA J. FORD

Join my email list for updates, previews, giveaways, and new release notifications. Join now: www.angelajford.com/signup

The Four Worlds Series (epic fantasy)

A complete four-book epic fantasy series spanning two hundred years, featuring an epic battle between mortals and immortals.

Legend of the Nameless One Series (epic fantasy)

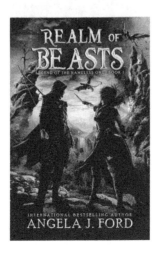

A complete five-book epic fantasy adventure series featuring an enchantress, a wizard, and a sarcastic dragon.

Night of the Dark Fae Trilogy (romantic epic fantasy)

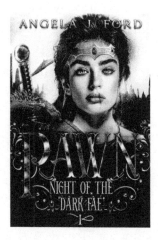

A complete epic fantasy trilogy featuring a strong heroine, dark fae, orcs, goblins, dragons, antiheroes, magic, and romance.

Tales of the Enchanted Wildwood (fairy tale romance)

Adult fairy tales blending fantasy action-adventure with steamy romance. Each short story can be read as a stand-alone and features a different couple.

Tower Knights (fantasy romance)

Gothic-inspired adult steamy fantasy romance. Each novel can be read as a stand-alone and features a different couple.

Gods & Goddesses of Labraid (epic fantasy)

A warrior princess with a dire future embarks on a perilous quest to regain her fallen kingdom.

Lore of Nomadia Trilogy (epic fantasy romance)

The story of an alluring nymph, a curious librarian, a renowned hunter, and a mad sorceress as they seek to save—or destroy—the empire of Nomadia.

Visit angelajford.com for autographed books, exclusive book swag and book boxes.

ABOUT THE AUTHOR

 Angela J. Ford is a best-selling author who writes epic fantasy and steamy fantasy romance with vivid worlds, gray characters, and endings you just can't guess. She has written and published over twenty books.

She enjoys traveling, hiking, and playing World of Warcraft with her husband. First and foremost, Angela is a reader and can often be found with her nose in a book.

Aside from writing, she enjoys the challenge of working with marketing technology and builds websites for authors.

If you happen to be in Nashville, you'll most likely find her enjoying a white chocolate mocha and daydreaming about her next book.

facebook.com/angelajfordauthor

twitter.com/aford21

instagram.com/aford21

amazon.com/Angela-J-Ford/e/B0052U9PZO

bookbub.com/authors/angela-j-ford